AN
UGLY ANGEL
VIETNAM 1967

Chapter 1

The sun reflected sharply off the silver metallic wing of the Boeing 707 as it banked to the left over the coastline on a final approach to Da Nang Airport, Republic of Vietnam. The multiple runways looked like long black asphalt fingers, beginning slightly inland, and stretching out into Da Nang Harbor.

On board was a new batch of young shaved tail United States Marines from the states. All had close haircuts, showing the typical shaved sides of new recruits. Their uniform was strictly stateside issued fatigues of heavy jungle green with web beige colored belt and brass buckle. Footwear consisted of black leather high top boots. Flights such as this had been going on since 1964 when Military escalation in Vietnam began in earnest. Every military personnel sent there would eventually call Vietnam just 'Nam. Now more than three years later, more troops came to replace those whose tour of duty was up and were now heading back to what troops called the real world. The occupants of this plane represented just another load of raw Marine recruits being sent to South Vietnam. The men on this plane were part of America's finest. Young Marines, some not more than 18 years old. Among the others, few had reached their 21st birthday. Each one of them looked somewhat alike; short hair, young eager faces, innocent looking boys who knew they were the best fighting men in the world. That's what they were told during three months of intense basic training and later infantry school, and that's why they joined. They shared a bond with those who passed before them, a special bond between Marines.

Vibration from the landing gears being lowered told the plane passengers that Da Nang was but a short moment away. As the plane approached closer to the runway, the landscape began to take on definition. The airport below contained small motorized objects moving about on the alternating, half sand and half asphalt floor of the runway. Immediately connected to the airport were numerous buildings taking on their importance regarding the closeness to the runway. On the outlining areas of the airport stood drab concrete buildings interconnecting with small shacks that were inhabited by Vietnamese.

Those aboard began to gather their gear and personnel belongings while attempting to gawk out the windows to get a glimpse of their home for the next thirteen months, the Republic of Vietnam. Four stewardesses were busy preparing for the landing, "no smoking please, fasten your seat belts, make sure that your seat is in an upright position." Pillows and blankets used on the long flight were returned to the proper place in the overhead compartments. Marines still sleeping were awakened by their friends so as not to miss the excitement of landing in Vietnam.

Activity on board the plane increased and anticipation was intense as the ground below grew increasingly larger upon further descent to the runway. A moment's hesitation was felt as the planes huge t-64 engines power was reduced and flaps extended to 30 degrees, then 40 degrees. The flying structure appeared to float briefly.

The pilot executed a perfect landing as the wheels of the Boeing 707 screeched upon touching down on the hot asphalt of runway 23. The planes flaps extended forty five degrees further downward to produce greater drag for slowing down. The twin GE Engines roared as the pilot reversed them to assist slowing down the Boeing 707. Like a giant tortoise, the plane slowly made its way to the tarmac and closer to the terminal. A young air force airman wearing aviation ear muffs directed the plane to turn first right and then left before coming to a rest at its berthing place at the airport terminal. The plane lurched slightly forward as the brakes were applied.

The pilot was on the speaker welcoming all on board to Vietnam and to remind everyone to take all their gear. The young Marines began to slowly stand and stretch. They gathered their gear and waited for the signal to disembark. When the plane was secured the stewardesses opened the plane door. Marines inside felt the rush of hot humid, sticky Vietnam air enter the plane. A gruffly Marine Gunny Sergeant barked an order for everyone to proceed in an orderly manner down the gangplank and into formation on the tarmac. The occupants slowly made their way out of the aircraft, down the metal steps. They immediately experienced the intense hot sun. The fresh state side issued fatigues worn by the newly arrived Marines quickly began to show signs of perspiration in the lower back and underarm areas. We're not in Kansas anymore Toto! Many squinted against the bright sun, putting a hand up to shade the eyes to get their bearings.

A veteran Marine Sergeant, showing no awareness of the intense heat, walked briskly from the terminal towards the plane with a clip board under his left arm. The Sgt. was no more than 22 years old with a hard and tough appearance that was no doubt the result of strong discipline and a no nonsense approach to his duties. When the Sergeant was within talking distance he shouted, "All officers and non-com personnel, Sergeants and above, may proceed to the terminal for travel assignments. The rest of you follow me," and directed the new arrivals to a nearby shelter. The structure was nothing more than an A-shaped roof having no sides. It was supported by several steel girders on 6x6 wooden posts to hold up the structure. A large overhang extended out acted as a staging area. Wooden benches provided the only relief from standing in the hot sun. A canvas top sheltered the new arrivals from the scorching Vietnam afternoon heat.

The Marines were only off the plane for fifteen minutes and their fatigues, soaked with sweat, were becoming very uncomfortable under the Vietnam sun. Perspiration formed easily on the foreheads and upper lips of the new arrivals. The fatigue caps were being used more like a handkerchief to wipe the sweat off the faces than a cover for the head. The starched fatigues wilted under the assault of the hot, humid Vietnam climate. The hot asphalt of the airport floor seemed to increase the intensity of the sun, some thought, much like standing in an oven. The heat penetrated the thick leather soles of the heavy black stateside combat boots, making standing very uncomfortable.

The airport itself was impressive to look at with the numerous types of aircraft activity. Many of the planes not being used were housed in open U-shaped metal and concrete stalls to protect against direct enemy assault. The stalls rose ten feet in the air and shielded the planes on three sides. There were groups of planes clustered in adjoining stalls. The size of aircraft went from the large working horse C-130's, down to the small versatile attack helicopters known as Huey's. Somewhere between these two sizes was the fast and deadly Phantom F-4 jet fighter. When the Phantom was taking off everyone would watch. The swept back design of the wings made the plane look fast just standing still. As the F-4 took off the jet engines increased in intensity followed by a quick roar and flash from the tail section as the after burners kicked in creating more speed. The formidable weapons on the F-4 protecting the Da Nang airbase provided a sense of security appreciated by the military personnel of all branches, Air force, Army, Navy and Marine Corps.

The new arrivals began to settle down. Each Marine started to find a comfortable spot in the sparsely furnished terminal shelter. The only accommodations were unpainted wooden benches with no backs. This was definitely not a place of comfort for those who arrived here and would be leaving in a short time for their final destination.

Finding a resting place was the order of the day for the Marines. Much like a hound dog circling a spot before settling down. the men made a small ceremony pounding their duffel bags to make a soft spot to lay against. Once they laid their heads on the bags, they made a small adjustment of their head covers so the brim of the hat protected the eyes from the sun's glare.

The shelter gradually became less noisy as the excited voice of the newly arrived Marines settled down to a low dull mummer of private conversations. A number of men fell asleep, affected by the jet lag from the exhausting 18 hour plane flight from the States. Others talked in broken sequence of their new surroundings or reached into their gear to find the half read paper back book, worn and tattered from being passed around the barracks. The Sergeant who had escorted the men from the plane to the shelter had finished comparing trip vouchers with the disembarkation officer. He headed towards a small stage podium under the shelter. "All right listen up! When I call out the following MOS's, men with that military occupation specialty pick up your gear and stand by the designated exits over on the west side of the building. A truck will be along shortly to take you to your outfit. Now stay put and don't go wandering off somewhere,, we got no time to grab ass looking for anybody. Now, here we go, 0311's, 0145's & 1320's, getcha gear and move out." Upon that command, a bunch of Marines grabbed their belongings and edged towards the west side of the shelter.
The Sergeant yelled out, "now the next MOS's, park your ass over on the north side of the building near the plane ramp." After being called the Marines rose and moved near the plane ramp. The once quiet building came alive with the roar of yelling, laughing and joking young men as they prepared to move out to meet their destiny. With both groups of men heading toward different sides of the building, the whole scene reminded one of a subway crowd during rush hour.

Many of the men stopped to exchange goodbyes with their friends who they had been with since basic training at either Marine Corp Recruit

Depot at Parris Island SC or Camp Pendleton California and then onto basic rife training, and still later, guerrilla warfare training. "Take care guy, maybe we'll get together on R&R."

"Ya, take it easy Mike, don't get shot in the ass."

"Hey O'Rourke, where ya going to be stationed?"

"I don't know, some corporal said we'd be going further up North in the I Corp area."

Pfc. Sean Michael was just one of those men who waited by the plane ramp for delivery to his outfit. He was a 19 year old kid from Boston, six feet, 185 pounds of raw muscle, sculpted courtesy of the USMC. His hair was short just like the rest of the men who arrived today. A slightly round face showed his Irish background. He was the youngest of nine children from an Irish Catholic family. The saying was, "If you're not Catholic, ya not Irish". He joined the Marine Corps just like four older brothers. Two served during the Korean War, one served during the cold war. Sean enlisted a year after graduating from high school. He was the first in his family to graduate straight thru to the 12th grade. All his older siblings had dropped out of high school to work. This was pretty much the way it was back then in their neighborhood. You graduated or left school, went into the service, came out got a trade or union job. The military background of Sean's family was due more to the low income of the family than any desire to be in a war. When a person came from the low income neighborhood of Boston, military service was the first step a guy took after leaving high school.

Few in Sean's neighborhood made it to college and if they did they never stepped back into the old neighborhood. Sean tried a semester at a community college but just wasn't focused. He wanted to explore the world some, so he enlisted in the USMC like his older brothers. Now he was on the other side of the world involved in the Vietnam conflict.

Chapter 2

It was near two o'clock in the afternoon, the Da Nang terminal was pretty much deserted except for those Marines who would be going further north. The other Marines had already left on large semi-trailers converted into troop carriers. The sides of the truck had five small windows along the length of the vehicle with a folding door in the center. Wooden benches acted as seats and in the center of the semi were four metal poles going from top to bottom. These poles were equally spread out in the semi to hold onto. When loaded with troops the semi's could carry 60 men. Four of these vehicles arrived and had taken the Marines to their new outfits around the Da Nang area.

Those Marines still waiting transportation were laying about trying to catch a quick nap, to shake off the effects of jet lag from their long plane flight from the states. All Marines knew that when you're idle, catch up on sleep because you never knew when another rest will come along. So most new arrivals slept.

The Vietnam sun was lower in the horizon than when the Marines had first arrived. A cool afternoon breeze made the shelter occupants more comfortable. The morning sweat, now dried, had stained the fatigues with a white line of perspiration salt on underarms and backs of the young men. Except for the bugs and flies buzzing about the sleeping men nothing seemed to move in the terminal. Many Marines would say that flies were the national bird of Vietnam. With no activity, it seemed like the whole airbase was taking a nap to relieve itself of the morning's heat.

It was at this moment that Pfc Michael began to seriously look around at his new environment. Sean noticed how well laid out the airport was. The top of hills surrounding DaNang airbase were dotted with brown patches where sand bag bunkers were laid out, and tall steel towers for radio communications pierced the sky. The bunkers surrounded the airbase in a semi-circle with one exposed section facing the ocean. The hills guarded the base on three sides and the ocean protected it on the fourth side. The airbase was fairly well protected from any attack. Except for the control tower, no building was more than one story high to prevent damage from rocket attack. All planes were well protected in three sided bunkers. Roads were zigzag to prevent weapon fire from going far during an attack. To Sean it appeared the military gave some thought into the setup of the airbase, which to Sean seemed unusual for the military to have an original thought. So this is where it starts for us, thought Sean. Periodically a half ton green military truck rambled by stirring up dust from the roads. Looking towards the right, one could view the Vietnamese fishing boats lazily floating out in the distance ocean. All around the base was the makings of war. Men in combat fatigues carrying assorted weapons, trucks with armor plating to protect the driver and passengers, even the local base buses that drove by had screens on the windows to protect against a carefully thrown grenade by a Viet Cong. The entire airfield was divided into sections according to aircraft type. At one area repairs were being done on camouflaged painted helicopters. Other helicopters from different bases could taxi to that area to let off Marines or Army troops, or take on cargo. In another area C-130's, the large workhouse planes, were having engines repaired or being loaded by forklifts through the planes large rear cargo doors. The plane's doors lowered to the ground acting as a ramp for loading. Maintenance vehicles of various types were idle or scurrying about busy with their duties.

Sean sat back against his sea bag and began to wonder how the hell he found himself in this place. Two years back Sean felt he would never join the military service like his brothers did. What was the use? Why spend three or more years in the service when nothing was going on. College and better things were on his mind. After high school he took a bartender job down in Hyannis, Massachusetts, working nights and enjoying the

Cape. He shared a small three room cabin within walking distance of downtown Hyannis. The cabin was sparely furnished. A kitchen table, a ratty old couch, a broken down soft chair an end table and three beds. A lot of beer drinking was done on the weekend. So much beer that someone hung a fishing net to the ceiling of the cabin to collect all the empties. At summers end, they'd moved to another cabin leaving the empty beer can net behind. During the days Sean would lay on the beach, at night he poured drinks for college kids. Fall would be soon enough to leave Hyannis and start college. Sean's' college career lasted one semester. He was smart enough to know he wasn't really college material at that time. Quitting college, he went from job to job. Tiring of dead end jobs, he took a friends advice and joined the Marine Corps. That was the very thing Sean did not want to do originally but saw no other recourse for a wandering guy unsure of where to go. So now he found himself caught up in a foreign war.

A newly arrived C-130 plane had landed and was taxiing over towards the terminal near Sean. The veteran Marine Sergeant who earlier that morning coordinated the newly arrived Marines, shouted "OK men, roust out, get your gear and be ready." The large plane stopped directly in front of the terminal and the four engines slowed to an idle. The planes rear cargo door began to open, yawning like a huge dinosaur. From within two crew members with flight helmets emerged. They made their way down the ramp and approached the embarkation Marine Sergeant. After comparing the passenger flight rooster, the flight crew members and the Sergeant nodded that all was in agreement. The Sergeant walked back towards the terminal and the flight crew walked back up the planes ramp. "OK, you guys," yelled the Sergeant, "line up near the terminal door here. When I call out your name, answer up and proceed out to the rear of the plane. Adams, here! Anderson, yo! Ascot, here!" Each Marine picked up their gear and walked out to where the crew members were standing.

Entry was through the large cargo doors. The interior of the plane was half full with supplies of ammunition in large wooden crates. The crates were strapped down by webbing straps and anchored to the floor of the plane. Sides of the plane had collapsible red nylon seats that were supported by hollow aluminum struts fastened to the planes floor. The rear half of the plane was divided in half by a series of those collapsible red nylon seats. These seats were supported not only by short aluminum struts but they also had strong nylon cargo straps that went from the seats to the roof. The crew member directed each man where to sit in the plane.

When all the Marines were on board, the veteran Marine Sergeant walked on with his clip board to take a final head count. Once this was done the planes' crew chief signed the manifest , took a copy , and the Sergeant walked off. The crew chief raised his hand and pushed a lever activating the shutting of the cargo ramp door. Some Marines took a last glimpse out the slowly closing space of the cargo door. With the cargo all secured and assured that each passenger had a seat belt on, the crew chief walked to the front of the plane to the cockpit intercom to inform the pilots. The C-103's four engines began to rev up and the huge bulky plane slowly taxied out onto the run up area. The pilots went through the flight check list. With all systems functioning, the flight tower gave an OK to take off. "Flight 330, proceed for a left pattern take off due north." After a slight pause the plane was taxied onto the runway. With increasing speed, the C-130 roared down the runway and slowly lifted up and was airborne, gaining altitude, banking for a north bound traffic pattern. The cargo of newly arrived Marines
was on their way to their next destination, Phu Bai, Vietnam on the south border of I Corp area.

Chapter 3

The landing zone of Phu Bai was nothing more than a concrete based runway covered with iron matting. A three story concrete building acted as the control tower, with a single controller.

Three Marines were waiting for a truck to carry them across the runway. One was a Sergeant who talked with the radio dispatcher inside a wooden hut, the other two Marines waited by a sandbag bunker. Sean Michael was looking down the runway at nothing in particular. The third guy was a colored Marine named Ford. He was six feet tall and weighed 175 pounds.

"Think it will be long before we get picked up," said the Sergeant. Ford turned slowly as if he wasn't sure he cared to answer.

"No."

Sean looked at the Sergeant wondering why a higher grade enlisted would ask a Lance Corporal about time schedules. The only conclusion was to make the Marine more at ease. Ford did appear to be apprehensive and weary of his surroundings. If he was nervous, the Sergeants question didn't help.

Soon a small green camouflaged pickup truck with a canvas back came down to the runway. The truck kicked up a small storm of sand as it left the asphalt and drove onto the sand. The pickup stopped alongside the hut and a small dark tanned Marine yelled, "hey if you guys are going to HMM-362 hop in". All three Marines threw their gear in the back of the truck and climbed in under the truck canvas canopy. The men didn't say anything as the vehicle made its way to HMM 362. The driver stopped for two checkpoints manned by Marines guards in green fatigues, armed with

M-14 rifles. At each station the guards checked the back of the truck to assured no unauthorized passengers were inside.

It was dark when the pickup truck stopped outside HMM 362 administration hut. Once the three Marines were inside the hut, they gave their travel papers to the on duty administrative Corporal who was behind a counter. The Corporal was dressed in an off white sweat stained T-shirt showing signs of many washings. A combat knife, called a K-bar, hung on the web belt. It was the usual survival knife issued to all Marines in a combat zone.

"Welcome to the Ugly Angels gents. You are officially attached to HMM 362, God help your souls. You guys can sack out in Hut 36, there are blankets & cots inside." The colored Marine Ford asked "what about sheets?" The Corporal smiled and said, "Ya, right!" Just be glad we have clean blankets. Besides you won't be in there long. If you want some chow, the mess hall is down past the flight line. Follow the yellow runway lights and watch out for the guard dogs."

The men went outside and were caught off balance by the total darkness. No light pollution, just darkness. It was easy to see the yellow runway lights that was for sure.

When they reached hut 36, they went inside and put their gear beside a green cot. The Marine Sergeant turned to the other younger Marines and asked, "you guys gonna get some chow or sack out?"

Ford laid down on his cot with a sigh and answered "no, I'm going to sack out."

"Me too" said Sean, "I'm tired." With that Sean looked over at Ford and said good night. The Sergeant turned and walked out of the hut.

The next morning Sean woke up and immediately felt the hot humid climate of Vietnam pressing upon his body. He rubbed his eyes and slowly looked over to the Sergeant who was already up and folding his blanket.

"Hey, what time is it?" The sergeant responded "0800."

"Been to chow yet?"

"No, I was just going to rouse you two and see if ya wanted to eat."
"Hey, Ford you wanna get some chow?" Ford nodded his head as he rubbed the sleep from his eyes. "Well come on, the chow hall closes in 45 minutes."
The three men walked out of the hut, turned left past a row of more huts. The flight line was lined with UH34D type helicopters parked twenty yards from each other. These were piston choppers, last of their breed with many years of duties in Vietnam. The choppers looked like giant tadpoles with swollen heads. The men reached the flight line and walked straight to a canvas tent the size of a house. The men walked inside grabbed a metal food tray that had four shallow food compartments. They also picked up metal field type eating utensils and a coffee mug. The chow hall still had a few late arrivals to breakfast and the food line was empty. The food for today and every day was powdered eggs and SOS. The SOS was available to pour over the eggs to cover the taste of the eggs or poured over toast. This concoction was referred to as shit on a shingle, thus SOS, because of its appearance and usually served over a piece of toast. It was a simple gravy made of butter, flour, milk and chipped beef or ground beef. Many military personnel made fun of SOS but when they got discharged and sent home, the first thing many missed was the SOS in the morning. SOS was a staple in military mess halls, it was cheap to make, would stick to your ribs and provided for a good start to the day. Besides, you would have to go out of your way to screw up SOS.
The Sergeant went to sit with the other higher ranked non-commissioned officers other wise called NCO's. Sean and Ford just sat at an empty table.
"Where you from Ford?"
Ford looked up from his tray, "Ohio......Cleveland."
"What about you? Sounds like a Boston accent to me."
"Ya, I'm from Boston, actually Dorchester. Boston is the business area, other towns surround Boston, so we just answer Boston when someone asks where you're from."

"Whats your MOS Ford?"

"Helicopter mechanic."

"Me too."

After chow Sean, Ford and the Sergeant washed their metal trays in a fifty gallon drum filled with hot soapy water. Then the tray was rinsed in another fifty gallon drum of plain boiling hot water, then stacked on a wooden table for newcomers to use.

The trio made their way back up to the administration hut where they had checked in the previous night. The same corporal was behind the wooden counter. In spite of it only being early morning , perspiration was already showing on the clerks t-shirt. The clerk turned when he heard the three men enter.

"Morning." The three Marines returned the greeting.

"Here's your orders and who to report to. When you pick up your gear in the hut, fold the cots and blankets and leave them there."

Outside the administration hut the men opened the manila envelopes, looked at their orders and walked toward the hut. Sean and Ford were assigned to HMM 362, the Sergeant to the third Marine division just down the road from Phu Bai.

The Sun was higher in the sky and the heat more intense. Ford and Sean walked down to the flight line near the chow hall they were at earlier. Flight crews were making their way to the helicopters. These were the UH34D utility Helios used as working horse by the Marine Corps. Each bird had an 18 cylinder Wright R-1820 engine, capable of delivering 1525 lbs of thrust. The choppers were armed with two sixty caliber machine guns, one out the open cargo door, the other out the opposite window.

After a quick inspection of the craft by the pilots, each climbed onto the wheel strut and up into their seats. The planes crew chief signaled the pilot to start it up. With a puff of black smoke out the engines smoke stack, the 18 cylinders came alive with a deafening noise. This went on repeatedly down the flight line as choppers initiated preparations for the runway and takeoff.

Sean and Ford found the administration shack of HMM 362 and walked inside. A young Marine wearing nothing but a green military issued t-shirt and trousers said, "Hi. You the FNGs'?
Sean and Ford looked at one another, neither one not knowing what the clerk meant.
"Fucking new guys. FNG means fucking new guys." Sean smirked a bit and said, "Ya, we just arrived last night."
"Good, we need more guys. Too many rotated back to the world this month and we're shorthanded" the clerk said.
"Both you guys mechs?" Sean and Ford nodded yes.
"OK then, Sean I'm gonna put you in hootch 15, Ford you're in hootch 10. Only one space available in each hut so I have to split ya up, that OK?" The NFGs nodded yes, as if to protest would make a difference. With each Marines' personnel folder handed over to the clerk and necessary transfer papers completed, the clerk directed Sean and Ford to the supply hut for blankets and sheets.

Sean looked at the stained sheets, which at some time in the past may have been white. The supply clerk spoke, " look this is not the Hilton, we're lucky to have sheets at all. Helps keep the wool blankets from being scratchy. But most of all we have new blankets, courtesy of a supply run that never made it."

Apparently while on a supply run down south, some of HMM 362 choppers didn't drop off all of it's supply, which was a common practice for Marines in the I corp area. The I-Corp was closest to the DMZ and further up North than most military outfits. So by the time supplies were handed out to the Marines in the I Corp area they got little if nothing at all. It was referred to as logistics problems by the supply outfits in Da Nang. To get by, most Marines procured their needed supplies via alternate channels. Basically they stole it from the Army or Air Force.

Sean said a quick bye to Ford and made his way to hut 15. The hut was up a slight incline, and sat in-between twenty other huts. The huts were

no bigger than most living rooms, most smaller than 12 x12. All were made of wood with screen side panels for windows. The huts stood eight feet high. Some huts had canvas tops others had corrugated tin roofs. All huts stood a foot off the ground to account for water drainage during the rainy season. The screen door slammed sharply behind Sean after he walked in. Ten cots were lined on each side of the hut, some with a mattress. In the far corner Sean spotted one guy laying on his cot reading a book. "Hi" the guy shouted over.
"Hi" Sean said."
The guy put down his book, rolled off his cot and walked over to Sean. He kinda limped more than he walked, hampered by a leg cast.
"Got hit two weeks ago, still a little sore, I'm Burt Jackson."
"Hi I'm Sean."
"Where ya from in the world Sean?"
"Boston, how about you?"
"Connecticut, actually Hartford. I 'll be back there in 30 days and a wake up. Rotating back and never coming back to this hell hole. Have a new Dodge Charger, all bought and paid for. Looking to run around in that. I get discharged when I get back to the States. That car will be a chick magnet." Burt smile as he turned and headed back to his cot. The sound of his cast marked his progress back to his cot.
Sean decided to check out the flight line and get his bearings. "Catch ya later Burt, I'm gonna check out the flight line."
"Ya, see ya."
The wooden hootch screen door made a loud crack as it slammed shut sharply against the hootch wooden door frame. Sean, turned left and made his way down the sloping dirt path to the flight line of HMM 362.

Chapter 4

The flight line extended some 300 feet along the ocean at Phu Bai. The largest of the building was the metal overhaul hanger. This was a metal half moon shaped structure open at the front and back. Inside were two helicopters in different stages of overhaul. The engine of one chopper was removed from the aircraft and secured to a mobile engine mount. The other helicopter had the main rotor blades removed and work was being done on the main transmission. The work was the usual semi-yearly pre-maintenance work. This was to get ahead of any potential mechanical problems before it caused an aircraft to crash.

A small crew of mechanics busied themselves with various activities involved with getting the aircraft back into service. Next to the hanger was the S-2 shack or intelligent shack. Here all vital material of operations and enemy movement and intent was analyzed. Next door was the S-1 administration shack where all personnel matters took place. Then next was the flight shack where flight and mission assignments were assigned. All down the flight line shacks were lined up ending with the armory, where weapons were locked up until needed and checked out by helicopter crews.

Sean walked into the administration shack and approached the clerk sitting behind a desk and typewriter. The clerk looked up and said "hi, you must be the FNG." Sean smiled.

"Everyone just coming in is called a FNG. Nothing meant by it just one of those terms."

"Ya I heard," Sean muttered. "Say, where or who do I report to for an assignment?"

"That will be Gunny Simmons," the clerk said. "He should be finishing his rounds of the flight line now." No sooner had the clerk finished when a large shadow covered the door. The shadow was a 6' 5" large frame that barely made it through the door. There stood the Gunny. A career Marine with thick jowls, very little hair on top and arms that looked like steel girders. "You the new guy?"

"Ya Gunny, Lance Corporal Sean Michael reporting in."

"Good, you get settled in alright?"

"Ya Gunny, I'm just reporting in now to see what I'll be assigned to."

"Have you worked on choppers in the states? You did just come from the states right?"

"Ya, except for school not a helluva lot. Kinda anxious to do a bit of flying, and see some action."

"Don't they all. Well ya have to crawl before you can walk. We need to get you some more mechanical experience before you get a bird."

"I was hoping to get flying right away."

"Look. I'm not sending you out in a bird unless I'm sure you can handle a breakdown in the field. And, that means knowing how to fix a chopper in the field. This means knowing your bird from soup to nuts. Got it?"

"Ya, I got it Gunny."

"Good, now report to the overhaul hanger and start earning your pay. You get through overhaul and you'll pretty much know how a chopper is put together. Then we'll think about getting you a bird."

With that, Gunny Simmons finished signing papers on a clip board, turned around and walked out.

"Well, guess Gunny doesn't waste words." Sean started heading for the door when the clerk spoke.

"Hey, Sean." The Gunny is right. He knows what he's doing. Listen to him and you won't go home in a black body bag."

Sean walked out of the hootch and slowly made his way down the flight line. Each hootch had a purpose; armory, electronics, S-2 Intelligence, and the flight room.

It was then that Sean came upon the Tool Room, small hootch with wooden sides and a canvas top. A tall lean Sergeant, came out of the hootch and threw water from a small pan onto the dirt. The Sergeant looked up at Sean and smiled. "How y'all doing? I'm Tommy Collins. You one of the new guys?"

"Hi and yes. I'm Sean, just reported today. Thought I'd make my way around before reporting to the overhaul hanger."

"Well come on in for a cup of coffee. They won't miss ya for a while. Hell they probably don't even know ya coming."

"Thanks I guess." Sean slowly made his way into the tool room. "So how long ya been here Tommy?"

"Hell, just call me TC, everyone does."

"Have been in country for about 26 months. I fly a few times a month to keep my flight pay, but most of the time I'm in here. There's another guy, a Corporal Dolman, he's at lunch now."

Tommy Collins was a tall thin guy. Easy going type from Austin, Texas with the typical Texas drawl. He had a youthful appearance about him which contrasted with the responsibility his Sergeant stripes placed on him.

"Where ya from Sean?"

"Boston."

"Ah, bean town eh? Wonder why they call it that when it has mostly sea food. It does, doesn't it? Have all sea food?"

"Well it has a lot of sea food but we have all types of food just like in Texas I suppose."

"So where have you been stationed before they sent you to 'Nam?"

Sean sat on one of the many boxes in the tool hootch. "Well this is my real first duty station. Before that it was Parris Island for boot camp and Camp Lejeune for infantry training. Then I was shipped right to here. Actually I asked to be sent here."

Tommy Collins turned suddenly and said, "why the fuck would you do that?"

Sean looked down at his feet and kicked some dirt on the floor. "Guess I figured if I was gonna be in the Corp I might as well get some fighting in. Didn't seem to make sense of being in the service during peace time."

"Shit!" TC said as he turned back around to face Sean. "If y'all can keep from coming to this rat hole, more power to ya. No sense in volunteering."

"I don't know TC. I have five brothers and all but one was in the Marine Corps. Three of them were in during the Korean War. The other one was in just after and served during the cold war. Seems a waste of time to be in when nothing is happening. Besides, in my neighborhood, everyone went into the service. Ya either graduated from high school and entered, or you were kicked out of high school and entered the service. That's just the way it was. After the service, the guys would come back, get a union job or something like that and settled down. That's what they did in my neighborhood. I felt like I should do the same."

"Well ya could of gone to college."

"I did, but it just wasn't for me, or maybe I just wasn't ready. Anyways I'm here."

"Ya sure are, for the next thirteen months. Just another day in paradise. I tell ya Sean, all the guys in the outfit are pretty much in the same situation. Either college drop outs or graduated from high school and then they just joined the service. Many were drafted, but few. The college drop outs were smart enough to get into college, but not smart enough to stay in. Went to college myself. Didn't like it. Most guys in the outfit are from NY, Chicago, California of South Philly. Everyone's a bad ass or knows someone in the Mafia. Bunch of bullshit. They got drafted or joined and they're here just like you and me. Only the rich assholes are still in school. Assholes don't give a shit about us. They're more worried about the Vietnamese. Don't know shit about what the NVA and Charlie do to these people."

"What's the NVA and Charlie?"

"You don't know? Charlie are the Vietcong, farmers by day and fighters at night. The NVA are the North Vietnamese Army. Many Vietnamese don't like the commies. They fight them, or they run from North Vietnam, kinda voted with their feet. Anyways we got involved and you and I are sitting here."

Just then the wood door to the tool hootch opened and Gunny Simmons walked in. He started to address TC when he saw Sean.

"Thought I told you to report to the overhaul hanger!"

TC spoke up quickly. "Hey Gunny, Sean here is getting himself a tool box for the hanger. No sense going there with no tools of his own."

"Well make sure you get there soon, we're short handed there and need to get those choppers out, up and flying."

"As soon as I get the tools Gunny," Sean said.

"Good. Hey TC, tell Dolman that I want to see him about his R&R."

"OK Gunny." Simmons left as quickly as he came.

"Shit, thanks TC, I thought he was going to hang me."

"Naw, Gunny is a great guy, old corps. and all. You ever get into trouble; you want him in your corner. He looks out after the troops. His bark is worse than his bite."

"Well maybe so, but he scares the shit out of me, too many stripes. Guess I better head to the overhaul hanger and report in. Thanks for the coffee."

"Hey Sean , don't forget a tool box. You walk outta here without one and Gunny will skin us both."

"Thought you said his bark was worse than his bite?"

Tommy Collins turned and smiled as Sean walked out of the hootch.

Chapter 5

   The overhaul metal hanger was fifty yards down from the tool hootch.
It was a three story tall metal pole shed type. It was rounded at the top and
had two large metal sliding doors on each end. Sean was making his way
toward the hanger when he spotted a familiar face.
"Hi, you're Ford aren't ya."
The guy stopped and looked at Sean and was trying to make out who he
was.
"I'm Sean, we came in together last night, up from Da Nang."
"Ford seemed to recognize the face now. "Oh ya, all you white guys look
alike. Didn't recognize you at first."
Sean looked at Ford in wonderment, not knowing how to respond.
It was then that a smile began on Fords' face and started to show some
teeth.
"Oh. Good one Ford, wasn't sure how to react."
"All you white guys react the same."
"So where ya been assigned?"
Ford said "I'm with HMM 362 , gotta report to the overhaul hanger. I
had to finish up some personal work before I got down to the flight line."
"Hey this is great, we're both assigned to the hanger. Guess they put all
the FNG's there."
"C'mon, I was headed that way".
Sean and Ford walked off towards the hanger.
"Bring that damn cherry picker over here. For Christ sakes, you guys are
slow as shit. I gotta get this bird inspected, out, and flying by tonight."
The voice came from Sgt Ervil T. Bonville, a Georgia boy with black hair.
Hell, Bonville was lucky he had any hair at all. A twenty year man

working on his 14th year before retirement. A former infantry grunt who got tired of hiking gear over the country and decided to get assigned to helicopters. Bonville figured if he was going to travel he might as well fly.

"Hey Sgt, what the hell the rush? This bird is not going anywhere and it's unassigned."

"Well that's how much you know dip shit. This chopper is scheduled for a mission tomorrow, soooo any more stupid remarks Gordon? Good! Now move your ass and get that cherry picker over there. Jeez, the idiots they send me!"

Sean and Ford entered the hanger and made their way to the only guy with Sgt stripes,

Sgt Bonville.

"Hey Sarge, we're assigned to the overhaul crew. I'm Sean and this is Ford."

Bonville looked up from his desk and said, "put your shirts over there and give those guys help getting that transmission back on."

A UH35D helicopter stood at the end of the hanger. The rotor blades and transmission were missing. A transmission for the rotor head was nearby hanging from a cherry picker. A cherry picker was nothing more than a large manual crane used to host heavy chopper parts on and off the aircraft. It stood some sixteen feet high with cables to lower or raise the helios' machinery. The crew was maneuvering the cherry picker over to the chopper. As they did, the transmission swayed slightly. Two guys were on top of the helicopter and three were maneuvering the cherry picker into position, getting the transmission directly over the chopper. Sean and Ford went over and helped push the cherry picker into position. A Marine on top yelled down, "OK, now start lowering the transmission. Slowly, slowly, that's right, real good, slowly, OK now stop! Jack, get the bolts and start putting them in to secure the transmission to the chopper. Good job guys." When the transmission was secured, one of the Marines yelled,"lets go get some chow and finish up afterwards. Hey Sarge, we're going to chow."

Bonville looked up from the paperwork and mumbled, "dammit, we'll never get that bird up at this rate."

As Sean walked out of the overhaul hanger, the flight line suddenly came alive with guys running. He looked to see the cause of the commotion. High in the west sky coming in fast were three helicopters heading towards the flight line. One of the birds had smoke coming up from the engine compartment, another had its landing strut and wheel hanging like a broken branch on a tree. A third was making an emergency landing over at the medevac pad. Even from a distance one could see the side of the chopper riddled with bullet holes and the tail of the aircraft had part of it torn open. A green ambulance with a large white cross painted on it was rushing towards the medevac pad.

A crash truck had already parked near where the first chopper was attempting to land. Men in white fire fighters outfits were perched on the truck. Two men were ready to hose the incoming aircraft with white fire retardant foam. Other men in similar outfits were on the ground next to the truck, waiting to assist the helicopters crew. This was a dangerous process. Any explosion from the aircraft fuel cells would destroy anything within twenty five yards.

The helicopter with the broken strut hovered five feet off the ground. "C'mon, get that skid under the wheel strut, and watch out for the rotor blades," Gunny yelled! A large metal skid was placed under the choppers strut by members of the crash crew. With the choppers strut now resting on the skid, the Gunny motioned for the pilot to shut down the aircraft. The four rotor blades slowly started to wind down. The helicopter crew jumped from the side door, the pilots scrambled down from their seats. All wanted to get away from the chopper and let the crash crew do their job of extinguishing any secondary fire that might occur. Over by the medevac pad, two Marines were carried out on stretchers and placed inside the ambulance. The crew chief and door gunner of the chopper stood nearby talking to the pilots.

The third helicopter landed and taxied to its berthing slip amongst protected sandbags and sand filled fifty gallons drum barrels. From the chopper, Lance Corporal Dunn stumbled out. He fell against the side of his aircraft and slid to the ground. Gunny Sgt Simmons ran to his side and helped remove the Marines ½ inch thick armor vest. The vest had a large dent in the front, the fabric was ripped. Dunn grabbed at his chest and ripped his shirt open. Gunny Simmons saw a grapefruit size black bruise on Dunn's chest. Dunn was having hard a time breathing.

"Can't breathe!" escaped from his lips."

The Gunny yelled out for a medic. Doc Duvas ran up with his medevac pack and knelt beside the Gunny.

"He's having a hard time breathing. Looks like he got hit good in the chest."

"Ya got yourself a bunch of broken ribs, plus your sternum" Doc Duvas chimed in.

Cpl. Richard Camron, picked up Dunn's armor chest plate and did a slow whistle. Camron, was a big guy and thus ironically called Lil' John. Big guys always seemed to be nicknamed Lil' or Tiny. Lil' John walked over to where the Gunny was and said., "look at this!" The Gunny looked up and spotted the large dent in the center of Dunn's armor. "Looks like he was hit with a fifty caliber. Shit no wonder he can hardly breathe. I'm surprised he's alive."

Another medic arrived and was administering oxygen to Dunn while unbuckling Dunn's belt. "This should make his breathing a bit better." Dunns breathing started to be easier now, color came back to his face.

"Holy shit, I felt like there was an elephant sitting on my chest. Whoa crap, that really hurt."

"What the hell happened, Simmons said?"

"We came into the landing zone for the second time to pick up more wounded. Then all hell broke loose. We took fire from every direction.

Charlie took his sweet-ass time to zero in on us during the first trip to the LZ. Looked like the fourth of July. Rounds were hitting us everywhere. Had Mortar fire too. The grunts ran for cover and I just opened up and returned fire. I sprayed every tree and bush with cover fire. Capt. Nelson got us in the air. YL 43 was damaged by a mortar round landing close by and hit his strut. I thought for sure they were going down. That's when I was hit. Felt like a Mack truck hit me, knocked me down. Was so numb, didn't feel anything till a bit later, when my chest started to hurt like hell. All I could do was lay back and suck air. Jesus, it seemed like forever to get back here. How's Rubio and John Nord? They must of gotten hit bad, they were still on the ground when we took off. And what asshole said it was a friendly zone? I'd like to kick his ass! If that's a friendly zone, what does he call hot zone?"

"Take it easy," Simmons said, "let's get you to sickbay and see how bad you're hurt. Hey Sean, Ford, move your ass and get a stretcher over here quick!" The two Marines grabbed the green canvas stretcher and ran to Dunns side.

"OK, take Dunn to the Ambulance."

Once the ambulance was on its way, the Gunny made his way over to the chopper with the broken wheel skid.

"So how bad is the damage, Simmons said to no one in particular."

Corporal John Nord spoke up. "Well it's damaged good, that's for sure. Guess we'll be down for a while till we can replace it."

"I meant the two Marines who were taken away on stretchers, asshole! How bad are they hurt…..and I thought you were one of the injured?"

"Naw, Sarge. I was lucky, the shit hit all around me, but nothing connected. Rubio is OK, just pissed his pants that's all, but we're OK! The two Marines taken off are not so lucky. Bad wounds, not sure if they'll survive. One's gonna lose his leg for sure. Guess they were in a fire fight outside the LZ and ran for cover inside the perimeter wire surrounding the LZ."

Simmons looked angry. "Who the hell said that area was friendly? The assholes in S-2 intelligence, don't know their ass from their head! Hey, Capt Nelson how you guys doing?"

Capt Nelson was rubbing his head, he looked over at Simmons. " I never want to go through that again. They had us in a cross fire. Waited till we landed and were loading wounded. No way could we have taken off any faster. I don't know how we got out of there. Now the co-pilot and I have to be grilled by S-2 as to what happened. Not sure if I can hold my temper. Friendly zone my ass! They'll try to blame it on us. That we should of acted with more discretion coming into a LZ. Friendly zone, shit!"

Capt Nelson and the co-pilot made their way to the S-2 shack.

Gunny Simmons directed Nord and Rubio to get some chow and then head to S-2.

"My boys eat first, screw S-2 and debriefing."

Sean and Ford stood nearby, taking it all in. First full day in Nam and they got a taste of things to come.

Chapter 6

   The sounds of activity woke Sean. He rubbed his eyes a bit and looked
around. There were five Marines dressing, faces he never saw before.
"Hi, you're Sean the new guy huh?"
Sean looked to his right and a guy with a handlebar mustache was looking
at him.
"Ah....ya, just got in yesterday."
The Marine extended his hand, "I'm Jack Rubio, most just call me Rubio."
"Hey, you came in on that beaten up chopper yesterday. You seemed to
recover pretty good."
"Well, I wasn't exactly hit or anything, just shook up once the adrenaline
wore off. That's when you start thinking about what if. What if I got hit?
What if we went down? Up to that point, you're too worked up, to think
about everything else. It's when things calm down that the nerves take
over and a guy gets a bit scared. I don't give a shit who they are, everyone
gets scared....afterwards."
"You know who you look just like?"
"I know a young Clark Cable. I hear that a lot. No relation. Might be the
mustache that sets people off."
"Ya I can see where that might be the case."
"Hey, why don't you meet me at the beer tent tonight. We'll shoot the
breeze and I'll introduce you to a few guys."
"Great, where's the beer tent, and how much are the beers?"
"Tent is down by the chow hall off to the left. Small green military type,
one each. As far as the beer cost, a buck or two would be good.   They
only charge a dime a piece. Guess the Corp is trying to keep us drunk

hoping we'll stay here. Catch ya later, gotta run to the flight line, my bird is up and running."

Rubio turned quickly and went out the wooden screen hootch door with a slam. Sean looked around and saw the other guys getting dressed. Some didn't notice him, others just didn't care. Sean threw off his blanket and sat up on the edge of his bed. He scratched his ass and gave off a yawn.

"Sean." Sgt. Bonville was standing by the hootch door. "Hurry up, get dressed. After you get some chow, report to the overhaul hanger. We got a bird to get out and we need every available swinging dick." With that, Bonville walked away.

"Don't mind him, he's an asshole who couldn't make it as a grunt."
Sean looked and saw the big guy from yesterday they called Lil' John. He was standing belting his trousers and reaching for a shirt.

"I saw you down at the flight line yesterday. How's the guy that got hit in the chest?"

"Oh, Dunn? He'll be fine, sore for a while, but good. He'll get a Purple Heart out of it. Easy pezy Purple Heart. No blood or lasting scars, just a bruise. Still he is lucky he had his vest on. Lot'sa guys don't like to wear them 'cause they're heavy and ya sweat like hell. But Dunn is smart, he wore his. He could have had a five inch hole through his chest from that fifty caliber round that hit him. Dunn's a good guy, glad he wasn't hurt."

"Say, when does a guy get his own chopper?"

"Get your own chopper? Hell it'll be a while before they let you fly. Ya gotta pay your dues. Get to know the aircraft. Get checked out with the M60 Machine gun and a bunch of other shit just to be a door gunner. Then ya have'ta take the crew chief test and get checked out. That's all the easy part. The hard part is getting Gunny Simmons to let you fly. Doesn't matter if it is as a door gunner or crew chief. He doesn't let any of his boys fly if he thinks they might get hit. Ya gotta win him over".

"What's the difference between a door gunner and a crew chief?"

"Well the door gunner basically mans the M60 on the left side window on the aircraft. He's not really at the door, they just say that. He also helps wounded into the chopper, loads supply, does whatever the crew chief says.

The crew chief is responsible for everything else except flying the bird. He's kinda like a traffic cop, he decides who or what gets on the chopper, what weight we fly with, how many guys we get on, all that kind of crap. Most of these guys know their shit, others don't know shit, some don't give a shit, lot of shit going on here." Lil' John laughed at his last comment. "If their chopper went down some wouldn't know what to fix. Somehow they slipped by the requirements. But those who did were here before Gunny Simmons came. Gunny don't let nothing go by. He's screening out those who fuck up, and promoting others who deserve it. He's a good Marine, watch and do what he's says. Gunny is old Corps and he takes care of the troops. But you screw up and he'll hand your ass to you on a plate."

"Well, I know it's my second day, but I didn't come over to watch on the sideline."

Lil' John laughed, "you didn't come over. Hell Marine, you were sent over just like the rest of us. Don't worry, you'll get your turn. C'mon, lets get some chow."

After breakfast, Sean reported to the over haul hanger. Ford was already hooking up a tractor to a chopper ready to pull her out of the hanger.

'Hey Sean, Bonville was just asking about you."

"Ya? Where is he now?"

"He went to get the pilot for a test hop. Give me a hand getting this chopper out. Keep an eye on how much clearance I got."

"Ya looks good Ford keep coming, you're almost clear of the doors." Just then Sean heard Bonville. "Hey Sean, when you guys park that bird get over to the armory hootch. You and Ford are being assigned to perimeter patrol. Besides, you need to check out a weapon."

With the chopper parked and the tractor returned to the hanger, Ford and Sean walked to the armory hootch.

Outside the hootch ten Marines were hanging around holding M14 rifles. A thin corporal was reading names off a clip board. As soon as Sean got close he heard his name. Sean shouted out "Here" and blended in with the other Marines. The corporal looked up and muttered, "oh new guys, and the other guy must be Ford." Ford said yes and got in line with Sean.

The corporal put down the clip board. " OK listen up. You guys with weapons can go but muster here at 1800 hours tonight for a drill. All of you are on perimeter patrol and will be for a while. Anyone without a weapon come inside and we'll issue you one."

Sean and Ford were the only two who walked inside. The armory was small but had crates of weapons and ammunition. Sean and Ford walked up to the corporal.

"OK you two, I'm gonna issue a rifle, magazine clips and ammo. Each magazine can hold twenty rounds of ammo. Ya get 4 magazines. Once I issue the rifles and ammo, its your responsible till ya leave 'Nam."

Ford spoke up. "what about a side arm? Won't we need one for flying?"

"Ya, you'll get a pistol when you get to fly, not before then. Now count your ammo, check your rifle and sign this form." After the weapons were checked and the forms signed the corporal turned away.

"Oh ya, don't forget about tonight, 1800 hrs and don't be late, Lt. Dowswell doesn't like to be kept waiting. Hell, he doesn't even like being in charge of the perimeter patrol. See ya tonight guys."

It was just before 1800 hrs when Lt. Dowswell showed up.

"OK corporal everyone here."

"All accounted for Lieutenant."

The Lieutenant turned and faced the group of Marines assigned to perimeter patrol.

"Men, my name is Lt. Dowswell, I'll be in charge of the perimeter patrol. Periodically we'll have an alert to test how fast we can assemble. I expect everyone of you to be here fast. Our mission is to help out the regular grunts on the perimeter in case of an attack. In a day or so, I'll take all of you around and assign a fox hole. Some will be assigned to a bunker. But for the most part, each will have a fox hole. In case of an attack, we'll assemble by the armory hootch and then go to out fox holes. Any questions? OK dismissed!"

Sean and Ford went back to their hootch and stored their weapons.

"Hey Ford, it's past chow time, let's go to the beer tent."

"You go ahead, I have a few items to square away, I'll meet you there."

"OK guy, catch ya later."

Chapter 7

Sean followed the direction Lil' John gave him that morning. The beer
tent was easy to find because of the noise coming out of it and the voices
of Marines sitting on the sand bag bunker next to the tent. Sean was two
steps inside when he heard his name. Over in the corner was TC, Lil'
John , Rubio and another Marine.
"See ya found the beer tent alright. Grab a beer," Camron said. On the
table in front of them were 15 cans of beer. It was hot enough that the
cans were sweating and leaving a small water puddle on the table. Sean
took a deep gulp from one can.
"Wow, didn't think I was that thirsty."
Tommy Collins spoke up. "Well take it slow. Easy to get dehydrated here
and alcohol doesn't help. A Marine can get heat stroke and dehydrated all
at once. I mean, hell it's past 8 o'clock and the temp is still in the high
nineties. Besides, you're still not acclimated to your new surroundings.
Give yourself some time."
Sean nodded as he took another gulp.
"You guys come here every night?"
"Well not many other places to spend time," Rubio said.
"Sean meet Dolman."
Sean saw the one Marine he didn't know and nodded his head. "Hi."
The other Marine smiled and returned the nod. Dolman was a heavy set
guy,sort of athletic looking with a strong face and a heavy beard shadow.
"Dolman works in the tool shed with me. A good worker." Tommy
Collins sat back and took a swig of his beer.

"So what's up with the squadron? Any action happens up here?" Sean asked.

TC looked at Sean and said , "well...., we had a guy taken out by a grenade last week."

Sean paused as he was about to take a sip of beer. "What happened?"

TC went on to tell how a guy named Monte was on a troop insertion mission. When a grunt jumped out of the chopper, one of his grenades came loose, the pin popped out and the grenade went off. Caught Monte and filled him with shrapnel. TC went on, "He didn't have a chance. Monte was a good guy. We don't lose many but we do lose them. I mean, it's not like being a grunt and spending weeks out in the bush. They get more than their share of action. Then it may be quiet for a while. Most of the time when we fly into a zone we take fire of some type. Mostly automatic weapons, other times mortar fire. Seems someone always flies back with bullet holes in their bird. That's just the way it is." TC took another sip of beer.

"Wait a minute" Rubio said, "we go on a few General chase which are fucking fantastic or nothing happens."

"Ya that's what I said." TC spoke up, "most of the time we take fire, other times we don't."

Sean asked, "what's a General chase?" Rubio grabbed another beer and with a slur said, "that's when some fucking General wants to get out of the command post and see what the front line troops are doing. Looks good on their record. Anyway, we ride them around, two birds, one for the General and a second for back up in case of trouble. Most times we fly down to Da Nang and wait for the General while he meets with his staff. We get to hit the PX down there till the General comes back. It's a nice run and counts as a mission. A real tit run."

The heat of the day was replaced with a wet, warm, dampness of evening. The beer tent got a bit louder as more Marines started to feel the effects of many beers consumed. Much of the conversation was talk of the days mission or bragging of hometown sports teams. A few fights were averted by level heads that didn't drink as much. Combatants ended as friends with arms around the shoulder of the other. Reasons for any argument were long forgotten, replaced by calls for another round of beer. Some guys were carried out by their friends who could walk better or at least navigate their way back to the hootch.

Sean found his hootch, it was quiet except for the sound of snoring coming from his hootch mates. Sean took his boots off and pulled his blanket over him and fell into a drunken sleep.

The next day sounds of movement woke Sean. "Morning sleepy, how ya feeling?"

Sean looked out one eye to see Camron putting his boots on.

"You had quite a night for a FNG, how ya feeling?"

Sean struggled to open his eyes, blinked a few times, raised his head to look around the hootch. Half of the guys were already gone and the rest were getting dressed.

"Well, I've felt better. Why the hell did I drink so many beers?" Sean heard himself mumble.

"Well you actually didn't drink that much, maybe six and a half. It's not how much you drank, it was when you did it. New to the country, its been hot all day, you're somewhat dehydrated, lots of reasons. Of course the beer didn't help, but you'll get use to the heat and drinking. Look at me, I drank way more than you and I only feel a bit hungry" Lil' John finished putting his shirt on. "Ya wanna get some chow? Hell your already dressed , just put your boots on."

Sean looked down and saw he was still in yesterday fatigues. With a scratch of his head he pushed the green wool blanket off himself and got his boots on. The screen door to their hootch had just shut behind them when Lil' John started in. " Guess you and I are on the same shit detail, cleaning out the shit barrels and burning them."

"WHAT? What do ya mean shit detail, Gunny assigned me to the overhaul crew."

Lil' John smiled, "ya well that was yesterday and Gunny does that with all the newbies. We have to take our turn. We're replacing NFG's that came in last month. Their time is up and so is ours, so to speak." Sean kicked the dirt, "aw man that sucks, I didn't come here to burn shit. What the hell did they give me a rife for, to shoot shit?"

"Well, the shit burning is the good news."

"What the hell do you mean good news?"

We, that be, you and me, get to go on patrols tonight to ambush Charlie. Last night's beer drinking will be the last for a while, 'cause we be ambushing. And that's the facts Jack."

"Christ Camron, this keeps getting better and better."

Sean held the door to the mess hall while Camron got two mess trays.

"Clever devices don't you think? Instead of dishes we eat off a piece of metal with four indented compartments for food, nothing to break here," Camron said as he handed a tray to Sean.

Breakfast was the usual for the Marine Corps, eggs with SOS poured all over them and burnt toast.

Sean looked down at the SOS and eggs and felt his stomach churn.

"Don't look at it, just eat it quickly, Camron said " salt and pepper helps."

Camron and Sean found a seat over near Ford.

"Hey Ford."

"Hey guys. I see you got the house special of the day. Can't these guys cook any other fucking thing, even the eggs are fake. Whoever invented powered eggs should be shot, or worse yet, made to eat them," Ford pushed his half eaten food tray away.

"I don't know Ford, once you get past the look, the smell, and the taste they're not so bad."

Ford and Sean looked at Camron at the same time. Sean spoke up.

"You've been here too long, you're taste buds have no taste, they don't call it shit on a shingle for nothing."

"Nope, just making the best of a bad situation," Camron said as he shoved back another mouthful of SOS.

Sean turned to Ford. "Guess I won't be joining you in the overhaul hanger, they put Camron and me on the shit detail."

"Well I got it a little bit better, I start KP this afternoon and turn out for patrol tonight"

Ford said. "All FNG's get on detail the first month, Gunnys orders." Ford stool up, grabbed his metal food tray and started to head for the exit. "Catch you guys tonight for patrol."

Sean turned to Camron, "we're on patrol tonight also."

"Nope" Camron replied. "You replaced me on patrol. I was on it for the last two months. FNG's replace those already on it. When we get some newbies then you'll get replaced."

Sean looked surprised. "Shit! I thought you and I would be on it together. Was hoping there would be someone that I knew with experience. Someone I could hang with on patrol. Now it will be Ford and I with no fucking idea what the hell's going on."

Camron looked up from his food. "Fucking eh. That's how it works. Newbies replace those before them and so on. It won't be bad, just stick in the center of the patrol, watch others. Just don't do anything stupid and don't make a sound. You'll do alright. We only came up on the VC a few times. They scattered before we could get set up. Best case scenario is you lose some sleep." Camron grabbed his empty tray and got up. Sean followed Camron to the wash area to clean their trays and placed them on a table.

"Catch ya later Sean. I'm going to the tool tent and talk with TC."

"Ya, see ya at the hootch, Camron."

Chapter 8

Nineteen Marines were milling around by the time Sean arrived at the Armory hootch. It was slightly past 1800 hours and still hot. Those gathered had sweat marks on their shirts. Some Marines were wiping their faces with their covers.

Lt. Dowswell came out of the Armory hootch. "OK ladies form up." At that command the Marines began lining up beside each other. Each extended out their left arm at a right angle from their body. The next Marine stood at the finger tip of the Marine to the right. This provided equal space between each person. When everyone was satisfied with the spacing they put their arms down. There were four rows of five men each, twenty men in all.

The Marines were equipped with a semi-automatic gas operated M-14 rife. Once the trigger was pulled, the rifle would fire and eject a round using the spent gas from the previous round fired. Every man had four magazines of 7.62 mm steel jacket NATO approved rounds. Each magazine contained twenty rounds. The men wore a camouflaged helmet, a flak vest and a web belt holding the four magazines. The twentieth Marine was armed with an M-60 machine gun. The M-60 was a gas operated belt feed weapon. It would fire 500-600 rounds per minute with a muzzle velocity of 2800 ft/sec. It used the same 7.62 rounds as the M-14 and operated on the same principle to fire.

The armory Corporal was going around and handing out strips of electrician tape to each person. "Men I want you to wrap the tape given to you around your two dog tags. This will prevent the tags from jingling like a cow bell as you walk. No sense giving away our position to Charlie."

Sean turned to Ford. "I wonder what the little notch on each dog tag is for?"

A Marine in back of Sean spoke out. "That's in case you get killed. They take one dog tag and jam the notch between your teeth. This identifies who you are. The other dog tag goes with the Sergeant so later they can keep track of who's been killed."

"So much for keeping up on my dental work," Sean muttered.

Ford turned to Sean. "What do you care, your not gonna be smiling."

Lt. Dowswell spoke. "At ease. We move out at 1900 hrs. For those of you who still think of themselves as civilians that's 7:00PM. Don't go grabassing and wander off."

Lt. Dowswell walked back into the hootch.

"Shit Ford, you worried about possibly getting hit?"

"Look Sean, let's walk behind that big guy. He's a bigger target and might block a round."

"Man that's cold Ford."

"It might be, but ya gotta think of looking out for number one."

"Damn Ford 'am I number one or two?"

Ford turned and smiled at Sean.

At 1900 hrs Lt. Dowswell came out of the hootch.

"Listen up. We're gonna be heading out to my right and head down to the perimeter. Once we pass the perimeter keep a distance of 15 to 20 feet from the guy in front of you. In case we take fire, not too many will get hit. Keep the same distance, and don't, I repeat don't, spread out. I'll be in the lead with the Sergeant. The Corporal will be at the rear to make sure we're not strung out. There are a number of rice paddies we have to cross, which means for a short while we'll be exposed. That would be a good time for Charlie to hit us. If we take fire don't jump into the rice paddies. Just hit the deck and slide in the water. Charlie has a habit of putting punji sticks in the paddies for you to fall on."

"Hey Lieutenant, whats a punji stick?" A Marine in the back asked.

"Good question. A punji stick is nothing more than a piece of sharpened bamboo stuck in the ground. You go ditty bopping along and step into a hole or jump into a rice paddy and it stabs ya. Those things are sharp! Worse thing is, Charlie stuffs the punji stick with Buffalo shit. That shit is shoved into your wound and can cause a mean infection. One injured guy causes two more to carry him. This limits the effectiveness of a patrol. So just be careful and always be alert! Also, once we set up an ambush no talking, don't so much as slap a mosquito. Sound travels far at night and one sound compromises our position."

Sean thought back to his basic training at Marine recruit depot at Parris Island, South Carolina. He remembered his drill instructor coming down on any recruit who killed a mosquito with a slap.

"Why are you killing my mosquito fuckface?" The drill instructor jumped on the recruit. "You don't kill my mosquitoes! Get down and give me 30 pushups scumbag! If I see one more of you girls kill a mosquito the whole platoon does pushups for an hour. When you see a mosquito on another guy in front of you blow at it! The guy behind you will do the same for you. One alternate is to let the fucking thing eat! One mosquito killed can get you shot in combat."

The sound of Lt. Dowswell voice snapped Sean back. "We'll be out most of the night so check your canteen for water. If you need water fill'em now. We move out in fifteen minutes."

Some Marines went to top off their canteens.

Once the patrol was ready Lt. Dowswell gave the sign.

"Alright in a single file, move out!"

With the Sergeant and Lt. Dowswell in the lead, the patrol headed to the perimeter.

Once the patrol reached the perimeter the Lieutenant. stopped. "Men, chamber a round and put your weapon on safety. From here on out, until we get back, keep your mouth shut! Stay alert and watch my signals. OK lock and load."

Ford was the ninth in line to pass the perimeter wire. Sean was right behind. Ford looked back at Sean, pointed to the big guy in front of Ford and gave Sean a thumbs up. Sean just smiled.

The terrain surrounding the Phu Bai area was mostly flat and cleared. Absent was the heavy jungle most expected of Vietnam. The country, like most, had various types of terrain, some flat, some jungle and others mountainous. The Phu Bai countryside area was flat with lots of rice paddies. An area could be laced with many plots of rice paddies, similar to a checkerboard. Each paddy was a square of ground surrounded on four sides by a mount of dirt that prevented the water from running off. Rows of rice plants ran the length of each paddy like rows of corn. Each plant stood a foot or more out of the water, water as dark as the dirt which held it in. The Vietnamese fertilized the rice paddies with water buffalo dung.

The patrol had been walking for an hour, crossing several rice paddies on top of the dirt mounds. Each Marine made sure they kept their distance form the guy in front of them, just as the Lieutenant instructed. Effort was made to step in the exact footprint of the guy in front, to insure no one steps on a booby trap. The patrol cautiously made its way off the rice paddies and into the bush for one additional mile. Lt. Dowswell raised a fist in the air to signal the patrol to halt. He motioned those behind to kneel. The word was passed back to spread out and find cover. The ambush was to be set. Sean found a shrub with a clear view. He laid down and watched as others carefully selected a suitable site for cover and view. The moon was high with some clouds. Not a bad time for an ambush. There was some light to outline any one walking but with some cloud cover to hide the Marines. Time seemed to creep by as they waited in ambush. Sean immediately felt the onslaught of mosquitoes, thick as dust. It felt like every crawling insect found the need to explore Sean. It took unimaginable effort not to swat them. Sean's' mind went back to his training of not slapping the buzzing mosquitoes. He knew the next day he'd be covered in mosquitoes bites. No sense using repellant because the scent could be smelled in the dense foliage. A foreign scent would be a dead give away against the natural smell of green vegetation. Sean carefully checked his watch and was surprised they had only been in ambush for a few hours. It was slightly past ten which meant he'd be lying here for another four hours. Unknown to the patrol there would be an eclipse of the moon that night. If things seemed dark in the absence of any light pollution, things were to get more dark. At midnight the moon was at its highest point. Sean felt an unquenchable thirst. He realized he was breathing a bit harder due to anxiety. Reaching down his right side, Sean felt for his canteen. Slowly he undid the two metal snaps of the green canvas pouch which held his canteen. As he started to remove the metal canteen from its metal case he could hear the scrapping of sand that was wedged inside his canteen cover. In the darkness of night the noise appeared loud. Sean thought best and decided not to remove it. His thirst grew intense yet he knew he really was not thirsty, it was just the sensation of thirst. The buzzing mosquitoes, crawling insects and sense of thirst was unbearable. Sean knew he had to bear up under the elements, nothing was worth giving their position away. The smell of green foliage and dirt permeated his nostrils. It was an earthy, natural smell of vegetation. From a distance the aroma of buffalo dung whiffed thru the air. He knew a farm or village was not far. A place the VC would use for refuge during the night.

The sky began to darken. Sean looked up and saw the moon slowly going into an eclipse. This was a time to be extra alert for sounds. Noise would be his only reference to any activity. Any one walking about now would go unnoticed in the darkness of the eclipse. The patrol waited out the eclipse and after a short period the moon again began to show itself. When the moon was totally free from the eclipse Sean did a double take on the rice paddy forty meters away. He felt his eyes were playing tricks on him. His first thought was that the bushes were moving. As trained for night operation, Sean looked briefly away and back again to where the bushes were. His heart jumped. They were not bushes but men walking along the rice paddy. Charlie had miscalculated using the eclipse as cover. Half of their patrol made it off the paddy, but half were still exposed. Sean pushed his head deeper into the ground, his breathing increased, his mind raced. What should I do? No sooner had he thought those words when the sounds of rifle fire erupted. He wasn't sure where it was coming from or who was doing it, his reaction was to press further into the dirt. Shouts of "fire" came from his right. He recognized the voice of Lt. Dowswell. Sean slowly looked up and saw that the whole patrol was firing at the walking bushes. To Sean it almost looked like watching fireworks on the fourth of July. White flashes lit the area. The sound of an M60 machine gun pierced the night's silence. Sean realized that the white flashes were coming from the direction of the VC patrol, breaking branches and ricocheting off the rocks and dirt all around. Again he pressed his face into the dirt. He felt if he could just lay there he'd survive the moment. Automatic weapon fire and grenades blowing up continued as Sean hugged the ground.

He knew he couldn't just lay there and let the others fight while he was safe. He thought of his family back home unaware of his situation. Maybe they were having tea while watching TV, maybe they were asleep. All he knew was that he might die tonight and his family had no idea. Sean felt anger, a surge of rage. No one is gonna do this to me or my family. Sean pressed the safety off his rifle and started to fire rapidly. His first magazine was empty and Sean was loading the second before he realized what he was doing. He stopped firing, and started to see the outlines of Charlie. He didn't know how many were there, just that they were firing at the patrol. There was one figure Sean did see. A figure slightly outlined by the moon. He carefully sighted down his rifle. Taking careful aim. He slowly drew the trigger back, slowly, very slowly, careful not to jerk the trigger, just as he was trained in boot camp. The distance figure disappeared quickly, no longer in his sights. Sean looked in amazement. "Shit"! He rolled over on his back holding the rifle close to him like a girlfriend. He was angry, frustrated. Waited too long, should of fired quicker, dammit!

All these thoughts raced though his mind. More pissed at himself than anything, he rolled back over and began to fire. Taking the moment to focus on where the light flashes were coming from and firing in that direction He was alone in his own world now, the only sound he heard was that of his rifle. Each round fired had a distant sound, almost like noise in a tunnel. The sound rolled slowly after each discharge. Sean could almost see his bullets leave the rifle muzzle heading towards its target. The slow rolling distance noise kept up.

He felt a heavy blow on his right shoulder. "Fuck I've been hit," Sean rolled onto his back waiting to feel the pain. He looked up and stared at the Sergeant looking down at him. All he could see was the Sergeants lips moving. Then Sean started to hear a voice to match the lips. "What's your fucking problem Marine! I said stop firing. It's over, listen up when you're given an order!" Sean realized he wasn't hit. The force on his shoulder was the Sergeants boot knocking him off balance. Sean slowly looked around as if he just realized where he was. He was not alone. Sean slumped back into the dirt, breathing heavy. He closed his eyes and reopened them. Others were starting to move out. Sean looked over to where Ford was standing. Ford motioned with both hands up as if to say, what the fuck were you doing? Not knowing what happened, Sean got up and followed the others as they marched off. Sean heard Ford call to him in almost a whisper. "What the hell happened to you? You were firing in a knelling position exposing yourself. When it was over you kept firing, The Sergeant yelled at you twice."

"I guess I don't know, didn't hear anything, just kept firing." Sean said.

"Hey Sean, by the way nice shot!"

"What do you mean!"

"Nice shot. You nailed Charlie good with that first shot, he went down quick. You're one mean Ugly Angel."

Sean was trying to process what Ford said.., nailed Charlie? It began to sink in that the distant figure didn't disappear, didn't get away. Sean didn't take too long in shooting as he thought his aim was right on. Slowly as he pulled the trigger, the rifle went off without his knowing it, just the way it was suppose to happen. He had no idea that he hit anything. As the patrol made its way back to the perimeter, Sean thought about that distant figure. Did I kill him, did I wound him? Did he have a family, what did he look like. How many others did I hit just firing? Sean just hoped that whoever that figure was, he was only wounded. That the figure would eventually go home and see his family again. Just like Sean wanted to do.

Chapter 9

Gunny Simmons was hunched over his desk. A green towel was laid out before him. On that towel was a field stripped Colt 1911 .45 caliber hand gun. The .45 cal. is a single action, semi-automatic, magazine-fed, recoil-operated pistol chambered for the Colt 45. The gun was the long time standard sidearm for the United States Marine Corps. The Gunny was cleaning the gun using a thin wire brush to clean inside the guns barrel. A cloth was nearby to wipe excess gun oil off the weapon. The door to his hootch opened and Sean walked in.
"Hey Gunny, Sgt. Bonville said you wanted to see me."
"Ya Sean come on in. How ya doin?"
It had been two weeks since the patrol and Sean was keeping to himself. Moments of that night were still fresh in his mind. The main issue for Sean was why he zoned out while firing. If this happened again, would he be aware of action around him? Was he so focused that he had tunnel vision? Doubt was swirling in his head.
"Heard you have a new name the mean Ugly Angel!" Sean thought 'great,... new to the outfit and already I have a nickname'.
"So hows the shit detail going?"
"Well its not my favorite activity and surely not what I thought I'd be doing."
Gunny put down his pistol, "Ya, it's not exactly what I wanted my Marines doing, but until we get flushing stateside type commodes we do our best. Believe it or not it is a valuable job. During the Revolutionary War and the Civil War, the lack of proper hygiene from open latrines sometimes killed more of our troops than the enemy did."
Sean looked down and then back up, "I suppose but it's not something I want to write home about."

Gunny chuckled, "no I suppose it's not exactly a John Wayne type moment. Look Sean the reason I called you in was I'm getting word that you're still living your patrol from the other week. Some said you mention it in passing then go to the beer tent and get drunk. Also you've been keeping to yourself. Drinking and isolation are not a good combination. So what's goin' on?"

"Gunny I get what happened that night. We go on patrol, set up an ambush and hope to catch Charlie snooping around. I get it that we may end up shooting at them or them at us. I get it. That night I was so focused on shooting I lost awareness of my surroundings. Hell, the Sergeant had to yell at me twice to stop shooting. Charlie coulda' come behind me and hit us from behind. I might of put the whole patrol in jeopardy. Guess I feel I just lost it."

"Hell Sean you're not the first Marine who questioned if they put their patrol in harms way. Just think of the Sergeant and Lieutenant leading the patrol. Every decision they make could get one of their guys wounded or killed. Maybe its natural to question what we do. But once we make and execute that decision don't go back and second guess that decision. Based on information at hand we make a decision. Now sometimes that decision might not of been the optimal choice. But it was made and carried out. No one has the mind of Solomon, we will make mistakes. The best we can do is learn from our decision and trust that the next time we improve on our choices. In the heat of battle or at times under duress the decision we make is what we live with. Now I'm a career Marine, not a politician. I believe being a Marine has a more honorable status. A military person serves to protect. A politician more often than not is advancing their position. This whole Vietnam thing wasn't caused by the military. It was caused by those politicians. We're the tools politicians use to pursue their policies. Ya ever see a politician out on the front line? Hell no, they're well insulated by the troops on the front line. We Marines will cover each others back, and ya we'll stumble at times, but not because of our intent. Your intent that night was to protect your patrol. Whether you knew it, doesn't matter. The training you received prepared you for combat. Even the best troops can only hope not to fall, not to stumble. We cover one another and trust everyone comes back safely. You're no different from those who started the Marine Corps back on Nov 10th 1775 at Tuns Tavern in Philadelphia. Did ya know the Marine Corps is older than the United States? For over a 192 years the Marine Corps has been called into action time and time again, from Tripoli until now. We have a proud history of backing up what we say. Hell, we not only look good in our dress blues, but we can kick ass! Many Marines can have second thoughts on their action in combat but no one can question their intent.

Sean you'll do alright, so will the other guys in the outfit. Do your job and learn from what you do. Stay true to yourself and your fellow Marines. Just don't beat yourself up
about it. Got it?"

"Ya Gunny. I'll do my best but........"

"But what?"

" Well I shot that guy that night...."

"Hold on Sean. Ya did what ya had'da do! You don't think for one minute that if given the opportunity Charlie wouldn't done the same to you? Hell they were firing at you guys! This is not a party, it's war plain and simple. They shot at us, we shot at them. The only question is who's the better shot."

"I know Gunny. And every thing you said is right on. Guess it was a bit too much, too soon. After that night, being on the shit detail doesn't seem so bad." The Gunny smiled

"Good , now get the hell outta here and let me get some work done. If nothing else, I can put this pistol back together."

Chapter 10

"Hey Sean over here." Sean's' eyes were still adjusting to the darken interior of the beer tent but he did recognize the voice. Ford and five others were at a corner table. The top of the table was already covered with empty beer cans.

"Damn, what time did you guys start drinking?" Sean said to Ford.

"Well, Sgt. Bonville went to Da Nang, we finished working on YL-43 and decided to take the rest of the afternoon off."

Sean looked at Ford, "ya but what time was that?"

"Oh just about noon chow." Ford and the others laughed and slapped each other on the back. "Well you guys are doing just fine." Sean raised up a beer can and the others followed suit. "Hey Sean, give us one of those Irish toasts of yours," Ford yelled.

Sean looked up for a second and pondered. Then he raised his beer can, " May the good lord keep Sgt. Bonville far away from us and may he never come back!"

Everyone broke out into more laughter and took a swig of beer.

Rubio spoke up. "Tell me Sean. I heard that you and Gunny had a nice talk about the ambush a few weeks back. How did that go?"

"Well he gave some good advice and sent me on my way."

"That's it?" Camron asked.

"Ya, it was the same old bullshit they mouth to get you back into the game."

Rubio said, "if it came from the Gunny it ain't no bullshit. Listen to what he says, it'll keep you out of trouble." Sean put down his beer and scratched his head, "Ya I suppose it just caught me off gua....." No sooner had Sean spoke when three loud explosions went off, one after the other.

"INCOMING! HIT THE BUNKERS!"

There was a large exodus from the beer tent as Marines scrambled to find cover. The three explosions were followed by six more. Sean and his group found shelter in a bunker next to the beer tent.

"God damn mortar rounds. Charlie has us zeroed in but he still can't hit us" Rubio yelled.

Each mortar round had a low thump as it left the tube, followed by a "voormph" as it exploded. The movies have it all wrong when it comes to simulating a military explosion. It sounds nothing like the movies, no crackle, no crack. Just a dull loud noise followed by a wave of air pushing you. Most guys were injured by the rocks and debris the mortar round explosions showered the area with. Even small pebbles can cause damage when traveling at high velocity.

All of a sudden it was very quiet. It was over as quickly as it began. Men shook their head as if to get the noise out of their ears. In the distance someone yelled "all clear."

One by one Marines came out of the bunkers, brushing dirt off their fatigues and out of their hair.

"Damn I hope they didn't spill my beers," Rubio smiled as he walked towards the beer tent. "Well another day in paradise."

Except for the mess made by guys running out of the beer tent, everything was intact. Chairs were put up right and tables put back in their place.

"So Sean you were saying?" Rubio took a swig of beer and wiped his mouth with the back of his hand.

"Well nothing really, Gunny just pointed out the obvious. That was it, I left and the Gunny went back to cleaning his pistol."

"Ya that be the Gunny, short and to the point," Camron said as he got up to get more beer.

It was a long night of drinking and the Marines helped each other as they staggered back to the hootch, each taking turns guiding the way in the dark. The next day was a bitch as the temp hit 98 degrees by 0700. Beer sweat oozed out of the pores of the drinking buddies from the previous night.

"Holy shit Camron, I can get drunk on my sweat alone," Sean said as he wiped his face with his cover.

"Ice cold Pepsi!"

Sean turned his head in puzzlement, "what?"

"Ice cold Pepsi.." Camron lifted a sandbag he had filled. "That's what I take to mend last nights drinking and the heat of today. It seems to work better than water at first. Then I followed up with lot'sa a water during the day. Helps makes ya right with the universe."

"You guys do that all the time?" Sean said as he shoveled another load of sand into a bag.

Camron stopped and leaned against the half completed bunker. "Well like I said before, only a few things to do here in 'Nam; work on the chopper, drink or get killed. Not necessarily in that order. Once you get your own bird you'll be flying all the time and getting shot at. Then it's a matter of time before ya get shot. Some stats indicate that a chopper gunner has a life expectancy of 30 seconds in a hot landing zone. That's why they say 30 in the Z. Its about as much time you want to be in a LZ. Now if you heard a mortar round the life expectancy drops to 8 seconds. About enough time we figure it takes Charlie to zero in on you. And that's if you hear the mortar round. So ya more than three times as likely to get killed than the infantry because of all the hot LZs ya go into. But who knows, plenty of grunts would argue that point. But I figure everyone's life expectancy is counted is seconds. An AK-47 round can reach over 2000 ft per seconds. So it doesn't matter what ya do, your time is limited to seconds in a hot LZ."

"How the fuck do you know all that shit" Sean quizzed.

"I read a lot, try it sometime," Camron smiled.

Sean made a face, "who the hell wants to fly at all if ya just gonna get wasted by a mortar round, Christ no wonder you guys drink so much."

Chapter 11

Hour upon hour, day by day little seemed to change for those not on flight status. The only consistent element was the hot sticky climate. Marines walked around with sweat soaked t-shirts or jungle fatigues with the sleeves cut off or rolled up. Always adjusting the shirt so as to pull it away from sweated bodies. It was as if some one poured syrup inside a shirt and walked around on a hot day. Clothing stuck to the skin. Humidity was the culprit and it never let up. If not flying, the day was spent on keeping aging helicopters in an up status. Sand got into everything, so rotor heads had to be constantly greased, and the chopper cleaned of loose debris. Bullet holes were mended. Some choppers looked like they had a spotted paint job where all the bullet holes were covered.   Choppers damaged by Charlie's ground fire or mortar rounds had around the clock repairs to be up and running. Day in and day out chopper crews came back exhausted from 8 to 10 hours of flying in and out of hot LZ's, that were suppose to be friendly. Ground crews did a quick repair and the chopper was ready for another mission.

At night the temp wasn't as bad but the humidity hung like a curtain. Squads of Marines assigned to perimeter control would muster and get checked out for patrols. Most patrols would set up an ambush for four to five hours, just waiting for Charlie to make an appearance. Patrols would eventually make their way back inside the perimeter. Marines would be dismissed, store their gear, head for some hot chow and back to working on the choppers. Flight crews who worked half the night getting their bird ready would be preparing for that day's mission. Getting enough ammunition just it case, checking out the operations of the M-60, plus other vital equipment. The temp would be back up high early and most

Marines would be sweating already by 0800. If ya weren't flying, the monotony of the day dampened your spirits. Some duties, or meaningless details were meant to keep Marines active, it sometimes caused discontent. Yet, a bitching Marine was a good Marine, according to some Sergeant. It kept their mind active and they were united in their bitching. A blind eye was given to all the drinking, it was a release for many. In between the work, patrols, flying and drinking there was the constant mortar rounds or rocket fire from Charlie. Filling sandbags for bunkers was a second occupation for many. No one wanted to be caught with a poorly constructed bunker.

Some Marines slept in the bunkers at night instead of inside their hootch's. The bunker not only provided protection but it was much cooler inside. Sometimes they shared the bunker with Mr. Rat. The rats in 'Nam could be as big as a cat, and always hungry. More than one Marine had been bitten while sleeping. It paid to sleep in the middle of the bunker if possible. Some farm kid said "rats move along the wall". That was dispelled when a rat ran across a guy's face. The little foot of the rat slipped inside the guys mouth. So much for farm wisdom. Every so often there was one or two rat carcases outside a bunker with a .45 cal bullet hole in it.

Marines kept as busy as possible with any duty. Even the hated shit detail was a relief from the boredom. Any job or activity kept one's mind occupied from the boredom of day to day same o' same o'. Grunts in the field were bored at times. Guarding a hill that no one was interested in at the time. Yet there was always the knowledge that 'Charlie' would want it sooner or later. But until then, the work duties were the same. Day after day. Support duty was lackluster but essential.

Between the every day duties and perimeter patrols, many sought refuge at night in the beer tent. Sean, Ford, Camron, TC and others washed away the days sand and heat with lots of cold beer. The conversations at times could get philosophical, girls in the states had a saying, "girls say yes to boys who say no." Many guys got 'Dear John' letters from their girlfriends. Seems separation makes the heart go wander. Married guys could find a divorce letter in the mail. It just appeared that we were fighting and support from the states was thin. In the beer tent all we had was each other. The bond between Marines grew as war protesters ran around college campuses. The talk was usually about what we'd do when we got back home. Rubio brought the new Dodge Charger from a home town car dealer. It was parked in his parents garage. All he wanted to do was go home, get a job and drive his new Charger. TC wanted to go back to college and get a teaching degree. Ford wanted to join his father's plumbing business in Cleveland Ohio. Sean was up in the air as to what he'd do, maybe enroll in college, maybe travel for a year. All were in agreement that they never wanted to talk or hear about 'Nam again. Politicians lie, and people in the states were unsure about there feelings on 'Nam. The newspapers gave the idea we were losing. Losing! Hell we were kicking ass, doing what we were trained to do, then we get yelled at for being in a uniform at home. Ya we bonded with our distrust of those back in the world; college kids, politicians, and people in general. Felt like they sent us to 'Nam to fight a war and then turned their back on us. So we'd look our for each other, the hell with everyone else. As the beer was thrown back more guys would bitch about our dilemma. Sent to fight a war with no support. But we did the job and did it well.

Some drunk guys started singing;

"We're a bunch of Bastards, scum of the
world born in a whore house, pissed on,
shit on, fucked all over the universe. Of
all the bunch of bastards, we are
the worst, we are from 362, the scum

of the universe.

Everone downed their beer and threw the empty can outsize. TC yelled,
"if no one will support us, we'll support ourselves.
    The next day, many were hung over but at their station. The day
would begin again, sand, heat, endless details which seemed to be useless.
Boredom is a Marines worse enemy. But just when you thought you
couldn't take another day of boredom, things would heat up. HQ came
down with a rush operation. All choppers had to be up and running. No
one got any sleep. Each bird had to be fully operational and armed
accordingly. A large operation involving a large troop insertion was on
the schedule. This is what the troops were waiting for, action! The
opportunity to perform the duties they had been trained for, duties
instilled in them from days of monotonous practice. This is where the day
to day activity paid off.

Chapter 12

The early morning of an operation was almost poetic. Flight crews mustered up early and went down to the flight line. Support crews had choppers fueled waiting for the occupants. Once the Pilots and crew received their instructions they headed to their assigned bird.

The crew chief and left door gunner checked out the M-60. They squared away and tied down any loose equipment. A good pre-flight, then the choppers were cranked up and running. The ground crew would give instruction to the pilots to roll. One by one the choppers would taxi out of their protected bunkers and follow one another to the taxi area. The lead bird would taxi onto the runway, building up rotor speed. The chopper would start rolling forward, increasing forward momentum. The tail of the bird would lift and tilt the chopper slightly forward and with a final upward pull by the pilot on the collective stick the bird gradually was airborne. Those that took off would circle the base waiting for choppers still on the ground to take off and join the others. During the grouping of helicopters in the air, the ground crew was hustling about removing wheel chokes from waiting birds, filling up those low on fuel, doing whatever it took to get the entire squadron in the air. It reminded one mid-west boy of a flock of geese heading south. The sky was full of helicopters and the sounds of their Pratt and Whitney 18 cylinder engines permeated the air. Eventually all were airborne. The lead bird would strike off towards the northwest, with the rest following behind. They headed for the assigned LZ, picking up US Marines.

Before long the area was quiet again. All operational birds were airborne and heading in harms way. It would be seven to eight hours before results of the troop insertion would be known. The entire base settled down into waiting mode. Those Marines on the ground would go about their assigned duties. It was now all a waiting game. Who would make it back , who wouldn't. There was always the possibility of a ten percent mortality rate on an intense mission, other missions did better. Yet it was a given that there would be a lot of damage, as well as casualties. It was a numbers game. You throw as much into the operation as possible, hoping for a successful outcome. How much damage there would be was anybodies guess. Ten percent was a rate from past missions. It's just a matter of waiting it out till they came back.

Chapter 13

It was about 1700 hrs when the first sound of chopper blades was detected. Sean and Ford came out of the overhaul hanger and looked Northwest to the whoop, whoop sound of the chopper blade cutting through the air. A small dark spot in the sky got larger and individual choppers could be seen. As they flew closer the sound of the chopper engines grew louder. The lead bird circled first down wind, then cross wind and then on to final approach for runway 01. Others followed suit, creating a conga line extending 5 miles back. Gunny Sgt. Simmons was the first one out of the the flight shack, trailed by the operations officer. Three ambulances came racing across the runway, siren blaring away. Right behind them was the crash crew in a large white truck with men, in white fire protected suits, hanging on the back .
As the birds got closer, the engines of one helicopter sputtered, black smoke belching out of the engine compartment.

The lead bird flown by Capt DeWay was the first off the runway and pulled into it's bunker. The damn chopper had more holes than swiss cheese. Another chopper stopped shot of the bunkers, shuting down quickly the crew and pilots ran from the helicopter getting just far enough away before it burst into flames. The crash crew trucks descended quickly on the burning chopper, spraying flame retardant on the burning aircraft. Other aircraft in the group upon landing pulled into their respective bunkers.

Gunny Simmons was over talking to Capt DeWay. "Hell Gunny, they were waiting for us! The coordinates S2 gave us were behind Charlies line. We got the troops out fast and they were taking fire. We lost three birds, two in the zone, no one got out. The third crashed 25 miles out from here. Capt. Bergman and his crew flew cover to watch for survivors. Doesn't look good. Probably two dozen choppers are riddled with bullet holes."

"Damn it" Simmons yelled. "Again with the crappy intel. That zone was suppose to be good for troop insertion."

"Well Gunny, even with our losses I feel real bad for the grunts. They're having a bitching fight. I suspect before long we'll get beaucoup emergency medevac calls. Wouldn't be surprised at a high casualties rate. I'm gonna get some chow and get ready for those calls. Gunny we lost three good crews. The shit is hitting the fan."

Capt DeWay walked off to the flight shack with the co-pilot.

The gunny saw the door gunner and crew chief sitting by the chopper, head down and smoking a cigarette. "Hey Marines, looks like a bad one. Leave the chopper for later, go get some chow and coffee."

The door gunner turned around as he was walking away. "Gunny I don't want to fly anymore. He choked on his emotions. I'm done. I'll go on patrols, be on shit details, work on the birds, but I'm not flying! I rotate home in three weeks. I'm too short for this." With that the gunner continued walking. The Gunny slightly shook his head. Lost another one he thought.

Ch 14

The screen door to the S2 shack was kicked open with a loud bang. In the doorway stood the imposing figure of the Gunny. "OK which one of you fuckers drew up the LZ coordinates to that operation?"

As the highest ranking NCO, Corporal Howl slowly stood up looking intimidated. When the Gunny was pissed, it was not a good thing for anyone. The Gunny was not prone to outburst, but when he did, Marines got out of his way. Howls eyes darted around the room looking for some support. Those in the S2 shack averted their eyes. Howl was on his own. In a somewhat quivering voice Howl spoke. "Gunny those coordinates came down from Headquarters in Da Nang. We just passed them along to the pilots."

"Well hell, didn't anyone check the coordinates before issuing them? Maybe see exactly where it put the LZ. LIKE BEHIND VC LINES!!!!"

Lt. Janhs hearing the loud shouting came out from his office. "Wait a minute Gunny, calm down. No need to get excited."

"No need to get excited? Hell! I've got four confirmed dead, maybe eight. Plus another half dozen shot up. Maybe six to ten birds out of commission and you're concerned about me being excited? I passed that point right after the choppers landed. You and your crew better get their shit together or there will be some major ass chewing!" The Gunny turned and left as quickly as he came in.

"Jeez Lieutenant, he shouldn't talk to you like that, you're an officer," Howl blurted out. "Ya I know Howl, I'm an officer, graduate of Annapolis no less. But the Gunny has more time on the shitter than I do in the Marine Corps. I found out a short while back that an officer may have rank but it's guys like the Gunny who run the Corps. You take your Marines with three stripes and above away and you have no Corps. I have no intention of going up against the Gunny. Besides he's not angry at us, he's frustrated. He just had some of his men shot up, some killed. I don't blame him for how he's feeling. He's thinking of his men. Ya can't fault him for that."

Out on the flight line the wounded were carried off and sent to triage for care. Later they would be flown to the Da Nang hospital for indepth medical care. Small groups of men were assessing the damage to the choppers riddled with bullets. The Gunny and his NCO staff made notes of which helicopters would be attended to first. Gunny's voice could be heard barking out instructions. "OK, lets get the least damaged in first and and repaired. I need these birds up and running by tomorrow. We have missions to fly and I'm not reporting that we can't do our job". The Gunny started to turn away when Sgt. Bonville spoke up. "Say Gunny, it's gonna take more than a day to fix these birds. Maybe the time line is a bit short?"

"Look Bonville, we'll work all night if we have to. We have people out there depending on us to support them. Bring them ammo, medevac them, pick up emergency recon extractions. We don't have the luxury of time, because they sure as hell don't. I know I set the bar high, but the men will perform. Now do your job or I'll get someone else to do it and you'll be supervising shit details. We're in a war zone man, we're in a war zone!" With that the Gunny walked away.

Bonville knew the Gunny was right. Hell, he was always right. The Gunny knew his shit. A quick sigh and Bonville yelled out, "OK, Brown, Sean, Ford and the rest of you start pulling those choppers over to the hanger for repairs. We're gonna pull an all nighter." Sean and Ford looked at each other, in unison they said, "Damn!"

Ch 15

The last of the six choppers were parked by the hanger. Sean leaned up against one and wiped his face. "Ya know Ford this all sucks and it's sad for those who got hurt. The squadron is gonna be short of crews. This may be our chance to get into action." Ford looked at Sean in astonishment. "Are you shitting me? All those guys got shot up, some killed and all you think about is being the next ones? What'da ya have a death wish?"

"C'mon Ford, we've been on shit details, patrols and working in this crappy hanger since we arrived here. Is this what you want? Is this what you joined the Corps for? We're both qualified for door gunner and crew chief. When is it our turn? When do we get a chance to be something other than hanger monkeys? I want out, I want to fly, get into some action. You feel the same way so what's your malfunction?"

"I don't know Sean. Seeing those guys all banged up, seeing guys we drank with carried off in a black body bag kinda tempers my enthusiasm. Sure I want out, want to be on fly status, but I don't wanna get shot!"

"Well I'm gonna talk with the Gunny and see if I can get on one of those birds. Hell they're gonna need people. And we qualify!"

Sean headed to the operation shack and the Gunny was headed in the same direction.

"HEY GUNNY!"

Gunny Simmons turned in the direction of the voice.

"Say do you have a minute I can talk to you"?

"Make it fast Sean I have a meeting."

"Well, aw......."

"Spit it out Sean, I'm in a hurry."

"Well"......

"You already said that."

"I know, I know. Look Gunny, when we first arrived, you said you wouldn't send anybody on flight status until they knew the choppers inside and out, basically paid their dues."

"I said that?"

"Well not in so many words, but you did say we needed to know the workings of the helicopters before you'd even consider putting anybody in a chopper. We know those birds inside out, repaired and replaced parts that were done for. But we got them working".

"We? Who's we?"

"Me and Ford. We've worked hard, worked all night at times and did patrols plus shit details. Guess we feel we deserve a chance, maybe it's out time."

"Where's Ford, how come he's not here. Does he feel the same way?"

"Ya, Ford is over at the hanger washing up. Sorry to say but we figured you might be needing crews to replace those guys who....well you know." The Gunny paused a bit, he looked down, "ah, you might be right. I just haven't thought that far ahead right now, still trying to figure out what the hell went wrong with the operation. Tell ya what, you and Ford see me tomorrow. After you get those birds up!"

"Great, thanks Gunny."

"Have a good night Marine," reminding Sean of the long night in front of him. "Aw shit."

Ch 16

Coming out of the hanger Sean rubbed his eyes and then stretched his arms into the air. It has been a long humid night. Four of the six birds in the hanger were now operational. Sgt Bonville was asleep on a cot inside, and Ford went up to his hootch. Sean was the last one to finish up.

The heat of the day could already be felt. It was going to be another hot day. Sean scratched his ass and walked down the flight line to the chow hall. The place had a few Marines already eating breakfast. Sean walked over to the chow line and picked up a metal dinner tray. The menu today was pretty much the same, SOS, the staple of military life. Sean sighed in despair and held out his tray. The cook slopped eggs and SOS over a piece of toast already placed on the tray. Hot, black coffee rounded out the meal selection. Taking his pick of any seat, Sean sat down. The tiredness of the long night could be felt in every bone of Sean's body. His eyes would half close, open, close, open. Sean reached for the salt and pepper, a sure fire way to add some taste to his food. Then he grabbed the ketchup and lavishly poured it over his chow. After a few spoonfuls, the food hit Sean's stomach. He pushed his tray away. He was hungry but couldn't eat, tired but couldn't sleep, he was just exhausted. Sean felt a hand on his shoulder and abruptly looked up. Gunny Simmons was standing over him.

"You're not the first Marine that fell asleep sitting or standing up."
It was then Sean realized he had fallen asleep. "Morning Gunny, guess I'm a little tired. It was a bitching night." "Well you better grab a few hours of sleep. We still have two more choppers to get up and running.

Then I have to put you out on the perimeter. Headquarters is expecting some VC activity."

"But Gunny, I don't think I can stay awake. I'll be no good."

"Look Sean I'm down thirteen guys. I need every swinging dick available. Besides, it's during the daytime. You and Ford can take turns sleeping. Two hours on, two hours off. By the way, where is Ford?"

"He went up to the hootch to catch some shut eye."

"Well good, he can take first watch and let you catch up with your sleep."

"Aw shit Gunny."

"Sean, we're in a bind, I need this done." The Gunny walked away. Picking up his tray of uneaten food, Sean walked to the garbage can and emptied the contents. He washed his tray and left the chow hall. Sean found Ford sprawled out on his cot, belly side down fast asleep. The back of Ford's t-shirt was soaked with sweat.

"Ford wake up!"

"Whaaat?" Ford, slightly moved, trying to turn over. "What the fuck you want. Leave me alone."

"C'mon, Gunny wants the other two choppers up and then we go on the perimeter."

"Fuck that, doesn't he know we've been up all night?"

"Ya he does. I met him in the chow hall. If you have an issue, take it up with him. I'm just the messenger. Let's not screw up our chances of getting on fly status. We do good now and we're in. For all we know the Gunny may be testing us, seeing if we can hack it.

Let's not screw this up"

Ford rolled over and slowly got up. "OK, OK I'm up, point me in the right direction.

Shit it's hot."

Ch 17

It was close to 1400 hours when Sean and Ford arrived at their assigned bunker on the perimeter. It wasn't a real bunker, just a hole in the ground with sandbags stacked two feet high around the edge.

The work on the choppers went fast and was inspected. The Gunny signed off on them, nodded to Sgt. Bonville and left. "OK, Sean and Ford you have an appointment on the perimeter".

"Ah fuck you, Sgt'.

"Hey don't bitch at me, tell the Gunny. Besides you have it good, I'm on the perimeter tonight. At least you have it during the day."

That was an hour ago and Ford was now staring down at Sean in the bunker thinking, man that white boy can snore. The snoring reminded him of his father, John Ford Sr. That man could snore the roof off the house. Mr. Ford was a slight man with a big personality and character. He once told Ford Jr. "a man is judged by his character, don't make no difference what color you are." Ford Sr. was the son of a farmer, not a sharecropper as Ford Sr. would say. "My daddy bought his land outright with good cash money. He owed no man and paid cash on the barrel head." Ford Senior's father came from Trinidad. Signed on to a Merchant Marine freighter and sailed around Africa. Saved his money and eventually landed in New Orleans. Ford's grandfather. knew any future he had, would be in America. He traveled up to Ohio, which he could never explain why, except it sounded like a nice name for a state. He bought 60 acres and began farming. He married a housemaid who lived nearby and went to the same church. A year later Ford Sr. was born. As years went by Ford Sr. worked the land with his father. But Ford Sr. knew he wasn't cut out to be a farmer. He liked fixing things. He built a drainage ditch

and installed drainage tiles on the farm. He was able to do this from books borrowed at the library. He only went to the eight grade but was a voracious reader. If there were words on a cardboard, billboard or advertisement, he would read it. He always had a paperback book stuck in the back of his overalls. One day a neighbor asked Ford Sr. if he knew any plumbing, 'cause if he did she would pay him well. Ford said, "Yes ma'am, if it involves water and pipes I can fix it."
"Well that's good, you come over Saturday and get started, I need to install a water closet instead of using the outdoor privy."

Ford spent the next few days flipping through books on plumbing at the library. A fast leaner, Ford didn't see any problem. After a week working on the water closet he was finished and to his own amazement everything worked. The neighbor lady was so happy she paid him a hundred dollars. He would have to work a month of farming to make that much money. Now Ford knew what he wanted to do.

When Ford Sr's father passed away he sold the farm and moved his mother to Cleveland Ohio and worked as an apprentice with a local plumber. Ford Sr. learned fast and eventually did most of the plumbing work that his mentor was to old too do. His mentor decided to retire and made Ford Sr. a 'contract for deed' type arrangement for the business. Ford Sr. expanded his business from just doing work for color folk, to doing work for the white people in their fine houses. He was fast, reasonably priced and made enough money to buy a larger house to accommodate his growing family. In 1946 the last of his four children was born. He decided to leave a legacy and named the newborn boy John Ford Jr.

During the years he was growing up, Ford Jr. would work part time in his dad's shop. First it was just sweeping floors and stocking shelves with plumbing parts. Later his dad took him out to job sites doing plumbing. Ford Jr. was impressed with the attention to detail his father had. Ford Sr. would say, "there is no such thing as a small detail, every part of a job is important. Even cleaning up after yourself on a job is as important as the job itself".

When Ford Jr. graduated from high school he intended to work with his dad. Two months after graduation Ford was drafted into the Army. Three of his high school buddies had already signed up for the Marine Corps and encouraged Ford to do the same. Ford went down to the Marine Corp recruiter and told the Marine Sergeant that he had been drafted into the Army but wanted to be with his friends who had joined the Marine Corps. The Sergeant smelled new meat to add to his enlistment quota.
"Why sure son, there's no reason you can't join the Corps. Hell the Army has plenty of recruits to choose from and they wouldn't miss one getting away. You'll have a great time traveling with your buddies." So Ford signed on and landed at Marine Corps boot camp. Ford never did see his buddies and never would. After boot camp and advance infantry training, Ford was sent to aviation school for helicopters at Memphis Tennessee. Seems Ford scored high on his aptitude test. After aviation school Ford received orders for the First Marine Air Wing, Vietnam. The next thing he knew he was standing on a runway in Phu Bai Vietnam.

The sun was bearing down and the heat was intense. Ford had a headband to prevent sweat from dripping down his face. His fatigues clung to him with perspiration. The lack of sleep made his head bob up and down trying to stay awake. He took a look out over the perimeter. His head started to bob down when he stopped and looked up quickly, "what the fuc...?" Something wasn't right. The landscape didn't seem the same. What was it, what was it he thought! Then Ford saw it. Just a slight movement. Someones out there. He kicked Sean with his boot. "Wake up, wake up. Sean wake up!" Sean looked up at Ford.
"What?"
"Wake up, there's someone out there."
"Who?"
"Who, who? How the fuck do I know who, President Johnson! There's movement about fifty yards out."

"Ah, you're tired and seeing things."

"No, I saw something. There, there! Fifty yards out, about nine o'clock."

Sean looked out and got back down quick. "Ahh shit. Easy day the Gunny said, it's during the day he said. You can take turns sleeping his said. Well the Gunny was wrong this time."

As soon as the words were out of Sean's mouth, Ford opened fired. Sean felt a hot empty cartridge from Ford's rife hit his face.

"Sean start firing!"

Sean took a breath, grabbed his rifle, sat up and started firing.

The sandbags around them were being hit with small arms fire. Incoming rounds were ripping the sandbags open.

Ford estimated at least fifteen individuals firing in their direction. Ford ducked down.

Oh boy Sean, we're in deep shit now."

Other bunkers opened fire. Tracers rounds looking like red dotted lines passed through the sky. A dark figured jumped into the fox hole with Sean and Ford. The movement startled both men. It was Lt. Downwells. "Slow down your fire, your going through ammo too quick. Use short blast of three to four rounds. Try and pick your target or concentrate on one area." With that Dowswell was up and gone, running to another fox hole. As quickly as the fire fight started it was over. The VC had disappeared and the Marines had been shooting into empty bushes.

"CEASE FIRE, CEASE FIRE!" Lt Dowswell was yelling up the line. All rifle fire on the perimeter stopped. Ford and Sean slid down into their foxholes, breathing heavy and sweating.

"Holy shit, I don't think I hit a fucking thing Sean."

Sean gave a slight chuckle, smiled and said, "I killed a lot of bushes."

Both men laughed.

The night replacements came. The day guard grabbed their gear and headed back behind the perimeter lines. Ford turned to Sean, "I seriously think it's beer time!"

Ch 18

Sean and Ford found the rest of the Marines at their usual table in the beer tent. They plopped down and grabbed a beer. Ford said, "you guys been here long?"

"Naw, we've only been here 'bout ten minutes." Sean looked the case of beer already on the table... "ten minutes? You guys work fast."

Tonight's subject was the firefight early this evening. Everyone had their story of how fast it started and how quickly it ended. TC said, "kinda stupid of Charlie coming at us in daylight. Apparently they didn't think we would be out there in force."

Rubio put his beer down. "Why were we out there? Did S-2 get some scuttlebutt about an attack? Most of the time there's nothing more than a skeleton guard."

"Did anyone hit anything?" No one answered Ford.

"Hell, Sean and I tore up the landscape, no bush is gonna mess with us." The table busted into laughter.

"Ya and the only thing I messed were my trousers," with that Rubio got a cheer. No one at the table could actually say they hit any VC. Charlie came and went so fast it was hard to know how many there were. If any of them were killed they'd be dragged away so as not to give a body count. The beer drinking went on. Everyone was getting drunk and glad to be alive. Sean walked outside and bumped into Ford. "Heey! Watch it, man ya almost made me piss on myself."

"Sorry Ford, I have to tap a keg here, fuckin' beer is making my teeth float."

"Hey Sean, lets go for a swam."

"A swam? You mean a swim?"

Yas, a swam in the watar, looks great huh?"

"Awwwww.... O 'ta."

Working their way down the sand dune, the two drunks came to the waters edge.

"Awww shit wat'd the fuc.., barbwire. Whose putts thes shits here?"

Sean shrugged and climbed over the sharp barbwire and stumbled into the refreshing sea. Ford was right behind but fell in the sand before reaching the water. His head was covered in sand and he was spitting a lot of it out. Sean started laughing when a wave hit him, knocking him into shallows. He came up coughing and sputtering. Once in the water both men felt refreshed. The heat and sweat of the day was swept away. Just like two kids in a wading pool, the two Marines splashed the ocean water at each other. Then they laid back and floated, feeling really clean for the first time in days. That's when everything went completely white. It was as if the sun came out two feet in front of their faces. It came with a loud whopping noise and a strong wind.

"Wha the fuc.." was all Sean got out.

A siren could be heard and the sound of dogs barking.

Ford said, "whaat 'sa hells going on?"

Sean and Ford stood in the water up to their waist with forearms up over their eyes trying to make out the source of the bright light.

"OK you two get out of the water, NOW!"

The voice came from the shore where twelve armed Marines stood with three barking dogs, drooling for a meal.

"Uh oh. Ain't wooking good Sean."

The two Marines stumbled towards the sandy beach.

A Sergeant armed to the teeth yelled, "what the fuck are you two doing? You're over the barbed wire and almost got yourself shot!" Sean and Ford looked up to see a helicopter flying overhead with a spotlight which explained the sudden bright light.

"Get your asses over the wire, you're in a heap of shit now fuckers."

Both guys were marched up to the guard shack, processed and told to report to Gunny Simmons in the morning.

Morning came fast enough. Sean heard noise but had trouble opening his eyes. They felt like they were glued shut. Using his trigger finger on the right hand, Sean opened his right eye. The morning sun hurt like hell on the eyeball. He rolled over and tried the left eye using the same finger. That eyeball hurt as well.

"Well look who's awake, Aquanaut Sean. Morning sunshine have a good swim?"

Sean didn't know what the hell Rubio was saying.

"Whaat"?

"Did you and Ford enjoy your swim last night?"

Sean started to think. "Awww shit."

"Aw shit is right. But now ya gotta face the Gunny. You and Ford are probably gonna be on shit details till you leave. That's if they don't throw you in the brig first."

"Aw shut up Rubio," Sean threw his pillow. Rubio laughed as he walked out of the hootch.

Ch 19

Ford and Sean stood fast in front of the Gunny who was viewing a report from last night while drumming his fingers on his desk. His complexion seemed a bit red for this time in the morning. Slowly the Gunny looked up. In a steel cold voice he uttered "would one of you assholes care to tell me about last night?" The two men were silent. "No? Nothing to say? Before last night I thought you two were smart guys, almost intelligent guys, unusual traits for a Marine I know. But now I realize that you two have the IQ below that of plant life. WHAT THE FUCK WERE YOU DOING! One of you better speak or I'll be in the brig for murder."

"Aw, well Gunny,.... ah Sean can explain."

Sean eyes grew large, his Adams apple bobbed from trying to swallow. His eyes darted back and forth trying to think of what to say.

"Ah well, ah."

"Asshole, Ford already said that. Tell me what the hell you two were thinking. I got rousted out of the rack last night by the MP's. Told me two of my guys nearly got shot being outside the perimeter. They thought you were VC trying to infiltrate the wire. That section of the perimeter was on high alert because of today's scrimmage in which you were involved in. Colonel Johnston is beyond pissed, he wants your balls in a nutcracker. And when he's done cracking your balls he wants them roasted for good measure. Then he's gonna discipline you two, maybe some brig time??? Huh? How does that sound to you assholes. NOW! What were you two thinking?"

"Well Gunny that's just the point. We weren't thinking. We were drunk and at the time a swim seemed like a good idea."

"A good idea? A GOOD IDEA! Fuck man you got the perimeter on full alert, they were looking to shoot someone. The dogs were hungry and they wanted to eat something, a Marine, VC, a rat, hell they didn't care. I've lost six Marines already and can't lose more. The only thing that saved you was, the Sergeant heard you laugh. Being a sharp Marine Sergeant he knew no VC would come in laughing. Now tell me good, what were you thinking so I can hand your ass over to Colonel Johnston."

"Well Gunny."

"QUIT SAYING WELL!"

"OK, look Gunny we got drunk and stupid. We were settling our nerves from this afternoon. The beer got to us, we let the devil in our mouth and we got stupid. Can't say it will happen again, can't say it won't. Truth is I don't really remember much about last night, just a bright light shining down on us. Ford and I have been in the outfit a few short months, been on more patrols and ambushes. Plus we've already been in two fire fights. Never expected to be doing ground fighting. Will probably be doing some more I guess. Just wanted to be in flight status and fight from the choppers. Never expected to be grounded. We're sorry and will take what ever punishment is deemed necessary. We have no excuses."

"Starting now you two are back on shit detail. Now get outta here! I'll check with the Colonel to see when he wants to cut ya nuts off, before or after the brig!"

The two Marines left the Gunny's office fast.

The rear door to the Gunny office suddenly opened.

"How'd it go Gunny?"

Gunny Simmons looked up at Colonel Johnston.
A small smile was visible. "I don't know. Those two jackasses pulled a real boner. I'll keep them on shit detail for a while. Not getting to fly will kill them and will be their real punishment. I'll let them think about that for a while."

"So you are going to put them on flight status?"

"Hell ya, they're both sharp, both qualified faster than anyone I've seen, except for Tommy Collins. Besides, it's a Marines nature to get in trouble. Hell Chesty Puller might be proud of these guys."

"I wouldn't give them that much credit, they did screw up."

"As I remember it Colonel, there was an incident in the Philippines when a certain Marine officer tore apart the Subic Bay Officer club. In fact this junior officer punched out a Navy Captain."

"Now wait a minute Gunny, you gonna bring that shit up again? And how the hell did you happen to be outside that club?"

"One of the bartenders was a Corporal of mine. He called me when you went after that Captain for insulting that waitress. You had been drinking pretty good, but from what I was told that swabbie was way out of line. Besides, he didn't know who the hell you were, just another junior officer who had to much to drink."

"I really thank you for that help Gunny. It could've been the end on my career. You're old corps and I like that. Now that I think of it Gunny, why were you driving a Generals Jeep?"

"Ohhh,...ah well, that's another story Colonel. Maybe sometime over a glass of Jim Beam."

Colonel Johnston smiled. "OK, Gunny another time."

When Ford and Sean had left the Gunny's office, Sean hauled off and threw a punch catching Ford on the shoulder. Ford stumbled over a box and hit the ground laughing.

"Why the fuck did you give me up in there? You set me up you bastard."

Ford was still laughing. "I'm sorry Sean." He tried to get up but fell back down laughing. "Christ if you could of seen your face. I'm telling ya it was worth it."

"Damn it Ford I almost shit myself. You put me on the spot, threw me under the bus. And it was your fucking idea to go swimming in the first place."

"Ah yes it was Sean, and you enjoyed it as much as I did. Look Sean I'm real sorry."

"Ya well you're still laughing."

Ford smiled. "I know, but the look on your face was priceless. And you did a great job. Your college mind came into use after all. The Gunny respected the honesty."

"Honesty? He put us on shit detail till we die. Now we'll never get to fly."

"Never say never Sean. C'mon, Sgt. Bonville's not expecting us back. Let's go to the beer tent, I'm buying."

Sean looked at Ford. "You're a piece of work, ya know that, a real piece of work."

With a smile Sean said, "OK one beer ,....but no swimming!"

"I knew you couldn't stay mad at me."

"Asshole."

Ch 20

The S-2 hootch was hot but had shade. Those seated were; Colonel Johnston, Lt. Dowswell, Gunny Simmons and S-2 Officer Lt. Janhs. Squadron Commander Col. Johnston took the floor.

"OK gentleman we need to run over the events of the past few weeks. In particular, the dismal operation in which six of our men were killed and eight shot up plus the loss of 3 planes. A very ineffective return on careful planning, but most of all my sadness over the men we lost. We need to discuss how that operation went sour on us and to prevent future occurrences. Sorry to put it so bluntly and crude, I find myself at a lost for words. I'll let Lt. Janhs S-2 guy rundown the sequence of those losses. Lt. Janhs."

"Well like Col. Johnston, I'm saddened by our lost of good men. There was no reason for those losses based on the intelligence we were given. Headquarters in Da Nang.....".

"We've had three bad intelligent report from Da Nang these past few months involving so called friendly LZs." The gruff voice came from Gunny Simmons. "I've had good men injured and killed. Helicopters put out of commission or badly shot up. I can't hold with that!"

Col. Johnston spoke up quickly. "Gunny we need to give Lt. Janhs the opportunity to report on his finding."

Lt.. Janhs shifted a bit. "Gunny we all feel the same way and no one is content with what has transpired. But the facts are the intel was good. What wasn't counted on was the enemy's ability to move around so fast."

"Well isn't that what S-2 is suppose to count on, the unknown as well as the known?"

"Yes Gunny, it's just that lately things have been spiraling fast and Da Nang now feels that something big is brewing. More than just troop movements. I just received information this morning that might explain the situation."

Col. Johnston took a drag on his cigarette, "go on Lieutenant."

"I was gonna cover events leading up to the most recent VC attack on our perimeter but it might serve to jump right to the latest findings."

"Go ahead Janhs."

"The attack a few days ago was strange that it took place during the daytime. Plus it began and ended so fast. This was not just an isolated incident. It was, from our latest intelligence, more of a probing element. Our defenses were being tested. If you gentlemen will look at the handouts going around the table. You will see that headquarters intelligence reports similar incidents around, not only I-Corp above Da Nang but South as well. In the I-Corp area, Khe Sanh, Quang Tri, a few outpost like Camp Carroll, as well as here at Phu Bai were all hit. Gunny Simmons jumped in," so what, we're always getting hit, some bases at the same time as us."

"Yes Gunny but what was unusual was they all happened at about the same time and the same way. A quick attack and it was over. No real motive or reason for the attacks. Small unit attacks and it was over. S-2 Headquarters think something is in the wind. That the attacks were in preparation for something more, something big!"

Lt. Dowswell spoke up. "I don't see it. Surely the enemy doesn't have the resources to engage in multi-attacks on numerous fronts?"

"That was the prevailing attitude in Da Nang All resources point to a weakened enemy. The general consensus is that Hanoi is weak and lacking the ability to engage in any large scale military action. Yet S-2 put together a report of increased movement on the Ho Chi Minh trail along Laos. Reconnaissance flights show beau-coup trucks and troop movement more than usual. This has been going on for a month."

Grabbing his coffee mug Colonel Johnston stood up and walked across the S-2 hootch to the coffee pot. With a slight agitation he looked at Lt. Janhs.

"Why the hell are we getting this information now?" Col. Johnston's cigarette glowed red as he took a deep puff and leaned against the table.

"Colonel, intelligent gathering is a slow process, only not as slow as interpreting what it means. First of all, the massing of supplies,troops and trucks down the Ho Chi Minh Trail didn't make sense."

"Isn't that your job?"

Lt. Janhs feeling a bit uncomfortable from the pointed questions, shifted his feet.

"Ya Gunny, but it takes a while to make sense of what we're looking at. It's kinda like looking at one of those pictures with the scrawling lines and if you look long enough an image appears. Well it's like that. You look at the intelligence till an image or trend appears."

Col. Johnston scratched his forehead. "So what triggered the latest appraisal that something big is due to happen?"

"The synchronized attacks did. All of a sudden it makes sense. Why the increase of trucks, supplies and troops? Hanoi is planning a major attack. Not at one place but multiple places."

"So why don't we attack?"

"Gunny we just don't know when and where. Hitting numerous targets would be like
playing whack-a-mole."

"What?"

"Whack-a-mole. Like those games at a carnival. You keep hitting with a hammer at a mole popping out of a hole. Only thing is when you hit the mole, another pops out of a different hole. We'd be using a shotgun to hit a fly. That would be a waste of our energy and armaments. What is needed is to find out when and where they intend to attack,
then we act."

Col. Johnston walked back over to the main table. "Lieutenant, when does S-2 believe Hanoi will attack?"

"Well, like I said, intelligence collecting is slow and the processing of it takes longer. I would suspect at least a month, maybe two before they come up with a plan. Hanoi has the same problem analyzing data as we do. It takes time and they will be just getting back intel from the field. Then they have to formulate a plan as well as mass troops and equipment. Since Hanoi doesn't have the logistic equipment as we do, it'll take a while. There are over 300 provinces in Vietnam. The North Vietnamese will have to decide on which ones to attack. It's not an easy task. It'll take them quite a while."

"Thank you Lt. Janhs. At least now we have an idea of whats going on behind the recent attacks two days ago. It also provides us with a ballpark time frame."

Lt. Dowswell had been sitting silent taking everything in. He said, "Colonel I think it might be wise to increase personnel at the perimeter and increase patrols." Also call for more infantry to assist us".

"Good idea on the first two suggestions but the third is going to be hard. Being that a major offense is expected, the infantry is going to be in short supply. They'll be assigned to Capital Provincials and Da Nang itself. Plus we lost six men and have eight more in the hospital recovering from wounds suffered during the operations a few days ago. No men, I'm afraid we have to relay on our own resources for now until something happens. Sorry gentlemen. Any other questions? OK let's dismiss. Gunny Simmons please stay behind, I have an item to go over."

Ch 21

Sean took his cover off as he entered the Gunny's office. "Sgt. Bonville said you wanted to see me Gunny?"

"Ya, sit down Sean."

Sean pulled a chair over by Gunny's desk and sat down.

"Where's Ford, I wanted to see him also."

"He'll be down shortly. Sgt. Bonville sent someone up to his hut to get him."

"So, hows the detail going? You guys learning anything?"

Sean look down a bit and turned his cover over in his hands. "Well it's no picnic that's for sure. We stink so bad at the end of the day, the other guys won't sit near us in the beer tent."

The Gunny had a little smile.

"I guess we had it coming, so we can't kick."

"Ya damn right you had it coming. You know I could've of thrown you two in the Brig for a few days. But that's not what I wanted to discuss with you guys. Had a talk with Col. Johnston the other day. With the flight personnel situation gone sour because of our recent losses, we're in need of replacements. I understand that both you and Ford have qualified as door gunners and passed the crew chiefs tests."

Sean's head came up quickly and the Gunny now had his total attention. "Ya Gunny, we qualified with the M-60 machine gun, and Tommy Collins helped us prepare for the crew chief's tests. Working in the overhaul hanger really got us to know the choppers inside and out." Sean's heart was racing a bit. There was a glimmer of hope rising in him that he was going to get out of the shit detail and onto something more substantial.

Gunny leaned back in his chair. "Well the Colonel wants me to put you two on flight status as door gunners. This is against my better judgment. I'd prefer you two pay another pound of flesh because of the swimming incident. Yet we're shorthanded and facts is facts. My intent is to assign you and Ford as door gunners. TC will be your crew chief and Ford will fly with Rubio. It won't be for two weeks. We need to get choppers for you men. Overhaul is instructed to get two choppers up and running ASAP."

Sean couldn't believe his luck. Here he was looking at weeks of shit detail and now he was getting out. Better yet, he was gonna fly, see some actions. He was gonna do what he wanted to do when he first arrived. It had been months since that first day. During that time he was in fire fights, ambushes, numerous patrols, been under rockets and mortar attacks. Now he was gonna see some flight action. Use the skills the Marine Corps taught him. He'll be part of a crew flying around "Nam. doing troop insertions, medevacs, ground cover, the whole enchilada. Damn, things were loooking up.

"That's not the only thing I wanted to tell ya." Gunny handed Sean three sheets of papers stuck together with a staple. "Those are your orders. You have filled the requirements for R&R and a billet opened up. You're going to Australia. That is if you want to. You did request Australia right?"

Looking at the papers, Sean was speechless. This keeps getting better and better.

"You and Corporal Rubio took up two recent opening spots."

An uneasy feeling came over Sean. "Gunny you said these two openings were recent. Hows that? I mean, why are they just recent now?"

The Gunny looked down at the paperwork on his desk. "Doesn't matter, you want it or not?"

"Ah, ya Gunny I was just curious. Ya I want this bad. Never thought I'd get a chance to go on R&R to a place I requested. It doesn't seem to be the Marine Corps way."

"Well your ass belongs to the Corps son. It tells you when to shit, where to shit and how high. Now get out of my office, I got paper work to do. As Sean was walking out the Gunny yelled "you leave in two days, I suggest when you're down there stay out of the water."

Sean bumped into Ford outside the Gunny's office. "Christ Ford we've been saved."

Ford looked strangely at Sean. It was then that Sean saw the Gunny drop six dog tags into a brown envelope. Paper work huh? Sean walked away feeling like crap. Here he was going on R&R to Australia, because two guys won't be going there. They'll be going home for good. One misfortune benefits another. That seems to be the way in war. Bad things happen and you just hope it doesn't happen to you. A guy gets killed, yet the man next to him goes untouched. It could have been you that was killed, but it wasn't. Luck, fate, the luck of the draw? What difference does it make? Dead is dead. One escapes, one doesn't. This was an unknown beginning for Sean. A protective shield descended around him. An emotional shield keeping him from attachment to others. Don't get too close to anyone. They may get killed and you have to deal with the loss. More get killed, more losses. If you keep thinking about it, it can tear you up. Make you second guess your actions. Can weaken your resolve to stay alive. Dead is dead and no amount of thinking about a guy killed will help. Just move on, stay alive so you can go home. No attachments, no emotions. Sean walked down the flight line with the seed of a thought planted , don't get to close to any one.

Ch 22

It was Sunday. The Gunny was making Sean work on a damaged chopper shot up on an emergency medevac extraction gone wrong. The helicopter had made a crash landing and was pretty banged up. Gunny Simmons told Sean, "this is gonna be your bird. But I don't have the personnel to work on it, so you and TC have to do it. This will be the only way you'll get flying. Do it right, 'cause your life depends on it."
Sean totally had a lack of attention to maintenance on his aircraft.
Tuesday couldn't come quick enough. On Tuesday he was scheduled for R&R in Australia. He and Rubio qualified for the last two remaining slots for down under.
"Hey TC, throw me up a ¾ inch wrench. I got a one ragger up here on the transmission hydraulic line." Sean reference of a ragger was how chopper crews measured the seriousness of a leak. Anything more than one rag was serious enough to replace the line to insure proper operation of the hydraulic system. The hydraulics controlled the pitch of the rotor blades to create lift, the direction of the aircraft or descending for landing. It took a few minutes for Sean to tighten the hydraulic line. For good measure he rechecked the tightness of the other lines, *'cause your life depends on it*. Then he got down from the chopper main rotor head platform.
""Where's the rag?" TC asked
"Ah shit, I left the damn thing up there. I tell ya TC I can't think of anything except getting the hell out of here. Christ I'm gonna have such a fucking great time in Australia. I took out $250 bucks last payday to blow on this trip. And I ain't coming back with anything. Say its almost chow time. What d'ya think of calling it a day and go eat, I'm starving."

TC yelled back, "sounds like a plan man." Sean and TC were ten feet from the chopper when TC stopped.

"Hey what about the rag?"

Sean made a face. "Ah shit!" He walked back to the aircraft.

That night Sean, TC, Ford, Camron and the usual bar flies were sitting on a sand bunker outside the beer tent. It was too hot to sit inside. Outside was hot also but at least here was a slight breeze from the ocean. The ground was littered with crushed Hamm's beer cans. Sean and TC went straight there from the chow hall. They had a two hour beer buzz going.

"OK!" TC said. "I'm buying." And with that staggered to the beer tent holding up a five dollar script note. The flap to the tent gave him problems as he tried to get past it. He finally gave it a full slap with both hands and pushed back the flap and went inside.

"So you ready for Australia." Ford asked.

"Is the Pope Catholic? Hell ya! And the hell with all of ya. Rubio and me are gonna have a blast. Gonna get drunk, then find some round-eye girls and get laid."

"Well, don't have too much fun. Rubio almost got locked up in Bangkok."

"No shit!" Sean slammed his beer can down.

"He took a bath in the hotel lobby water fountain pool thing...buck naked." Ford said.

"No shit. Did he really do that? Naaa, you're full of crap, Rubio's a pretty mild dude."

"I'm not kidding. He got hammered on Johnny Walker Scotch, walked down to the lobby with a towel wrapped around him. He dropped the towel and got into the fountain with a bar of soap. The zipperheads went ape shit. They were jabbering at him to get out. Of course he didn't know what the fuck they were saying. Didn't understand a word. They were calling him a crazy American, throwing stuff at him."

"Holy shit, I don't believe it." Sean said laughing as he slapped the palm of his hand to his forehead. What happened to him?"

"Well Rubio comes from a wealthy family. A little pay-o-la to the police and they let him go."

"I still don't believe it."

Ford smiled and laughed back. "Go ahead and ask him, he's sitting over there."

Sean yelled out. "Hey Rubio how was Bangkok?'

Without looking up Rubio flipped Sean the bird. The whole group burst into laughter. TC came staggering back, his arms full of beer. He looked strangely at the guys laughing. "Whaaat I'd miss." This made everyone laugh louder. TC puzzled, glanced over at Rubio who still had his arm raised casting a finger at the group. TC thought it was for him. "Ya, well fuck you too Rubio."

Sean and Ford rolled off the sand bunker onto the empties on the ground laughing. TC was still confused as to what he had missed.

The beer tent closed up for the night leaving Sean, TC and Ford staggering arm in arm up the path to their hootch's. TC stopped quickly. Ssssh, that's Sgt. Bonville going into the shit house to take a crap. Lets go up and tip the fucker over."

"Ohh that's sick man." Ford laughed.

"Sssh he might hear ya. C'mon."

The door to the outhouse closed. The drunken trio waited for Bonville to get settled in. They got behind the structure and TC silently mouthed; *one, two, three.* With as much might as the drunks could muster, they pushed against the outhouse tipping it at an angle. From inside a voice yelled out. "Hey, hey,hey...what the..! Who's doing that. Ya sons of bitches, I'll kill ya." As the outhouse was tipping over, Sgt. Bonville struggled to get his trousers up, yelling all the time. "Ya bastards, I'll get whoever it is. I'll get ya, ya sons of bitches!"

The trio struggled to find the strength while laughing and howling. But finally the shit

house tipped over spilling it's contents onto the occupant.

"Ya bastards." Cough, cough. "Awww, I'll kill you cocksuckers. I swear I'll kill you bastard. Oh God, this sucks..ohhh damn."
As it was reported three men were last seen stumbling and laughing as they ran up to the hootch area.

Sgt. Bonville was later than usual coming into the overhaul hanger the next morning. Sean, TC and Ford looked over and saw a mean, pissed off look on the Sergeant's face. It took all their effort not to laugh out loud. TC walked over to Bonville. "Having a rough morning Sergeant?"
"Fuck you TC, what do you know?"
"What? I just asked if you're having a rough morning."
"Well back off and get back to work."
TC turned and walked away. Smiling, he looked up at Sean and Ford. He thought it was all worth it. Rumor had it that when ever Bonville went to the shit house he posted a look out while he took a crap. It was also rumored that because of the outhouse incident he got the nickname, The Turd.

Ch 23

"Hey bad ass Ugly Angel, drop your cock and grab your socks. Time to get up."

"Whaaa?"

"C'mon Sean, you need to get your gear and catch a flight."

Monday had gone quick. After giving Sgt. Bonville a hard time about his outhouse adventure, Sean and TC made progress on rebuilding their damaged chopper. During his absence, TC got permission for Ford to assist on the rebuild. Sean hit the rack earlier than usual Monday night for a morning flight to Da Nang.

"Shake it out man, ya don't want to miss your R&R. I got a jeep outside with two other lucky bastards also heading for R&R. Let's not keep' em waiting."

Sean came alert and got up quickly grabbing his trousers. "Oh man I can hardly wait. One blessed week in Australia with round-eye girls. No pigeon English and no crappy back ass country."

Ford sat down on the cot next to Sean, leaning back on his elbows.

"Hate to say it but I'm gonna miss ya company Sean. We've had some interesting times since we arrived; fire fights, rocket attacks, unauthorized midnight swims, drunk fests. Shit it'll be too quiet around here."

"Don't give me that bull, you'll be down at the beer tent tonight drinking my share of the brew."

"Well ya got me there. C'mon hurry up, the guys are waiting. Gunny let me have Col. Johnston's jeep to take you guys over to the tarmac area.

Sean lifted his travel bag and headed out of the hootch with Ford behind him. In the jeep were two other guys from his squadron.

"Hey. Where's Rubio?"

"Ah the poor bastard got food positioning yesterday. He snuck down to the gook village to see his honey. He ate something they were boiling in a pot. Should've known he can't eat that shit. Our stomachs aren't adjusted for whatever they put in their food. I heard his honey and her family are just fine. So he just can't take the food. Probably some small Vietnamese parasite done him in. Anyway, he's in sick bay. Lost out on his R&R though. Hop in the jeep."

The four Marines drove away from the hootch, crossing the small runway and over to the tarmac by the control tower. "OK, jump out guys, take all your gear. Here ya go Sean." Ford lifted Sean's bag out of the jeep and handed it over to him. "Well, gotta get the jeep back to the Colonel. Have a good time Sean, see ya in a week and don't go swimming." Both men smiled as Ford turned away and got back in the jeep. Sean felt a little sad as he watched Ford drive away. They had been together since they arrived in country. It didn't seem right to leave Ford behind. They worked, drank and ate together. Ford was a good guy, Sean thought, a real good guy. He turned to catch up with Jogda and Nord. All three walked to the embarking area.

The flight on the large C-130 cargo aircraft to Da Nang took an hour. The large aircraft lined up on the same approach for the runway as when Sean first arrived in country. The same downwind approach, same cross wind, same final approach. The plane crossed the runway threshold at 140 mph. The wheels touched the ground with a squeal with the pilot quickly feathering the props and applying the hydraulic brakes. The ground roll was 2463 feet and the plane took the first ramp into the disembarkation area.

After coming to a complete stop, the plane's crew chief hit a lever. The large rear cargo door slowly opened down acting like a ramp. Good for loading supplies. Sean and the other two men were met by the same back straight, thin Marine Sergeamt Sean had seen when he first arrive. Over the roar of the engine he motioned the men to head to the same A-frame shelter Sean encountered when he came into country.

"OK, men who's going where?"

Of Sean's party, Nord was headed to Bangkok, Jogda to Hong Kong. Each was assigned a different hootch with instructions to stow their gear and to make sure they're here at 0800 tomorrow morning. The following morning's flight would take them to Okinawa where each man would be allowed to access their personnel gear they'd surrendered when they arrived. They would be allowed to take limited civies from their stored duffel bags, or buy some at the Okinawa PX.

The men shook hands and left for their assigned barracks. Sean entered the empty barracks which was ten times larger than his hut back at Phu Bai. He threw his gear on the first rack and walked to the head. His eyes got big when he looked in. There were rows of toilets. Actual flushing state-side type, white porcelain with shinny handles. He walked over and ran his hands across the the top. Not being able to help himself, he flushed it, let it fill up, flushed it again. He muttered to himself, "state- side shitters,whoa."

"Impressive huh?"

The sound of the voice startled Sean. Standing in the doorway of the head had to be the tallest Marine Leprechaun ever.

"I did the same thing when I walked in. And it gets even better....HOT water in the showers. You can just stand there and let the hot water soak you to the bone. Hi, I'm Tom Sullivan. Got in about an hour ago. Heading back to the states. Finally rotating out of this hell hole."

" I'm Sean, down from Phu Bai. Heading to Australia for R&R."

Sean looked over Sullivan and pegged him at five feet five, about 135 pounds. Sullivan had brown slightly curly hair, a two day beard growth, and wore the basic jungle fatigues stained with perspiration. His face looked familiar.

"Where ya from back in the states Sean?"

"Boston."

"No shit, me too. Where abouts?"

"Dorchester to be exact."

"GET OUT! What Parish?"

"St. Ambrose. Up around Fields Corner."

"I don't believe this. I'm from St. Anns' Parish, down around Neponset Ave. Holy shit my last days in 'Nam and I run into a guy form my own area. Go figure. Hey, Sean when did you come over here?"

""Mmmm about five or six months...no six months next week."

"Well ya almost halfway there. I could never figure out why Marines have thirteen months and the Army serves 12 months.   Marine Corp luck huh?"

Sean now knew why Sullivan looked so familiar. He'd seen that face many times in Boston. That Irish look, that Killkenny Irish look.   Ya can almost picture Sullivan arriving off a boat from Ireland during the potato famine. Seen that face many times

"Say did ya have anything to eat?"

"Actually no. Never even had breakfast. Had to catch my flight."

"Well, what do'ya say we get a bit of the Irish before we eat?"

Sean thought, oh damn I'm back in the neighborhood and it's only noon.

"Ah, what the hell let's go."

Sullivan gave a big smile and walked out ahead of Sean.

Walking down past rows of barracks, small huts, and military buildings, the pair made their way to Freedom Hill. The area looked much like a strip mall with numerous buildings lined up selling anything from tailored suits to nuts. It was just a long row of shops, some by Americans, mostly by Vietnamese. No one was quite sure why it was called Freedom Hill. Probably some General's idea of instilling good ol' American democratic flavor to the area. Sean and Sullivan found what they were looking for, the beer garden. The place was just a crude store selling liquor and had an attached fenced- in area with picnic tables. The two buddies walked in.

"What did ya think we should get?"

"Old Thompson, get a bottle of Old Thompson". Sullivan licked his lips. "Haven't had any hard liquor since I left the States."

"I'm a beer man myself, but what the hell, might as just try something new. A bottle of Old Thompson my good man."

The good man behind the counter was an Army Sergeant, He was a bit shorter than Sean but way taller then Sullivan.

"Sorry guys, can't sell hard liquor to you. Can sell ya some beer though."

Sean looked at the Sergeant

"Why not?"

"You two are only Corporals and we have direct orders not to sell hard liquor to any Marines below the rank of Sergeant."

"Are you shitting me? We're in a combat zone. Hell I'm older than you. What do ya mean ya can't sell us hard liquor?"

Sullivan started to take a step forward but Sean put out his arm to block him.

"Easy feisty one."

Looking back at the Sergeant, Sean leaned closer to the counter.

"As you can see my Irish friend has been denied the nectar of our heritage. Now I'm not one for the spirits myself, but I'm willing to learn. Now why don't ya be a good guy and grab us a bottle of Old Thompson and there will be something extra in it for yourself..hmmm?"

"I'm really sorry guys, I'd really like to but we've had a few disruptions from some Marine who got out of hand. The guy who sold it to them was sent back to the line. And I have no intention to give up this easy job. I'm too short, rotate back to the world in a month. No can do."

Sean realized his easy approach was going nowhere. And this guy was not gonna jeopardize his easy way to get back home alive. Couldn't really blame him.

"OK, I don't like it but what the hell."

"Sorry guys."

Sean grabbed Sullivan by the arm and led him outside. Sullivan was looking back over his shoulder giving the Sergeant a mean look as he was escorted out.

"Well what the hell we gonna do now? Hell Sean, I was looking forward to a good drink.   Now we got shit."

Sean was looking down the dirt walkway and spotted an Army Warren Officer coming towards them. The guy was younger than the two Marines. Maybe nineteen or twenty. Made sense that this Army turd was one of the new Warren Officers created by the Army for guys right out of high school to fly helicopters. This helped the Army staff helicopters with pilots faster. They didn't want to wait for someone to graduate from college. The Army would train these kids to just fly helicopters.

As the Warren Officer got close to the Marines, Sean stepped in front of him.

"Hi, say we need a favor. Seems like the military doesn't trust Marine Corporals to drink hard liquor. The Sergeant inside won't sell us a bottle of booze. Ya think you can do us a solid and buy it for us? We'll naturally give you the money. What'da ya say?"

The Warren Officer was kinda taken back by the two Marines rapid approach.

"I'm sorry guys but I don't feel comfortable doing this. It's breaking military rules and all."

"Aw, c'mon. No one will be the wiser. We get the liquor and you could feel good knowing you've done someone a favor."

"Mmm,no I'm sorry, I just don't want to do it."

The Warren Officer started to walk around Sean. Sean again stepped in front of him.

"Look guy, we'll give you a few bucks to do us this favor. You come out ahead."

The Warren Officer got an indignant look on his face.

"Look, first of all, I'm not the guy. I'm a Warren Officer and out rank both of you. I believe I'm entitled to the respect of an officer."

"Well ya got me there. However, you've overlooked a few points."

"And what might those be?"

"First, you do out rank us,....true. But I'm taller and out weigh you, plus there are two of us and there is no one around. Oh ya, thirdly, respect should be earned, not expected. Do we have a deal?"

The Warren Office felt the presence of the other Marine right behind him, up close.

"Ahh, what did you men want?"

"My good man, just a bottle of Old Thompson. And here's a ten, get yourself something."

The Warren Officer went in briefly and came out with the goods.

"Here's your stuff. Oh ya, the Sergeant said to enjoy but don't cause any trouble or he'll call the Military Police."

"Sir, now you've earned our respect."

Sean and Sullivan made their way into the beer garden and sat at the picnic tables.

The men pour themselves a stiff short of whiskey.

"Ah Sean, like the man in the movie said, this is the start of a beautiful relationship. Slainte!"

It had been a while since Sean heard any Gaelic. "Cheers to ya Sullivan."

   The afternoon passed by rapidly and it was about 1700 hours. The contents of Old Thompson was rather low. The beer garden had filled up with mixed military personnel, Army, Navy, and Marine. Sean and Sullivan were feeling pretty good, almost drunk but still able to walk and speak.

"Say Sean let's get some chow. We never did eat."

"We don't have any transportation and I'm not sure if I could even drive."

"Oh hell I passed a nice restaurant on the way to the barracks when I arrived. And there's a jeep here right out side."

"Sullivan, it's not ours and if we get caught, it's the brig for sure."

"Look it's a military jeep, we're military personnel type. And we're just borrowing the jeep. Kinda like a taxi, only we're driving, c'mon."

The two got in the jeep quick and were on the road before any one inside knew it. Twenty minutes of winding around the area, Sullivan finally saw the restaurant. With the jeep parked in the ditch, unintended, they walked into the restaurant.

The occupants sitting by the door looked up to see disheveled, rank looking Marines. Both looked like they just came in from the field, and they weren't standing straight, more like leaning against each other. Those already there were dressed in more stateside uniforms or nice civies, clean, polished with no smell.

The new arrivals were shown to a table way over in the farthest corner. One more step and they'd be outside. But it was next to the restrooms. Sullivan made sure he said hi to everyone entering or leaving the head.

"Evening Capt'n, lovely lady there. Hello, Colonel, enjoying your meal?"

"Shut up Sullivan. You're gonna get us kicked out."

"Ah Sean these bunch of tight assholes got nothing on us. What are they going to do, send us to 'Nam? Besides, I'm heading home and getting discharged."

"Let's order and get the hell out of here."

After the steaks came, drinks spilled, reordered, utensils falling on the floor, Sean and Sullivan were having a great time. It was a great time until the MP's came and escorted the pair outside with a warning to go back to their barracks.

"That didn't work out as planned."

"Hell Sean, the jokes on them."

"What'da ya mean?"

"Sullivan laughed, we never paid our bill."

"Oh shit , let's get outta here."

"Wait Sean. Look, it's my last night in 'Nam. We just became good drinking buddies and will never see each other again."

"Where's this going Sullivan?"

"What do Marines do after getting drunk, and eating? Right! We need some companionship. There's a couple of Vietnamese guys over there, lets inquire about escort service."

"Escort? You mean hookers."

"Escort , hookers, what's the difference? It's all companionship."

The two paid for a trip to the local escort service. Riding on the back of a small 90cc Honda scooter, Sean's feet were dragging on the ground. The driver had a hard time getting it up to speed. Sean thought he may have gained some weight since he first came to Vietnam.

Twenty minutes later they arrived at the Play Boy Club. The so called Play Boy Club was nothing more than a typical Vietnamese shack in a long line of shacks. The only difference with this one was that it had a small sign stating 'The Play Boy Club', hand written of course.

Once inside Sean and Sullivan had their pick of five beauties, ages ranging from 18 to 60. The oldest had about eight teeth, four were on the necklace around her neck. Not the best selection, but ya make the best of what ya got.

"I'll take the mature one" Sullivan said, "I like experience." He was smiling as he walked off. Sean motioned for the younger one to follow him.

Within a half hour Sullivan pushed into Sean's room. "Hey you still in bed? C'mon, Mama-San has some great weed."

"Hell no that shit messes your brain up."

"No it doesn't. Look at me I smoke it all the time."

"Case made."

"Ah the hell with you Sean."

The two lounged around for another hour when they heard an explosion. "What the hell?"

Sean and Sullivan jumped up quickly and ran over to the window. Some Vietnamese were running across the street yelling at each other. The distinct sound of a Russian AK-47 rifle fire was heard.

"Shit I think we're in the middle of an attack."

Mama-San came running into the room shouting and motioning the men to follow her.

More rifle fire rang outside, both AK-47 and the sound of an M-16 American rifle. More explosion rocked the area. The two men ran fast to follow the old lady. She led them through the back door of the hootch into a narrow alley that had a small water ditch in the middle.

"Where the hell is she taking us Sean?'"

"Damn if I know, but a guy sobers up quick when there's an explosion and rifle fire."

The Madam led the pair through two other hootch's into a larger one about one story high. They were brought into a room and motioned to climb a small ladder into the ceiling crawl space. Sean had a T-shirt on, while Sullivan just sported a towel. They crawled into the dark space. Mama-San put a finger to her lips and made a shhh sound as she closed the crawl space cover. The men laid still on what seemed like a soft floor covering. Sullivan immediately started to move around, making noise as as if he was trying to settled in.

"What the hell are you doing? Keep still and don't make a sound."

"Something is poking me in the ass. Some kind of soft thing with a sharp end."

It was then Sean felt the same thing poking his back and legs. Whatever it was, was soft but hard to lay on because of the sharp object it was attached to.

"Damn, it's hot up here Sean, I'm sweating like a pig. Must be a hundred degrees in here."

"What the hell, it's feathers, Sullivan. They have the crawl space lined with feathers."

Below the sound of doors busting open and shouting was heard. All Vietnamese, mostly men's voices with female voices doing the loud shouting.

"Damn Sean, I 'm dying here, my ass is covered with feathers and they're in my ass, my crotch and all over, the sweat is making them stick."

"Shhh, they'll hear us below."

"Do you think they are VC or ARVN soldiers?"

"Don't know Sully, I just hope they don't fire into this crawl space whoever they are."

The shouting and noise below started to quiet down as the invaders seemed to leave.

"God, Sean I'm not sure I can take much more of this heat and feathers."

"Damn it Sully, shut up! We don't know if they're are friendlies or not below. We could get shot any minute."

"Well, I was just thinking in the right situation these feathers could be down right kinky."

"Oh you are a sick man Sullivan."

At that moment the crawl space door opened up and mama-San's head popped though.

"Come quickly."

"Damn Sean she can speak English."

Stepping through the opening onto the ladder, the pair made their way down. They turned around to find three women smiling with hands over their mouth trying not to laugh. As the men, puzzled, turned to each other, each one broke out laughing. Standing before the women were two Americans covered in white chicken feathers sticking to them. The sound of explosions and rifle fire could be heard at a distantance. The women guided the men back to the original hootch. The couch and tables were turned over, facing the windows. Everyone got behind the protective barricade. Sean was feeling a little breeze and looked around for his trousers. Sullivan was peering out the window from behind a curtain.

"Seems the streets are empty, nothing moving. How the hell are we gonna get out of here. In fact I don't recall how the hell we got here."

Sean asked the woman who spoke English if she could get transportation. She rubbed her fingers together indicating money. Sean found his trousers and gave her twenty dollars, then she disappeared. Distant gun fire was heard.

"Must've been a VC attack, trying to penetrate the area around here."

"Sean where the hell is here?"

"Don't know, but when Mama-San gets us a ride out of here, we'll know."
The women came back and told the two Marines a truck would come slowly rolling by and for them to run out and jump on. The ARVN driver would take them back to their line".

"Holy shit Sean, I wonder how far out into Da Nang we went?"

"Guess far enough that we need a ride back."

A dark military truck came slowly up the street. Mama-San ushered the men out the door just as the truck was near the hootch. Sean and Sullivan ran like hell towards the truck. Sean wearing nothing but trousers and boots, while Sullivan had a towel and one boot. Sean made it to the truck first and hopped in the back. Sullivan was losing ground as the sound of his one boot made a slapping sound on the pavement. Distant rifle fire motivated him to catch up and jump in. The driver took twenty minutes to reach the American perimeter. Behind the sandbag bunkers Sean could see Air force sentries. The men got out of the truck and made their way over to the bunker. An Air Force Sgt looked up and smiled. "Marines huh?"

Sullivan said, "how do you know we're Marines?"

"Happens more often than not and it's always Marines. Get your asses in here."

In the morning the Air Force guys gave Sean and Sullivan fatigues with Air Force insignias on them. "It's all we got guys, but it's better than what ya came in with."

"Thanks Sergeant, and we really appreciate your help. You Air Force guys are OK."

"Good to hear that. There's a truck out side to take you to your barracks."

"Oh shit what time is it?"

"0600, why?"

"We need to catch a plane at 0800."

"You're only fifteen minutes away so you'll make it."

"Thanks again Sergeant, adios."
Sean and Sullivan made it into the barracks just as the embarkation Sergeant walked in.
"OK you guys don't appear to be quite ready right now and I really don't wanna know about your choice of outfits. Must have been one hell of a night. There will be a bus outside at exactly 0730. Make sure you make it. And, oh ya, I'd change into something more to your style."
A quick shower and change of clothing, the two Marines were ready to begin the day. They made the bus and loaded onto the Boeing 707 aircraft to Okinawa. From there Sullivan would head to the states and Sean would be off to Australia. Two guys who never met before, had an adventurous night in Da Nang. They would soon part ways and never meet again.
This happens for military personnel. Ya make friends and then they're gone. Part of the military life style. The only thing remaining is a lifetime memory of events and men.

Lt. Janhs walked briskly towards the S-1 administration Hut. His head was down as he read from newly arrived reports. Colonel Johnston was just leaving the hut when Lt. Janhs saw him.

"Excuse me Colonel, I need to speak with you. Just received some news from S-2 in Da Nang."

"Sure, I was just on my way to the chow hall but it can wait, let's go inside, Gunny Simmons is here."

The Gunny was over by an area map of the I-Corp area which extended from just above Da Nang to the DMZ. The area covered the northernmost region of South Vietnam. That section covered five provenances; Qua'ng Tri Provence, Thu'ra Thien-Hue' Provence, Qua'ng Nya'i Provence, Qua'ng Nam Provence and the Qua'ng Tin Provence. The area was ground territory for the Third Marine Division.

"Say Gunny, Lt. Janhs has some news flash from Intelligence in Da Nang."

"Let's hope it includes correct information about what constitutes a friendly landing zone."

Lt. Janhs over looked the slight leveled by the Gunny and handed Colonel Johnston a copy of the new intelligence.

"Seems that the NVA and VC are moving a bit faster than previously thought. They've doubled down on their efforts to move troops along the Ho Chi Minh trail. It had been suggested we move up any flight operations immediately. Headquarters wants us to send out daily overflights to monitor any enemy movements."

"Isn't that what fixed wing aircraft do? Hell they're faster and can cover more territory."

Lt. Janhs looked at Colonel Johnston."

"Ah, yes that's true, but they feel the helicopters can fly lower and at a speed where things might be easier to see."

"Well what do ya think Gunny, can we increase the turnaround time for getting a full squadron flight worthy?"

Gunny Simmons looked at the man and said. "That's a lot of territory with our choppers. But ya Colonel we can work around the clock and get the remaining birds up but we're still short of flight personnel to man them. I was hoping to get Ford and Sean up flying next week. Sean won't be back till then. I can put Ford up now but that leaves us short in the overhaul hanger."

"Look Gunny we're expecting three new guys in a few days. Give them a crash course on being a door gunner. They don't have to know the plane that well, just shoot straight. I know your policy about making guys pay their dues in the overhaul hanger first before flying. But, this is different, we're caught between a rock and a hard place. We gotta do what the Corps always does, adapt."

"OK Colonel, I don't feel comfortable about this, but your right, we adapt."

Rubio saw Ford in the overhaul hanger. "Hey Ford."

Ford turned and walked toward Rubio.

"Guess you're gonna be flying with me. Gunny just informed me you're going on to be on flight status tomorrow."

"No Shit! What about Sean? What's going to happen to him when he gets back?"

"Gunny said he'll start flying right away with TC. Right now you need to check out a pistol from the Armory and get a flight suit, if there are any left. Ya can fly in what you have but the flight suits have all kinds of pockets, are lighter, and you will be cooler. So kiss Sgt. Bonville goodbye and get cracking."

"Thanks Rubio, you made my day."

Ford grabbed his shirt and left. Rubio looked at him as he walked away and thought Ford might regret this day.

Ch 25

Sean and Sullivan slept all of the six hours and thirty five minutes from Vietnam to Okinawa. It was an uncomfortable journey on board the Boeing 707. The noise of fellow passengers, cramped seating, plus recovering from the previous night of drink and sleep deprivation, made for a restless sleep. They arrived at the Kadena Air Force base where the entire plane disembarked. All walked without military precision, just like civilians, over to the terminal. Along the way Sean viewed a C-130 cargo plane taxi over to a hanger close by. As he got near the terminal he watched as the cargo was unloaded. Sean stopped suddenly and froze. Air Force ground personnel were lining up gray steel coffins side by side on gurneys. A Marine color guard in dress blues walked in slow unison over to the coffins. The color guard was headed by a Marine Sergeant. Each of the other ten men in the group were mixed Corporals, Lance Corporals and Private First Class. The Marines were standing at attention in front of the coffins. The Air Force personnel in turn draped an American Flag over each coffin. When the last of the flags was draped, Sean counted fifty. The Marine Sgt. barked an order, "Right face!." With that instruction each member of the color guard did a sharp right turn, clicking the heels of their shoes together. The sound of the Marines shoes made one loud snap sound. Two Air Force ground personnel stood by each coffin. At the Marine Sergeant's command "forward march!," the procession slowly moved alongside the coffin into the hanger.

Many who arrived off the 707 had stopped to watch the process. Some gave an inconspicuous salute. Once the color guard procession disappeared into the hanger, those watching started to move into the terminal. Sean didn't move. He was jousted by those passing by him in the tight quarters of the terminal ramp. All Sean thought about were the six dog tags the Gunny had put into that brown paper envelope.

Sullivan patted Sean on the arm, "c'mon Marine lets move it, nothing to watch here." "Did ya see that Sully?'

"Ya, it's the last damn image I wanted to see before going back to the world. Lets go."

Sean started to move his feet sideways as he looked towards the hanger. Finally he turned fully forward and entered the terminal.

"Listen up." It was the voice of an Air Force Lieutenant. "There are gray buses outside to take you to the storage hanger to retrieve your duffel bag. Extract those clothes you want to wear on R&R, secure the bag and leave it for storage. Those going back to the states take your duffel bag with you to the barracks. All of you will be transferred to an assigned barracks. You can clean up, go to the PX, or the Enlisted Men's Club. Just be ready at 0800 tomorrow for your destination flight. You have your orders with a flight number in it. Don't screw it up or you'll spend your R&R here in Okinawa on details. For those going stateside it'll be a while before the next flight. Now move out!" Sullivan turned to Sean. "Well friend, it has been interesting knowing ya, glad we met."

"Me too Sully, good luck back in the world." With that the men separated.

Once Sean hit the barracks he decided to walk over to the Enlisted Men's Club. When he was on his fourth beer, he heard a familiar voice. "Hey Sean, how ya doing guy." It was Lil' John Camron from HMM 362.

Sean looked up in surprise. "Hi Camron, what the hell are you doing here?"

"Going home man. Caught an unscheduled flight right from Phu Bai. Some politicians plane, forgot his name. They all look alike anyway. Camron smiled. Let's get another round."

After an hour, Sean was on his sixth beer and only half heard what Camron was saying. He heard something about his new car and what he was gonna do when he gets stateside. But mostly it sound garbled.

"Sean!."

"Huh?"

"What the hell is the matter with ya? I asked ya a question."

"Sorry Camron, I'm a little distracted."

"What's going on Ugly Angel?"

"Don't call me that!"

"OK,OK, but what's going on?"

"Did ya see those coffins outside?"

"Ya bad thing, but it's not me and I'm going home."

"Ya, well so are those guys in the hanger."

"Sean, Sean, ya taking it too personal. Ya have to blot out those things or it'll drive you nuts."

"I know. I've been sitting here drinking and thinking."

"Bad combination Sean."

"Ya. Have you seen the papers? Those assholes in the states protesting, calling us vile names. Calling us baby killers. You know any baby killer? I don't. And those poor bastards in those coffins, ya think they killed any babies, fuck no! I passed by the hospital coming to the E Club here. There are guys out there in wheel chairs. Some with an arm or a leg missing. Hell, some with no legs. There were so many guys at that hospitals with bandages, looked like a bunch of mummys. Guys all banged up, bodies in the hanger and these assholes protesting us. What the hell is going on Camron? They sent us over here. We get shot at, some get injured and some get killed. Ya know how many have been killed?"

"No, how many?"

"Fuck, I don't know. Lots. I can tell ya that, lots."

Sean was really feeling the beer, and it was the beer talking The more he drank the more pissed off he got.

"Why? Why the hell do they send us here and then criticize us. The politicians are starting to go against us. Some even running for President. Even they are criticizing us being here. They send us to 'Nam and then they criticize it. All those assholes back there, safe and having fun. Eating good food, going where they want, when they want, no barbed wire, no sandbags, no one shooting at them. They're living good and we're stuck in this shit hole 'Nam. They send us here, then they criticize us being here plus they call us names. Ya, know what the girls back there say? They say, 'girls say yes to boys who say no'. They're talking about those draft dodgers. I might have more respect for guys who go to jail rather than run. At least they stick by their convictions, instead of those fuckers who skip to Canada, chickenshit bastards. Well, piss on the girls, I wouldn't touch them with a ten foot pole."

"Sean I think ya may of passed your beer limit here. You have an early flight tomorrow."

"Ya, well I don't care! 'Member those six guys from our squadron killed weeks back? They could've been in them coffins. They wanted to go home, but not like that. Bastards back in the states, eating good shit , drinking and getting laid. Then all they do is protest us. They all turning against us. Go ahead. ask Ford, TC and Rubio. They'll tell ya the same thing. You heard them."

"I know Sean, it sucks but we got each other. And that's all we got."

"You're right on that Camron. But don't get close, 'cause ya lose one and it hurts. You have to put up that wall, don't let no one close. That way your mind stays right. You may go home without an arm or leg, but your mind stays right."

"C'mon, you're drunk, let me get ya back to the barracks."

"OK, OK, but those som'bitches back in the states suck a big one. College kids, politicians, all of them."

"C'mon Sean , the morning comes pretty fast when ya out drinking the night before."

Ch 26

The Taxi driver pulled up to the corner curb on Kent St, Sidney Australia. Sean stepped out to look up at a two story old colonial type building. The structure was the Lord Nelson Brewery Hotel, Sean's home for the next seven days. The hotel was built in 1841, and the pub used to serve the men who worked at the nearby sandstone quarry. Walking in gave one the feeling of history. It had a rustic decor, sporting a grand fireplace with a picture of Lord Nelson posing above the mantle.

It had been a long nine hour flight from Okinawa. Again Sean slept most of the way. He was awake when the Boeing jet flew over the Sidney Opera house. It's distinct design was familiar world wide. He did a quick disembarkation and scramble to get a taxi ahead of the other military personnel on R&R.

Walking up to the front desk, Sean got his room key and took the elevator to the second floor. Upon entering his room, Sean could hardly contain his excitement. He looked out the window at the busy traffic below. How normal everything looked. It felt like he had been in a long crazy dream and he just now woke up. There were no green military vehicles running around. No dirt road, no sandbags, no barbed wire, no trappings of war at all. Everything was normal. Sean had almost forgotten what normal looked like. Throwing his gear on the bed, he walked into the bathroom and turned on the tub faucet.

He walked out and stripped down to his skin. The small refrigerator next to the bed had cold beer inside. He took a beer, walked back into the bathroom. It had been so long since he had a proper bath. A lay down, stretch out your legs, hot water type bath. The water reached the overflow level and he turned it off. Slowly placing a foot into the hot water, Sean made a slight face. He brought the other foot in and gently sat down in the hot water, with an oooooooh sound coming out of his mouth. The hot water felt almost unbelievable. Taking a huge swallow of beer, Sean laid back and closed his eyes. There is no feeling as laying in a hot tub of water. It caresses the muscles and seems to penetrate the bones. Just being in the soothing water erased months of stress, heat and uncertainty. After a half hour, Sean stepped out of the tub and put a towel around his waist. Taking another beer from the fridge, he took a long swig, almost draining the entire bottle. Placing the beer on the end table, Sean laid on the bed, feeling the softest bedding ever. He could now feel the tiredness in his eyes and gave into it.

It was dark outside when Sean woke. Rubbing his eyes he just laid there. He felt a bit more refreshed but still a little groggy from the sleep. The clock on the end table showed 7:30 pm. His first thought was wow, I'm thinking in civilian time, that has to be a good. He rolled over and sat on the edge of the bed. Adjusting his towel, Sean got up and walked over to the window, letting the curtain block his scanty apparel. The sight of cars driving by was still amazing to view. The lights of street lamps and the cars almost looked beautiful to him. So normal, so much the way it should be. Sean's stomach made a gurgling sound. Damn he thought, when was the last time I ate. He decided to dress, go downstairs and get some chow.

The dining room had an attached bar area, just left of the desk where he had checked in. It was an open concept. If you sat at the bar you could view the diners. Just beyond was the fireplace with the picture of Lord Nelson looking down at the tables. The dinning area was not quite full and three people were sitting at the bar. Sean decided a drink would be nice before eating. He took the first bar stool as he walked in. Taking a small handfull of peanuts off the bar, he looked around. Amazing he thought, people eating, drinking, laughing, enjoying life. What a contrast from where he had just come from.

"Can I help ya mate?"

Sean turned to find the bartender in front of him.

"Ahh, ya, lets see. It's been a while since I ordered a drink at a bar."

"So you're the Yank huh? Heard we had one come earlier."

"How about a gin tonic."

"Gin and tonic it is."

Looking around the room, Sean's' eyes locked on a vision......a brunette with long hair, beautiful legs and a killer smile. She was younger than her happy hour group.

She looked up from her drink and gazed back at him. Avoiding further eye contact, he turned back to the bar, grabbed another handful of peanuts and took a sip of his drink.

Within minutes Sean heard a beautiful voice, "Gin tonic please."

Sean turned to the voice.... it was her.

"Hello."

"Hello," She responded."

Sean smiled, "seems we have the same taste in drinks"

Yes, well the weather determines what we drink, don't you think? Winter is for a heavy drink, a lighter liquor during the intense hot months."

"Well I' m not sure. I drink what I feel like drinking."

"Spoken like a true Yank."

As the woman picked up her drink, Sean thought it was unusual that her table had a waitress yet she came to the bar to order a drink.

"Nice talking to you Yank. Have a grand time in Sidney."

"Thanks. By the way my name is Sean...Sean Michael." She extended her small hand out. "Well welcome to Australia, Sean I'm Joyce Nagel."

"Well thank you, Joyce."

"Enjoy your stay in Sidney Sean."

Joyce turned with her drink in hand and walked back to the her table.

"That Shelia seems to fancy you mate."

Sean turned to see the bartender washing glasses behind the bar.

"She said her name was Joyce."

"It is. Here in Australia, Shelia is a common term for females."

"Why's that?"

"Well mate, back in the day Australia was a penal colony. People were sent here from England and Ireland as punishments. A common Irish name for females was Shelagh. Got shortened to Shelia. Anyway, that's what I heard. Eventually females here were just referred to as Shelia's."

Taking a sip of his drink, Sean nodded. He was looking at Joyce sitting at her table. She had a very nice face, not pretty, but attractive. Her long dark hair came down beyond the shoulders. The hair was in a long ponytail, draped over the shoulder resting on her chest. She had long beautiful legs, like a fashion model. Sean was captivated by the very short skirt she wore.

"Hey bartender."

"My names Thomas."

"OK, Thomas, what's with the short skirts Australian women are wearing?"

"Guess you have been away for a while. Those are the latest thing, they're called

mini-skirts. Pretty nice invention I'd say."

"I agree with ya there Thomas. Ya know it had to be a guy that came up with that idea."

Thomas continued to wipe glasses. "Some call them skirts, airplanes skirts."

"Why's that?"

Thomas smiled and said. "When they bend over you can see the cock pit."

Sean shook his head with a smile. "Really Thomas?"

"Sorry mate that's the best I've got. Excuse me, got another customer."

Thomas went to the other end of the bar to engage a new arrival.

Sean decided he wasn't hungry after all. Seems the alcohol deadened his appetite. When Thomas came back Sean asked where people go for drinks, dancing and music.

"Well mate, most of the Yanks seem to like the Black Hen just down the street. A lot of women go there because the Yanks are free spending guys on vacation like yourself."

"Black Hen huh?" Sean finished his drink and headed out the door.

Two blocks down the street Sean saw a rustic old style sign THE BLACK HEN. Inside the music was blaring. Couples were on the dance floor moving to tunes from Motown. The tables and bar were fairly crowded. Sean managed to grab a seat vacated by a couple leaving.

A bartender walked down to Sean. "What can I get you to drink?"

"Gin and tonic."

The patrons of the bar were definitely American servicemen. The hair style, clothing and the way they carried themselves, was totally American. The atmosphere of the bar was pretty much like that stateside, loud music and everyone talking loud over the music.

Sean noticed a few Australians at the bar chatting with Americans, smiling, laughing and having a good time. Damn it's great to be here, he thought.

On his second drink, Sean watched as a small group walked in. Among the group he saw a familiar face. She smiled when their eyes met and she walked towards him.

"Hello Yank, fancy seeing you here."

"Well this is a pleasant surprise Joyce. Extending the happy hour?"

"Kinda. My friends wanted to hear some music and we haven't been here for quite a while."

The bartender approached the pair.

"Hello Joyce, Gin and Tonic?" She gave an awkward grin and nodded her head.

"So you haven't been here for a while? You must leave a good impression."

Joyce sat down and changed the subject.

"So what do you think of the place Sean? Is this what your bars in the states are like?"

"Pretty much I guess. In the states the drinking age is twenty one so most of the time I sneak in."

"Well you look of age and shouldn't have much of a problem.

The bartender returned with her drink and placed it in front of them.

"So how long are you in Australia for?"

"They give us seven days, but some of that is taken up with travel. I'll be here for another five days and then head back. I'd like to see some of Sidney, but not sure what to see."

Joyce took a sip of her drink, holding the glass with one hand and using the other to grasp the straw.

"Well, I'd suggest that you visit the Australian Opera House, it's really quite nice and some what iconic. Many Yanks come here and just go to the bars. There is a lot to see. The beaches are great and there is a fine zoo here."

"I just might do that."

Sean's stomach made a grumbling sound.

"Oh, sounds like someone hasn't eaten."

"Ya, I probably should've of gotten something to eat at the hotel but my appetite was dulled by the drinks."

"There's a nice small restaurant around the corner, I could show you where it is."

"What about your friends?"

"Oh they'll get along fine without me. Besides they're already entertained by some Yanks."

Sean looked over and saw her group sitting at a table with some guys.

"OK then, show me the way."

They finished their drinks and left the Black Hen. Walking half a block they turned left. A few stores down was a neon sign that read Jerome's.

Inside were a half dozen tables with checker tables coverings. They sat down at a window table. A waiter came over and took their order and left. Time was lost as the two chattered. The waiter had brought the food and later cleared the table. Sean mostly listened as they drank coffee. He found Joyce to be captivating, her mannerism, in the way she held her head, her gentle laugh, and of course the blue eyes. He learned she was from a old Australian family. Three generation of Nagels, originally immigrated from England. Her great grandfather was a ship captain who set up a small Marine shop in Australia to service cargo shipments. The family successfully established itself and prospered. Joyce benefited from the family wealth. Yet the Nagel work ethic encouraged members to make their own way. Joyce choose a career while benefiting from a trust fund.

Sean found Joyce to be pleasant, interesting company. The time passed and Sean noticed the restaurant was slowly closing up.

Joyce spoke first. "Seems we should let these good people close up for the night. Shall we go back to the hotel? My car is parked there."

"Sure. It's been an enjoyable evening." The two walked the two blocks back to the Lord Nelson, but instead of leaving, Joyce suggested a nightcap. When they walked in Joyce headed to the elevator. Sean was unsure of her actions. At the elevator she turned. "I assume you have a mini bar in your room."

Sean just answered yes and pressed the elevator button. Once in the room Joyce took off her short jacket, removed her shoes and sat on the couch. "Anything will do."

Sean went to the mini-bar and took out two small gin bottles and mixed both of them a drink. He turned on the radio to a smooth jazz music station and joined her on the couch.

"I hope you don't think I'm too forward but I feel very comfortable with you and I just didn't want the evening to end."

Sean nodded and took a sip of his drink. The moon cast a dim light into the room. There was a little awkward moment as he leaned over and kissed her. He felt her soft lips, warm, and inviting. She gently pulled away, got up and walked over to the bed and sat down. Sean was treading lightly, unsure of how to proceed, yet he felt a basic urge stirring inside.

Joining her at the bedside, they kissed again, this time it was a long, slow, passionate kiss. Sean was aware of the faint scent of her perfume. He inhaled the seductive aroma of her person. Again she pulled gently away, stood up and very slowly took her skirt off, folded it slightly and placed it on a chair. Sean leaned back on his elbows, watching her from the bed. Reaching up, she methodically unbuttoned her blouse, folded it and placed it on top of the skirt. His mind was a little cloudy as he viewed the vision before him. Removing the remaining clothes she walked around to the side of the bed, folded the bedspread back and gently slid beneath the sheets. Sean sat there, mesmerized by her actions. He was a bit unsure of what to do. He stood up looking down at her.

She smiled at him. "Well, you going to stand there or join me?"

Sean hesitated, then made record time taking his clothes off and crawled under the sheets. He thought to himself, God I love Australia.

The love making was passionate and drained all of Sean's remaining energy. They laid there afterwards, her head resting gently on his arm. With his eyes closed he fell quickly asleep.

Ford had just checked out two M-60 machine guns from the Armory and walked to his chopper, YL39. Rubio was up on the transmission deck wiping off the last grease fitting of a rotor blade.

"Looks like we're all set to go," he said down to Ford. He closed up the transmission deck cover and climbed down the side. He turned to Ford, "pilots should be out in a few minutes."

Since this was only his third mission, Ford was a bit nervous. The other two missions had been a supply run to Da Nang and a Generals chase over to Camp Carroll, a small Marine artillery outpost. This next mission was a genuine entry into a potential hot landing zone. A Marine Recon team found itself in a North Vietnamese controlled area and needed to be evacuated immediately. Ford was uncertain how he'd react if they took enemy fire. He wanted to hold his own and protect the left side of the aircraft going in and more important going out where there was a greater chance of taking fire. Rubio sensed his new door gunners apprehension.

"Don't worry Ford you'll do OK. Just do everything you've been taught and keep your eyes open for any ground activity."

Ford nodded and loaded the M-60's into the aircraft.

The pilots walked out of the S-1 shack and briskly made their way over to the chopper.

"All set to go here? We'll be heading about 40 miles northwest towards Cambodia. Once there we will head north and contact the Recon team and get their coordinates. I don't want us to be in the LZ for more than 15 seconds. Get the team in quickly and we will be off. Keep yours eyes peeled going in and out. Any movement, shoot. There are no friendlies in the area. I'll take the heat for any indiscretions that occur. We're coming back in one piece."

The co-pilot finished the pre-flight and climbed into the left seat and strapped himself in, the pilot did the same on the other side. Rubio stood in front of the chopper with a hand held fire extinguisher. When both pilots were ready the pilot engaged the engine.

Rubio gave a thumbs up when he saw a small trickle of fuel drain from the bottom of the engine. This signaled the pilot that the fuel pump was working. The massive 18 cylinder Witt and Pratney engine turned a few times and came to life as belching black smoke came out of the exhaust stack on the left side of the chopper. Rubio ran and got in through the side cargo door. The chase bird YL-37 followed the same procedures, duplicating those actions of the chase bird. Yl-37 had a crew consisting of Sgt. Tommy Collins and door gunner Corporal Tom Post. Their pilots were Capt. Robertson and Lt. Smally.

Within minutes YL39 was taking off the Phu Bai runway, banking a left traffics turn to the Northwest. YL-37 was right behind as backup.

Once in the air Ford was enjoying watching the scenery pass by. The rural area was dotted with rice paddies, isolated shacks with water buffalo strolling about. Sometimes people on the ground would wave, most of the time they just looked up. He was in awe of how beautiful Vietnam was, green and plush with growth. A small river could be seen winding through the countryside. Vietnamese were paddling along in long wooden boats. It was idyllic in many ways for a war zone. Hard to think a conflict was going on in the lush green foliage below.

YL-39 and it's chase were already an hour flight out northwest of Phu Bai. The ground below began to show craters caused by previous bombing runs in that area.

The destination for the two helicopters was just below the high country leading to Khe Sanh. After another half hour Ford heard the pilot contact the recon team. "Alpha team, Yankee Lima, what are your present coordinates?" The radio was silent, "Alpha team, Yankee Lima, what are your coordinates?" The second request was answered with the assigned coordinates the pilot was given at briefing that morning.

Alpha team, Yankee Lima, in five minutes pop a smoke." At this request the recon Alpha team would pop a smoke grenade so the pilot could tell the wind direction but more importantly to report the color of the smoke. The pilot would tell the recon team what color the smoke was to ensure the correct location. It also prevented the VC or NVA, if they were listening, from popping a smoke and luring the chopper into a trap. Within five minutes the pilots reported, "Alpha team I have an orange smoke at my nine o'clock." The recon team responded, "Yankee Lima, orange smoke confirmed."

At this point the pilot instructed his crew. "OK guys keep your eyes open for any activity. We'll be coming in low and fast. I want that recon team on board and out in 13 seconds. Shoot at anything that moves outside the recon teams perimeter. Confirm this."

"Roger that Captain." Rubio nodded to Ford to be ready.

YL-39 went in first, coming in fast over the trees to a clearing smaller than a gas station parking lot. YL-37 circled low overhead as cover. The orange smoke spiraled upwards from the turbulence of the rotor blades. A rag tag team of seven Marines ran for the chopper. They had the look of both fear and relief in their eyes. The men jumped into the chopper fast, then the pilot applied power. YL-39 was less than two feet off the ground when they began to take fire. It seemed to Ford as if every automatic rifle in the world open up on them from the brush. Small bullet holes opened up on the fuselage of the chopper. The blast from a nearby mortar round pushed the aircraft sidewards. Rubio and Ford returned fire. Their M-60 machine guns raked the surrounding brush. The branches of the brush flew in all directions, the impact of stray bullets kicked up the dirt.

Even with his helmet on and the roar of the rotor blades, Ford could almost hear the impact of bullets hitting the chopper. The floor of YL-39 was filling up with shell casings as they returned fire. The chopper banked left to the southeast. The circling YL-37 was also returning cover fire. At fifty feet Ford felt an impact. He was thrown off his seat onto a recon Marine. He felt it hard to breath and was experiencing a burning sensation in his side. Another Marine jumped onto the empty M-60 and continued to return fire. The recon team medic laid Ford out and tore his protective armored vest off. Blood was coming out of Ford's mouth and he was staring up.

"Sir, Ford's been hit, we need to head to nearest hospital compound."

Rubio continued to fire. The chopper was in flight and out of range now when Rubio settled back and watched Ford laying helpless on the chopper floor surrounded by the recon team. Rubio yelled, "Damnit!"

On the way back the chase bird reported their own casualty. Their door gunner was dead. As in any fire fight, if the enemy throws out enough fire power, they'll hit something. Unfortunately for the door gunner it was him.

Ford was laboring hard when they landed at Phu Bai. An Ambulance took him directly to the aid station hospital.

Both chopper pilots and crew were directed to the S-2 shack for debriefing A lone figure was left standing by the choppers. His hand ran over the bullet holes of

YL-39. Gunny Simmons lowered his head and sighed, "God help us."

Ch 28

The turbulence from the 707 Boeing woke Sean. It took a second for him to remember where he was. He was having such a nice dream, just he and Joyce, laying on Bondi Beach. The Beach was a favorite of Joyce's growing up. It was just 4 miles east of Sidney. Its name was from an Aboriginal word meaning, water breaking over the rocks. They spent a whole day just laying in the warm sun. enjoying the sand under their feet.

The R&R in Australia had gone too fast from that first day he arrived. Sean was remembering that first morning when he awoke to the sun giving a soft, warm glow into his hotel room. He came out of his sleep blinking and getting his bearings. Reaching up with his left hand he rubbed the weariness out of his eyes. The long plane ride from Okinawa, plus the drinks from the previous night and the love making session caught up with Sean, putting him into a deep sleep.

He looked over to his right and saw the empty pillow. Raising his head, he called out, "Joyce!", no response. Slowly placing his feet on the floor, he cupped his bent head with his hands. Standing up, with his hands on his hips, he arched back. He startled himself with a loud yawn. Walking over to the mini-fridge, he opened it, grabbed a small ice tray and opened a beer. Shuffling his feet, he headed into the bathroom. Placing a small rubber cork into the sink basin, he turned the cold water on and added the ice. As the basin filled, he took a long swig of the beer. It was a shock to his system so early in the morning but awakened his senses. He turned the water off when the basin was filled. Taking a breath, he plunged his entire head into the cold liquid. It was a quick way to fully wake up. Taking his head out of the water he wiped with a small hand towel. The reflection in the mirror showed one sorry looking Marine. He reached over and turned the shower on and took another gulp of beer. After showering and shaving, Sean got dressed. He realized he was hungry now and decided to get some chow.

Since the hotel restaurant was not open, he asked the bartender for the nearest place to get a bite to eat. A few blocks down Sean found the quaint eatery, he entered and sat down.

When the food came, he ate thinking how the same food in the states could taste so differently. He never had a fried tomato that came with the meal, but it was quite tasty. Returning to the Lord Nelson Brewery Hotel Sean asked the desk clerk for his key.

"Here you go sir, Rm 202. Oh by the way you have a message." The clerk handed Sean a small envelope bearing the hotels name. He open the the envelope and unfolded the paper. It read, Dear Yank, Sorry to leave without saying good bye, had to go home, change and get to work. Give me a call, I can be free for the next few days. Always Joyce. PS: I kissed you before I left.

Included in the message was her phone number. Hot damn, Sean thought, things are looking good.

"Thanks guy. Say what is there to see during the day here in Sidney?"

"Well , as long as you're in Australia you really should see the Opera House. So few of you Yanks take the time and it is worth it."

"Thanks pal, think I will do that."

Sean took a taxi to the Opera House and spent much of the day on the tour. It really was a grand thing to see and he thought it sad that others on R&R passed it by. There were a few pubs around the area and Sean made it a point to throw one down at each one.

When he got back to the hotel he called Joyce.

"Hello?"

"Hi Joyce, it's Sean."

"Well, hello Yank. Did you enjoy the Opera House?"

"How did you know I went there?"

"I wasn't sure if you would get my message so I called the hotel. The desk clerk told me you were headed there."

"Mmm, checking up on me huh? Only kidding. Say would you be free tonight?"

"Actually I'm free for the next few days if you'd like the company."

"You're a women after my own heart Joyce."

"Sean let me pick you up in an hour and we can decide where to go from there."

"Sounds like a plan Joyce. See ya in an hour."

 Just after five o'clock Joyce pulled up to the curb of the Lord Nelson Hotel. Sean was sitting outside on one of the quaint benches, one leg crossed over the other and his left arm casually slung over the bench back support. When he saw it was Joyce he gave a low whistle. What he was looking at was a 1966 Mercedes-Benz 560 SL yellow convertible coup. Sean stood and walked over to the vehicle and gazed in admiration.

"You really know how to travel in style."

Joyce smiled, "You like it? Used to belong to my father before my mother got after him to act his age. She felt that a successful businessman should drive a black sedan and look important. So he gave it to me as a twentieth birthday gift. But it's still listed under the company's name for tax purposes."

"Oh I like it a lot. And the car is nice also. What is this a 6 or 8 cylinder?"

"Hell Sean I don't know, I just put the key in and start it up. Anything else the mechanic takes care of it."

Sean looked at Joyce, "well you both look fantastic."

"Shall we go? I have a list of places I want to show you." Sean went around to the passenger side and hopped in. He could smell the rich aroma of Corinthian leather seats.   "mmm, they should make a mans colonge of that smell."

"Well Sean if they did it might just attract men."

"Good point Joyce, should we go?

Joyce slid the Benz into first gear and merged with the traffic.

"So where we headed?"

"First I have to go home and change into something more casual. I just came from work and feel the need to change into something more casual. I only live a half hour from here and I'll dress quickly."

They drove east on Kings Cross Road, then north onto New South Head Road. The destination was Point Piper, a sought of penisula East of Sidney. The view was spectacular. Small costal towns, farm land, they were never far from the ocean.

Joyce turned left onto a dirt road that became paved after fifty feet. A white three board fence extended up to the main house. Seans eyes widen as he viewed the main house.

"Just who are you and what does your family do? This place is a mansion! Something like out of a 1930's movie picture. It's gorgious."

"My grandfather bought it years ago and added on to suit his nature."

"Well his nature has pretty expensive taste."

"I know. Sometimes I'm almost embarrassed by the way we live, but it was all paid for with hard work. Nothing came easy for my grandfather and my dad. Everything you see was paid for, cash on the barrel head. Oh maybe a small loan here and there, but for the most part, paid in cash. My grandfather never believed in going into debt. He always said the best way to get out of a hole was to quit digging. So everything you see was built and paid for in small increments over sixty years of hard work, eighty hour weeks, including the weekends."

Joyce brought the Mercedes-Benz to a stop on the circular driveway right in front of the house. She turned slightly to him, "c'mon inside, you can have a drink while I change clothes."

They walked up the ten concrete steps. The steps were two feet wide and twelve feet long bordered on each side by twenty foot high white columns. Seans head was swimming. He felt like he was entering a museum. Once inside, Joyce headed to a wide cicular staircase. "help your self to a drink over at the bar." She continue up the stairs.

Sean thought to himself, 'a bar'? He looked over at the staircase thinking, sure why not, every household should have one.

Sean barely had three slips out of his drink when Joyce came back down the stairs. He looked at her and felt she would look great even in a potato sack.

"OK, lets go to dinner. There's a great place just down the road from here."

"Is that a city block or a country mile?"

Joyce flashed that killer smile of her, "here you drive and I'll navigate."

In twenty minutes they arrived at the Catalina Restaurant on Rose Bay Harbor. A slightly modern structure with some rustic elements to match the harbor setting. They were escourted to the main dinning area. The room faced the harbor and marina. The wall was total glass from floor to ceiling, wrapping round in a semi-circle so every table got a view of the ocean. A person could not ask for a better water view. The attached marina had boat slips to accommodate sailing craft as long as sixty feet. A separate dock was for the motorheads.   Power crafts of fifty feet or more lined the dock. Some boats were moored in the protective harbor, using small dinghies to motor back and forth from the dock to the boats.

The evening was dusk and the sky was turning orange, red and copper with some yellow lines inbetween the strong colors. "Beautiful, just beautiful," Sean said.

They sat down. Sean was careful to hold out the chair for Joyce.

"Why thank you sir, I guess chilvery is not dead after all."

"My pleasure my lady."

Sean sat close to Joyce, closer than is normal in a restaurant. By her smile it was evident that Joyce approved.

"This place is incredible, the view is worth the drive alone."

"Yes, my girlfriends and I come here a few times a month, girls night out and all." A waiter in a white shirt, black vest and black trousers came over. He reached for the napkin on the table, fluffed it, and placed it on Joyce's lap. He did the same thing to Sean. "Good evening, I'm Maurice. Would you like to order something to drink?"

They both ordered Gin & Tonic.

"Very good, I shall place your order and give you time to review the menu." With that the waiter was gone.

"Wow, everything looks great" Sean uttered.

Joyce looked over to Sean with a concerned look and placed her hand on his arm.

"Yank, let me treat you to dinner. After all, I was the one who recommended this restaurant."

"Naw, I'm good, I can spot a lady to a good meal. Besides this place is fantastic."

"But Sean." He looked up quickly, it was one of the few times she didn't call him Yank.

"Sean you're in the service and I believe if it is anything like our military, they don't pay much."

"Oh, is that what it is? You worried? Look Joyce, it's very nice, you're concered about any food bill. What you don't know is, I came to Australia loaded for bear and I'm spending it all before I go back to 'Nam. So don't give it another thought."

Sean looked back down on the menu and spotted his choice. "I'm getting the Seafood Sampler. Look at what you get; oysters, shrimp, scallops, spicy olives and mushrooms,

prosciutte and cheeses. Oh ya that's for me." He placed the menu back down on the table and noticed Joyce had been looking at him with a smile. "Guess I'll try the Parmesan Crusted Sea Bass, sounds yummy." Now Joyce looked up and saw Sean smiling at her.

The waiter came with the drinks, took their order and left. Sean lifted his glass, "I have a toast. Here's to those who wish us well, the rest of them can go to Hell."

"Really Yank! Your Irish is showing." With that she smiled and clinked her glass against his.

The dinner was grand and the drinks hit the spot. Soft music was playing, when Sean asked Joyce to dance. On the dance floor Sean held Joyce against him. The scent of her hair and slight perfume aroma, was intoxcating to him. He felt she might be out of his league. She was pretty, smart but more so, she came from a very affluent family. Old money, they call it. Here he was, just a schmuck from a working class Boston family. He had nothing but the clothes on his back and no prospects. Ya, she was out of his league. But then again he was on R&R and he came here for fun, and fun it shall be. He'd only known her two days, he had no right to think beyond the R&R.

The music stopped and they walked backed to the table. The food and bar bill was nicely hidden in a black leather pouch with thin gold details along the boader. They both raised their glass and finished their drinks. Sean opened the leather pouch and restrained a whistle.

"Yank, you sure you won't let me treat you to the dinner?"

"Joyce I got this. Besides this will help pay for the last house payment for the owner."

Joyce flashed that killer smile and said, "lets go."

The Valet brought the Mercedes around to the front of the restaurant. Sean and Joyce got in with the assistance of the valet who received a nice tip for his efforts. Heading back down New South Head Road, Sean asked "where to?"

"Say let's go to Bondi Beach. It's beautiful there. I used to go there with my parents when I was small. There are some nice shops there and we can pick up bathing suits. It's a short drive."

"OK, Bondi Beach it is."

Sean continued on New South Head Road, then turned onto O'Sullivan Road. In took less than twenty minutes to wander through smaller streets to reach Bondi Beach. Since it was late they decided to rent a bungalow for the night and hunker down for the evening.

The next day they got up around nine, dressed and went to breakfast. It was close to eleven o'clock when they left the restaurant and drove down Main Street.

Sean parked the car outside a small apparel shop. Inside they bought two bathing suits and two towels then drove to the edge of the beach. There was a small changing booth where they exchanged their clothes for the swim suits. When they came out the sand felt warm under their feet. Taking Joyce's hand, they walked to a secluded spot. Sean whistled under his breath at the sight of Joyce in her swim suit.

Joyce smiled, "why are you looking at me like that?"

Sean sighed, "I guess you really don't know how good you look."

"Why thank you Sean. Now let's lay the towels down and test the water." They walked down to the water's edge and slowly entered. Joyce shreaked as Sean splashed her. "Sorry girl, just couldn't help myself."

"Oh you're going to pay for that." With a big smile she jumped on to him and pushed his head under the water. They laughed as they splashed around in the warm ocean water. He held her close and finally gave her a big kiss. Back up on the towels they laid down and let the Australia sun bathe them with it's warmth.

Joyce looked over at Sean who had his eyes closed.

"You know Sean, I don't believe I have ever felt so comfortable with anyone before. I mean there is absoutely no effort talking with you and I just enjoy being with you." Sean noticed she was using his given name more often instead of calling him Yank.

With a smile Sean said, "well Joyce I don't blame you."

She kicked some sand on him saying "ooh you brat." Then she gave that killer smile again. He rolled over to her and gave her a deep kiss. "I'm pretty fond of you too Joyce."

They laid back on the towels and enjoyed the sun, sand and the sound of the ocean breaking up onto the beach. It almost seemed that it couldn't get much better.

The afternoon passed slowly by and the beach was starting to empty. It was close to five o'clock and bathers were heading home.

"Looks like we'll have the beach to ourselvs pretty soon," Sean said.

Joyce rolled over on her side with her head on her elbow. "Do you think we should look for a place to eat? Or maybe a drink? It will help get the taste of salt water out of our mouths."

"Good idea girl, lets change and see what kind of restaurant they have here."

After changing they drove slowly around the beach main street. Most bars and restaurants were starting to fill up with beach goers. Sean pulled suddenly to the curb.

"Whoa, ya gotta be kidding me. Look Joyce they actually have a place called Sean's Panorama. This has to be fate."

Joyce smiled and made a small groan, "guess I'll never hear the last of this."

Sean parked the Mercedes and walked around the other side to let Joyce out.

"Thank you Yank."

Sean muttered, " mmm back to Yank huh?"

"What?" she answered.

"Nothing Joyce, just a small cough." They went inside and got aa table by the window over looking the beach. They ordered drinks, then dinner. Everything served was great. After paying the food tab they left the restaurant and headed back to Sidney.

It was dark out when they arrived at the Lord Nelson Hotel. The long day, drinks and dinner made them a little tired. They went to the room and in spite of the tireness, made
love. It was a slow, drawn out love making session. Afterwards laying back on the bed, Joyce turned to Sean. "I need to talk. We have only

known each other for two days but I feel quite an attraction to you. I don't ever remember feeling like this about a guy and I like it."

Sean turned to her. "Joyce I feel the same way. Not sure when I felt so free with anyone. But we have to remember that I'm just here for a few days and then I go back. No telling what happens after that. I still have a fair share of time to do in 'Nam and a lot can happen."

"I know Sean, I just wanted to let you know how I felt."

With that, he leaned over and kissed her. With their arms around each other.they fell asleep.

The next three days were a whirl wind. Sean and Joyce toured many of Sydneys attractions. Climbing Sydneys Harbor Bridge gave a spectacular view of Sydney. The Harbour Dinner Cruise was made for couples like them. The lights of the harbor against Joyce's profile made her look stunning. Sean got his first look at a live koala bear and a Kangaroo at the Tanaga Zoo. He and Joyce strolled through the zoo holding hands and acting like lovers. A walking tour of Sydneys historic district impressed Joyce.

"You know Sean I have lived here my whole life and never knew anything about this great history."

"It's not suprising. Many people who live in Boston have never been on the Freedom Trail. There's so much American Revolutionary History on that trail, yet it is lost to those who live in it."

Every night they would return from touring feeling exhausted. Each would complain how much their feet and legs were tired. They would have dinner at the Lord Nelson or head down to the Black Hen for drinks, food and music. Returning to the hotel late they would make love and fall to sleep holding each other. On the next to the last day, it was decided to take it easy, sleep late, have room service, lay around and just enjoy the closeness of each other. As evening closed in, Joyce suggested they go to Sydney's Tower Restaurant. It was on top of Westfield Centre on Caslereagh Street, not far from the hotel. Sean called and made the reservation for seven o'clock. By the time both of them had showered and got ready, Sean found he still had to wait for Joyce to change again. She wore no make up, but had a natural glow, beautiful skin. It was six thirty when they left the Lord Nelson, and arrived at the Tower in time for a drink at the bar before dinner. Sean was taken back at the view. "You didn't tell me this was a revolving restaurant. Look, you get a differant view just sitting still."

"Marvelous isn't it. I thought you'd enjoy this, it gives you continuing views of the city." The waiter came and guided them to a window table. "Wow, this is incredible Joyce, the whole place revolves 360 degrees. How the hell do they do that? A guy can get dizzy just eating his meal." Joyce flashed that killer smile. "Let's hope you can keep it together Marine."

The last evening was perfect; the view, drinks, food and her company. After the meal they strolled slowly back to the hotel and up to the room. Sean poured them drinks from a bottle of Johnny Walker Red. Each took a slow slip and said nothing. The silence in the room became awkward. "Look, Sean I really don't know what to say. This is our last night together and it's sad. I don't want this to end but I know you have to go back. I've grown so close to you over the last few days. You gave me so much joy, I'll never forget you."

Her voice started to quiver, a tear slowly rolled down her cheek. He reached over and grasped his hands around her's. Sean was looking at the floor.

"Maybe I won't go back. Maybe I'll stay here, go AWOL for a month. Shit, all I got to look forward to is getting shot or killed."

Joyce got real worried. "Sean, don't say that. You have to go back or you'll get in trouble."

"Ah hell, what are they gonna do to me, send me to 'Nam? I don't owe them anything. The only reason I'm here is because some guy got killed and I took his place. Just another cog in the wheel. Seems when you get close to people they disappear, so whats the use?"

"Sean, please you're starting to scare me." Both of her eyes were wet, she wiped at the tears with the back of her hand. Sean finished his drink and poured another.

"Ya, that's what I'll do. Take off for a month, you and me. We can travel around Australia. We'll have a blast."

"Sean no...I can't do that. I couldn't do that knowing you'd be in trouble at the end."

He looked at her. "So... All this feeling of yours was just talk? You didn't mean any of it?"

"I did Sean, every bit of it and more. It would hurt too much knowing in the end you'd be in trouble. I'd be worried sick for you. Believe me Sean, I'd go anywhere with you, but not if it would cause you harm. Please Sean, believe me." The tears came more freely now, her shoulders slumped and she held both palms to her eyes trying to stop the tears.

"I care a great deal for you. I know it has been a short time, but I can't go with you under those conditions, it's not fair to you or me."

Her wet eyes glistened as she looked up at him. He thought how beautiful she was, not just her looks but who she was.

"You're right Joyce. Guess it's just the realization that this is ending. We have to deal with the fact that I'll be back in 'Nam to finish my tour. Then they'll send me back to the States, if I get back. Then there's knowing you're here and I'll be over seventeen thousand miles away, over half way around the world. Maybe it's better to end it now, avoid the hurt."

Joyce started to sob, Sean sat down and held her.

Another jolt of the plane brought Sean back to his senses. He looked around at the other passengers talking and laughing. He looked straight ahead and remembered that last night of making love to Joyce. That next morning they drove to the airport in silence. He gave her one last longing kiss and felt her tears roll onto his cheek. His last memory was of her standing by the Mercedes tearfully waving to him. As Sean walked to the plane he started to feel his eyes water, he caught himself.

He thought,... never get close to anyone.

The C-130 cargo plane landed at Phu Bai. Sean got his gear, disembarked and hitched a jeep ride over to the other side of the runway to his squadron. He felt good to be back in familar settings.

It had been a long flight from Australia to Okinawa. He stored his civies back into storage and flew out the next day to Vietnam. It almost seemed to him as if R&R was a long time ago even though Joyce was still fresh in his mind.

The jeep let Sean off near the overhaul hanger. He grabbed his bag, gave a thanks to the driver and headed towards the hanger. As he passed by he could see Sgt. Bonville way inside sitting at his desk. Sean waved as the Sergeant looked up. Without acknowleging Sean, he continued working on his paperwork. Sean thought, what a prick.

He continued walking down the flight line. Up ahead were TC, Rubio and Dolman.

"Hi guys, how's it going?"

All three just looked at Sean No one said anything.

"You guys seem too serious."

TC spoke up, "the Gunny wanted to see you right away when you got back."

"OK, I'll just put my gear in the hootch and go see him."

"No Sean, the Gunny was pretty adamanant about seeing you right away."

"Wow, you guys need some coffee. You all look uptight. I'll head over to the line shack right now, watch my gear will ya."

Sean gave a quick knock on the screen door before walking into the shack. The Gunny was busy at his desk but looked up.

In a very solmen manner he said, "hi Sean come in and have a seat. You want some coffee?"

"No thanks Gunny, I'm all coffee'd out. TC said you wanted to see me right away."

The Gunny pushed away from his desk a bit, put his pen down and leaned back.

"Ya, I wanted to speak with you before you talked with any of the guys." Sean got a bad feeling, "oh shit Gunny, you're not gonna let me fly are you."

The Gunny shook his head, "no Sean I...."

Sean spoke up. "Aw Gunny I thought it was a done deal, that when I got back I'd get to fly. What the hell is going on? I was really looking forward to being on flight status. You so much as promised me and Ford would be flying."

"Sean will you just shut up for a minute!" The abruptness of the Gunnys voice caught Sean off guard. He never spoke like that to him except for when he and Ford went swimming outside the perimeter. Sean sat back, "OK, whats up?"

"Sean there is no easy way of saying this so I'll come right out. Ford is Dead.

With his mouth half open, Sean just stared at the Gunny.

"Whaaat?"

The Gunny looked away for a second then turned back to Sean.

"I said, Ford is dead."

With a quizzical look, Sean said, "what do you mean dead? Like dead, dead? Wha...how,when? What the hell you talking about. I left him a week ago. He and I were gonna get together when I got back. I got a bottle of Johnny Walker Red for him. He can't be dead!"

"Sean, calm down. I wanted to tell you before you heard it from the other guys."

Sean thought, that was why TC and the others were so serious.

"I know you and Ford were tight, thick as thieves. When I saw one of you the other was not far behind. I wanted to break it to you before the others did."

Sean got up, walked away, turned around, walked back, turned again, shaking his head. He was trying to process what the Gunny told him. "What the hell happened? When did he start flying? Where did this happen? How did it happen? Sean grabbed the edge of the chair and stared at the Gunny.

"Please Sean, sit down."

Sean came around from the back of the chair and sat, still shaking his head.

"After you left for R&R, we had to put Ford on flight status. We were short of qualified people to man the helicopters. I put him on with Rubio. They had already flown a couple of missions. An emergency recon extraction came up. Rubio and Ford were in the lead aircraft. TC and a new guy, Corporal Post, were chase. They got into a bad situation, beaucoup automatic fire coming out of the LZ. Ford got hit, as did a few recon Marines they picked up. TC's door gunner was killed immediately. When Rubio and the chase got back here, Ford was rushed to the hospital. He died on the operating table. Thats about it. Bad thing all around."

Sean kept staring at the Gunny. The silence was awkward. Sean got up without saying anything and slowly walked to the door. The Gunny called out his name. Sean stopped without turning around.

"Sean, I'm really sorry. Don't bother reporting back to the flight line. I'll square things with Sgt. Bonville."

Without turning, Sean nodded and walked out.

The back door to the Gunnys shack opened. Col. Johnston walked in. "How'd he take it?"

"Not sure Colonel. He walked out not saying anything. I'm sure it's a shock to him. Those two were really tight."

"Well get him up flying ASAP. It'll keep his mind busy. I've seen guys in Korea over think the loss of a buddy and they end up being no good to anyone."

"OK Colonel, I'll give him a few days and then assign him with TC."

The old beer tent had been taken down and replaced with a new wooden hootch. It had the dimension of a small house with a low tin roof. During a downpour, the rain made so much noise on the roof that it was difficult to talk. The hootch even had a wooden floor and large folding wood window shutters. All the wobbly tables and chairs from the old beer tent were still in use. It had the coziness of a country store minus the cast iron stove in the middle. The lighting was dim and would go out a few times during the night due to the old generator breaking down.

TC, Dolman and Rubio found Sean sitting in the rear corner. Four empty beer cans were already on the table and three full ones at the ready. Sean spent the last few nights drinking by himself. Gunny Simmons asked TC to check up on him.

"Hey Sean, mind if we join ya?"

Sean looked up and motioned for them to take a chair.

"Seems like progress has come to Phu Bai. New beer hootch, but same smell and crappy beer."

"You've been hitting it heavy the last few nights", TC said. "Missed ya on the flight line."

"Well Gunny said for me to take a few days and get settled in. I think he wants me to get my mind straight."

Rubio spoke up, "well we thought we'd come down and join ya ."

Sean stared at Rubio. "You should've looked out for him"!

"What?"

"You should of looked out for him."

Rubio appeared suprised by the comment, "you mean Ford?"

"Ya, who the fuck did you think I meant?"

"Wait a minute Sean, I'm not sure what your getting at but I was in that chopper as well. They were shooting at all of us. I was a target just like everyone else."

"You were the crew chief Rubio, you had a responsibility for your crew! It was only Ford's third mission, you should've better prepared him."

Rubio had an astonished look on his face.

TC could see Sean was getting agitated, "wait a minute Sean....." Before he could finish, Sean was out of his chair and on top of Rubio swinging with his fist. The action caught the others off gaurd.

"You son of a bitch I'll kill ya." Rubio tried to fend off Sean. The others grabbed Sean and pulled him off Rubio. He jumped up quickly, "OK asshole you want a piece of me? C'mon. If you're gonna blame me for Ford's death , then go for it."

TC jumped in front of Rubio. "Wait a minute, both of you"! He turned to Rubio. "Can't you see he's been drinking and pissed off? Now both of you calm down."

The others were still holding Sean.

"Let me go you fuckers." Sean wiggled to get out of the grasp of Dolman

TC spoke, "not until ya settle down. You've been drinking and quite frankly acting like the asshole Rubio called you. He had nothing to do with Ford getting shot. In fact if it hadn't been for the recon Marine sitting in front of him, Rubio would've been hit, so calm down, damn it!"

Seans body went a bit limp and Dolman let up on his grip, "alright, alright, let me go." With that, Dolman let Sean loose. TC looked at Sean. "Why don't you call it a night and go up to the hootch. You and I are scheduled for a mission tomorrow. Your R&R has offically ended. If you want me to pull rank I will. Now go!"

Sean staggered a bit, picked up his hat and brushed it against his knee. He started to turn away and stopped., "sorry Rubio, nothing personal."

Rubio stood there and smiled, "aw fuck you." Sean smiled and walked away.

TC clapped his hands and rubbed them together, smiling, "OK now lets drink some beer."

The three sat down with Rubio holding his jaw, "that Irish bastard can really hit." They all laughed.

It had a been a few weeks since the incident with Rubio. The day after, feeling like a jerk, Sean apologized to Rubio, TC and Dolman. Everyone chalked it up to the drinking and Sean's attitude at the time. The following days were a series of small missions, resupply, generals chase, and a few mild medevacs. Not one mission involved even a hint of danger. Sean was getting frustrated. Ford had run into a firefight on his third mission and yet Sean hadn't even fired his weapon over the past week. He watched as others would go off on emergency medevacs or recon evacuations. In some ways he felt cheated, maybe a small amount of guilt. Others were doing their part and he felt like he was on milk runs. TC had been good about teaching him the ropes. What to look for, how much weight to take on during supply runs. He even helped Sean add piggy back rounds to the machine gun belt for greater fire power. The piggy back round had two projectiles, one in front of the other. When fired, the M-60 machine gun would give out two rounds for each single round. Just for the hell of it, Sean attached a tracer round on the belt after every fifth round. The effect would be a red dotted line when the machine gun was fired. This helped sighting in on a target. With all the preparation, he was still yearning for some action. He started to hang outside the flight shack where fight missions were assigned. Noticing that missions were written with chalk on a blackboard, he got an idea. When missions were assigned, Sean would sneak into the flight shack and replace a choppers number with YL-37. This way he and TC would get missions that had more activity. The next day a call came in for an emergency medevac. After the mission was assigned, Sean went into the now empty hootch and switched the assigned aircraft sign letters to

YL-37. He hurried outside and headed over to his chopper. TC was standing talking to Rubio.

"Hey TC, I think we got a medevac mission."

"Really? How do you know?"

"I walked by the flight shack and saw us listed."

"Mmm, first I've heard of it."

"What'd ya think TC, should we get ready?"

"Guess so."

Within fifteen minute the line chief came over. "Saddle up guys your on in twenty minutes, medevac mission north of Hue' City. Seems some Marines ran across some NVA and took some casulities."

"We're on it chief," TC said.

The pilots were already headed out and coming their way. After the pre-flight and run up was done, YL-37 taxied to the runway and took off with a chase aircraft right behind. Their distination just west of Phong Dien, a small coastal city in the Thura Thien-Hue Provence.

The flight took less than 20 minutes to travel the twenty five miles. Sean was pumped for the coming action. He kept scanning the terrain for possible ground fire. TC was smoking a cigarette and smiling as he watched Sean. He thought that this guy was a Wyatt Earp, just looking for a shoot out. Five miles, out the pilot radioed the Marines in the LZ.

"This is Yanky Lima, I see a red smoke, confirm."

"Yanky Lima, Zulu One, roger on the red. We have four casualties, two on stretchers, two walking.."

"OK Zulu, watch our back, coming in low."

YL-37 came in at five hundred feet and descended fast. Inside the chopper, Sean and TC had their M-60 locked and loaded. TC spoke to Sean over the intercom. "Watch the tree lines, any sign of white flashes, shoot!"

The approach was smooth, casualties were loaded and the aircraft took off. At three hundred feet they took automatic fire from the tree line on Sean's side. He opened up and watched as the carefully prepared rounds in his machine gun belt gave off a red dotted line. It excited him to use the red line to zero in on his target. The vibration of the M-60 was all that he expected, empty shell cartridges littered the floor. They were well in the air when TC yelled at him. "Quit firing"! Looking over at TC, Sean realized he had gone on to long firing and knew he'd catch hell later. He sat back but could feel the adrenaline raging through his body. Looking at the floor, he saw a puddle of blood flowing back and forth as the chopper made directional moves. He could smell the mixture of blood and dirt. It was a wet, earthy dirt smell mixed with the stench of blood.

The aircraft had landed at Phu Bai, YL-37 taxied to the flight line. The calusities were unloaded and taken away by an abulance. After the aircraft taxied into it's assigned space the pilots shut it down and left for the briefing room. Sean tried to avoid TC's attention. Finally TC approached him. "Look, I know this was your first mission under fire. But get one thing straight. Never, and I say never continue firing the way you did. You kept your finger on the trigger too long. Ya do that, the barrel of the gun heats up and can cause a jam. Then where would ya be? Huh?"

Sean shurugged his shoulders. "Hell I'm sorry TC, I was excited and just trying to place cover fire."

"Cover fire? We were at five hundred feet and a mile away. There was no longer a target and you wasted ammunition."

"Guess I got caught up in the moment TC, it won't happen again."

"Well..., just use this as a learning moment. You'll need it in the furture. I'm going to the briefing room. Clean up the mess inside!" With that TC stomped away.

Sean didn't care. He was still pumped from his first action. He was high on the feeling. Leaning against YL-37 he smiled. Damn he thought, that was some shit. He turned and looked inside the aircraft. The still fresh smell of dirt and blood was exhilerating. Grabbing a cloth rag, Sean began the task of wiping up the mess.

The beer hut was half filled when Sean entered. He walked to the bar and ordered a half dozen beers. Grabbing the beers up in his arm, he looked for an table. Over in the corner was Rubio and TC. Sean took a deep breath and walked over. "Hi Guys."

"Hey Sean. TC was telling me you got your cherry broke today."

Sean looked at TC.

"Ya we ran into a bit of trouble but nothing we couldn't handle."

TC spoke up, "We got lucky. By the way there was some confusion in the flight shack. Gunny was pissed that we went instead of the chopper he assigned. He said he knew he gave that mission to YL-29 and was wondering how it got switched. You know anything about that?"

"Hell no! I saw the assignment and walked right out to you."

"Well Gunny is looking into it so no more screw ups like that occur again." TC took a swig of beer and stared at Sean.

Feeling a bit uncomfortable Sean picked up a beer. "Ya I can see where he'd want to check into that."

The three Marines sat, drank, and talked about missions.

The next morning Sean was still feeling the effects of last nights drinking. He was sitting outside the flight shack sipping on a cold pepsi to quench the dryness in his throat.

It was around 0900 when Gunny Simmons walked towards him.

"Morning Sean, heard you finally got your taste of action."

"Ya Gunny, was pretty exciting. I finally felt like I did something."

"Look Marine, everything you do here, no matter how small it may seem is important. These flight missions are just the point of the needle, But without the rest of it, it's no good. The whole thing is one package, from the overhaul hanger to the shit details. It's all important."

Sean looked up, "Got it."

The Gunny started to turn away.

"Ah say Gunny. YL-37 is all set to go. I got up early and greased all the fittings. Got the bird fueled up. We're ready anytime a mission comes in."

Gunny stared at Sean. "Don't be too anxious son, ya still have six months to go. Don't press your luck."

"Oh I won't Gunny. I just wanted to let you know TC and I are ready to move. Just say the word."

The Gunny walked away.

Ch 31

For the next few weeks YL-37 was seeing more than it's share of action. It was emergency medevacs, emergency extractions, anything involving going into a potential hostile LZ. YL-37 was always returning all shot up. The aircraft and crew were racking up missions after missions. The next day after it returned it was back up and running. The aircraft was patched, fueled and ready to go. There was some scuttlebutt around the flight line that YL-37 was just unlucky to be on so many missions.

Colonel Johnston walked into Gunny Simmons office.

"Afternoon Gunny."

"Hello Colonel, what can I do for you?"

"Say I was going over this months missions and saw that YL-37 has been on three to four times more missions than the other helicopters. Any explanation? I mean they come back shot up and they get sent back out."

"Well you're right on that Colonel. I was wondering about that myself. The bird comes back shot up and is back on line the next day. It's all fixed, patched up, fueled and set to go. Most unusual for the overhaul hanger. They have enough work to keep them busy for weeks. Yet they have time to push YL-37 back out onto flight status."

Colonel scratched his head, "well look into it will ya? I never knew an overhaul crew to be that efficent"

"Will do Colonel."

The Colonel walked out of the hootch as TC was walkng in. TC sharply saluted the Colonel, which was returned just as sharply.

The screen door shut behind TC. "Hi Gunny, you got a moment?"

"Sure TC, I just happend to be thinking of you, but you go ahead. What can I do for you?"

"Gunny I want off flight status."

The Gunny looked up and slowly lean back in his chair. He eyeballed TC for a few seconds. "Ya mind telling me why?"

"Gunny, I'm on my second extention. I'm due to rotate back to the world next month. Now I've done more than my share of flying and I feel like I'm pressing my luck."

"TC let me ask you. Does this have anything to do with Sean?"

"Oh no Gunny...well kinda. Look Gunny, Sean is a hell of a door gunner, couldn't ask for better. He's up and at the chopper before the flight line is awake. Planes always ready and clean. M-60 are mounted and at the ready."

"But what TC?"

"Gunny, he dosen't know when to quit. We've been on more emergency medevacs, recon extraction than anyone. Hell I've been fired at more this last month than twice as much as my whole first year in 'Nam. I have the feeling Sean somehows gets us assigned to ever shit mission. It seems like he's trying to prove something or get revenge at Charlie. He's a helluva of a crew mate but I'm too short." Like I said he's a hell of a gunner, if I had just started flying I'd want him on my chopper. But Gunny I'm to short."

"I know TC. I've noticed you and Sean seem to be always flying missions and coming back all shot up. Wasn't sure what to do. How do you discipline a guy for doing a job too good? I'm more concerned about his aloof atitude when others are hit or killed. It's like he's distant, doesn't want to acknowledge it."

"Gunny, Sean is a great guy, and yes he does put up a wall to maybe protect himself. He mentioned this once when we were drinking. He said it does no good to get close to people 'cause it kinda hurts when they go away or get killed. Plus to cope with the possibility of getting in harms way, Sean mentally figures he's already a walking dead man. In that way it dosen't matter how dangereous the mission is or if he gets shot. And yes, I think maybe Ford getting killed was the start of it. But Sean is a good man. It's just I'm too short in country and have played my hand way beyond what I should have."

"I got it TC. Let me find a replacement for you, but in the mean time you're still flying."

"Thanks for the talk Gunny."

TC walked out of the hootch and down the flight line. Gunny frowned thinking he was losing a good man. The more he thought of his talk with TC the more he started to develop a solution. He always felt better when he could formulate a plan on the fly. He picked up his pen and wrote, thinking to himself, this can solve two situations.

Gunny Simmons met up with Colonel Johnston regarding YL-37 availability the day after being shot up on an intense mission.

"I tell ya Colonel ya never gonna guess how YL-37 is back on line so quick.

In-addition to that hot shot Sean being up early and getting the bird ready, he's been bribing Sgt. Bonville."

"What the hell do you mean bribing Bonville?"

"Seans been giving the Sergeant a bottle of Jonny Walker whisky for working on YL-37 before any other helicopter. And Sean promised him a bottle each week if he worked on his bird first and get it out of overhaul for the next day."

The Colonel shook his head. "Well I knew Sgt Bonville was a boozer but this is wierd. Never heard of anything like this. What the hell, does this Sean have a death wish?"

"Don't know Colonel. Since the first day he arrived he has pushed to be in on the action. He works hard and always has his bird up and running. I kinda think that when Ford got killed Sean just got it into his mind to revenge his death. I don't know. Like I said, he works hard and he plays hard."

"What do you mean he plays hard?"

"Rumor has it that he's in the beer hut every night, stays to closing. But he's up and running the next day. He also has a tendency to stay to himself quite a bit. He mostly hangs with Rubio, Dolman and TC, but thats just for drinking. Like I said, he's up and at it the next day and his bird is always ready to go.

"Well Gunny, lets keep an eye on him."

"Colonel, I have close to a dozen hotshots out there like Sean. They're all eager and ready to go. Kinda hungry for action. The only thing is, Sean is more aggressive than the rest of them."

"Well put YL-37 on a mission less exciting, maybe it will dampen his enthusiam

Sean was at his usual seat just outside the flight line shack when the Gunny walked out. "Hey Marine, go gather up TC. Got a mission for ya." Sean got up quick. "What's its gonna be Gunny, medevac or recon insertion?"

"Your gonna fly some show girls around. They're part of a USO show. We've been chosen to give'em a lift."

The smile on Seans face disappeared. "But Gunny, can't someone else take that? Maybe ya want to keep YL-37 in reserve for something more important."

"What did I tell you before? No mission or detail is unimportant. It all works together for the good of our unit and the Corps." The welfare of the troops is important. If morale goes down so does our effectiveness. Seeing some female singing and shaking her ass around on a stage works wonders for the men. Now go get TC and get ready to saddle up!"

"OK Gunny if we have to , we have to."

"Oh you have to, now go get TC!"

Forty five minutes later TC, Sean and the pilots had YL-37 up and running and made their way to the runway for takeoff. Fifteen minutes into the flight the pilot came on the intercom.

"We're going to Camp Carroll to pick up some USO singers. We will take the female singers and the chase bird will carry the band members. Once we have the singers loaded and inflight I'm gonna pull a P manuver so watch for a reaction from the passengers."

Sean never heard of a P manuver. He unpluged his headset and took two steps over to TC. TC lifted part of his helmet to hear Sean. Sean shouted over the noise of the chopper.

"What the hell is a P manuver?"

TC smiled and shouted back over the noise of the chopper. "The pilot pulls up fast on the cyclic stick to get max lift. Once we get a quick ten foot lift he disengages the rotors. It causes a quick decent . Like being in a fast elevator. It really puts the stomach up into your throat so be ready."

Sean was still unsure what to expect or what was the purpose of a P manuver. He went back over to his seat, sat down and plugged back into the intercom. Forty minutes later YL-37 landed at Camp Carroll. All USO passengers were loaded and the chopper took flight. Within fifteen minutes the pilot came on the intercom.

"Ok guys get ready, I'm set to do a P manuver. Sean braced himself and felt an immeadate up lift followed shortly by a quick descent. Even with his helmet on and the helicopter noise, he heard the screams of the female singers. Sean thought, Christ no wonder they could hit high notes with lungs like that. TC was smiling and pointed to where the singers were seated. Two out of the five female singers had wet themselves and urine was soaking through the nylon web covered seats onto the floor.

Sean got it, a P manuver was actually done to cause the passengers to piss their pants. Thus the P manuver. The pilot came on the intercom for TC and Sean to hear.

"How'd I do guys? How many did I get?"TC responded smiling, "not bad Captain, two out of five. The look on theirs faces is priceless. I could hear them screaming through my helmet." Sean smiled and shook his head

"Well then, let's get them to Ky Hai for their first show and to dry themselves. With that the pilot switched the intercom on to Armed Forces radio. A new song came on, 'Light my Fire' by a group called the Doors.

YL-37 flew a zig zag pattern to Ky Hai. The music and the zig zag flight manuever seemd to go hand and hand. The organ solo of 'Light my Fire' was in rhythm with the aircrafts flight pattern. For once Sean felt relaxed with out the thought of getting shot at. Sitting diagonally from Sean, TC was smoking a cigarette and smiling. The music just seemed to make the mood for the flight. Some of the singers were still crying and trying to wipe themselfs. Ya this is a good flight TC thought.

The day was spent at two outpost, where the USO band gave female deprived Marines a much needed morale boost. Some lucky Marines got to go up on stage and dance with the singers while those in the audiance hooted and shouted. The pilots, TC, Sean and the crew from the chase birds spent most of their time at the steak cookout supplied by the host base. It had been a long time since they had tasted steak. Not too much of it gets north to Phu Bai where they were stationed. Sean had three steaks and later felt like the bulge in a pythorn after it had eaten. Since they would stay the night at Ky Hai they were allowed to have a beer, which TC and Sean managed to consume four apiece.

The next morning the singers and band were loaded and headed to Da Nang to drop them off for a USO show. From there another chopper squadron from Da Nang would fly the band around bases near Da Nang. As TC and Sean walked around Da Nangs'
Freedom Hill near the beer garden, Sean was reminded of Sullivan and the night they were caught outside the perimeter during an attack. He smiled and kinda missed ol'Sully. Sean also was reminded of his trip to Australia and Joyce. It seemed like years ago even though it was only a month and a half.

TC and Sean made their way throught the variety of small shops on Freedom Hill. Both loaded up with peanuts, kool-aid, lot'sa gum and of course they hit the beer garden liquor store for some Johhny Red and Old Turkey whiskey. This time, because TC was a Sergeant, the clerk didn't refuse them service. As they were paying for the booze the clerk looked at Sean.

"Say, don't I know you?"

Sean hesitated a bit, "ahh nope, never been here before."

"You sure? I have a good eye for faces and you look familar."

"Nope, sorry guy, you got the wrong face this time."

As they walked out TC turned to Sean. "Hey I thought you said you drank here just before your R&R trip. Told us some cock and bull story about stealing a Generals jeep, getting laid and almost getting caught up in a ground attack."

"Ahh, thats true except I didn't want the clerk to know. He might just be friend with the Army Warrant Officer Sullivan and I threatened."

TC smiled, "You beat all Sean , ya know that? You beat all." Sean shrugged his shoulders, "c'mon let's go."

With their new purchases the two headed back to YL-37 to wait for the pilots.

Within the hour YL-37 was in flight back to Phu Bai. During the flight Seans mind wandered to Sullivan and their night of debauchery. He also thought of Joyce. He thought it odd he hadn't given much thought to her in the past month. His ability to shut out past acquaintances was keen. Yet he felt a void without her.

Ford was gone, Camron went home, Sullivan was gone and Joyce was gone. He thought every time ya get close to some one they're gone. In his mind it reinforced the notion, don't get close to anyone. It's no good to experience the emptyness when they're gone.

The USO mission was great and enjoyable but it was time to get back to reality. In war people leave and die never to be seened again. Nope, it serves no purpose to get close. Keep that wall up and ya minimize the losses and the dreadfull experience of emptyness. Nobody got time for that hurt.

YL-37 landed at 1700 hours at Phu Bai. After taxiing to it's berth, the pilots and TC left for briefing. Sean stayed behind to get the chopper ready for what ever comes it's way. Sean was hoping for another mission, an emergency mission, something that would give him that rush again. He looked inside the chopper and saw some wetness where the USO girls had sat. Smiling he grabbed a rag and cleaned the area....P manuver, shit who thought that one up?

After cleaning up Sean took his purchases of peanuts, gum and Old Turkey whisky up to his hootch. He looked around before hiding the goodies under his canvas cot and inside a pair of boots. Next step was the beer hut and a few rounds of beer. Inside Sean found TC, Dolman and Rubio at the task of drinking. Rubio waved a hand at Sean to come over. At the table TC spoke up.

"Rubio and Dolman was telling me we missed all the action last night."

"Why, what happened?"

Dolman put his beer down. "Just before it got dark we got incoming rockets and mortar fire. Lt. Downwells called out the perimerter platoon. Every swing dick was on line. Seems the VC wanted to test our resolve and hit us fast."

"Ya", Rubio broke in. "No sooner did we get on the perimeter line than Charlie started firing at us. Never saw that much automatic weapons open fire on us. Charlie was laying down quite a barrage."

Sean took a swig of beer. "Shit, what happened, did anybody get hit?"

Rubio motioned over to the other table. "Remember those guys who sat there? Well, three are dead and four are in the hospital. Their sector was hit the hardest. Me and Dolman didn't get hit, but it was bad. I went through seven magazines. Dolman, didn't you use up most of your ammo?"

"Shit ya. I had one magazine left after the fighting. But Charlie kept lobbing mortars down on us. Someone called in Huey gun ships and nailed the bastards. Whole thing must've of lasted an hour and a half. Later those guys...." Rubio stopped and pointed over to the empty table. "They took the brunt of the attack. Poor bastards. Lt. Downwells found them all shot up."

Sean spoke. "Did you know any of those guys?"

"Ya." Rubioa said. "I went through bootcamp with one. Nice guy. He was an office
pinky, a typewriter was more his weapon. The other one was a cook.
Blond kid from Nebraska.   What a shame, he was gonna rotate back to the world next month."
Sean thought, thats why ya don't get close to any one. Hell a clerk and a cook, not really combat type MOS's. But in the Marines everyone is an 0311, a basic infantry guy regardless of their secondary MOS.
Sean looked over at TC who was staring off to the empty table.
"What you staring at TC?"
"Oh, just that I'm due to rotate back next month and I don't want to go back sooner. Ya catch my drift?"

Ch 32

Gunny Simmons was going over the casualties list from the previous nights attack, when Colonel Johnston entered the administration shack. Lt. Jahns was reviewing a map.

"Say Gunny you have a tally of casulties from last night?"

"Ya, I was just reviewing it. We got three dead, four shot up real bad and about ten with injuries ranging from mortar schrapnel to just cuts and bruises of various degrees."

Colonel Johnston sat on a corner of the Gunnys desk. "I just finishing reading the report from S-2 intellegence officer Lt. Janhs. It states headquarters expects more of these attacks. It all lines up with those sporadic attacks last month, when Hanoi was tesing our capabilities. HQ feels that the NVA and Charlie have restocked their supplies and are ready to rumble."

"But Colonel the Vietnamese will be starting their Tet year holiday soon. I mean it's like fourth of July and Christmas all rolled into one. The VC usually observe a cease fire or limited action."

"Well Gunny, anything can happen. Headquarters S-2 dosen't believe the enemy can muster a large scale attack. All we can do is wait and see, but be ready regardless. It's near the end of January and the beginning of Tet so anything can happen. The Vietnamese government has stepped up it's Chieu-hoi program. Sometimes pronounced Chu-hoi. It was designed to entice more VC to defect to our side. Quite a propaganda operation. Some of those poor bastards are nothing more than conscripts at gun point. They get taken away by force with the threat of harm to their families if they don't go. Once conscripted they rarely see their famiiles or hear from them in years. They get no pay to speak of, no R&R, crappy food plus they sleep out in the bush all the time. And some are given ancient weapons to fight us. They're a sorry lot those poor bastards."

The Gunny turned in his chair. "Well Colonel a lot of the enlisted don't like the Chu-hoi program. They tell of the VC shooting at us and when we capture them, they throw out the Chu-hoi card. One Marine outfit took one VC down. Charlie came out with hands raised yelling, Chu-hoi, Chu-hoi! Some one shot him. The VC went down and exploded. Seems he had a satchel charge strapped to his back. He was gonna blow eveyone up. So, many troops don't trust the Chu-hoi program. Some VC hang on to the Chu-hoi cards until they get captured and then pull the Chu-hoi thing."

Colonel addressed Lt. Janhs, "what the hell does Chu-hoi mean any way?" Lt. Janhs looked up from the map he was studying, "roughtly translated it means open arms or forgiveness in Vietnamese. All Charlie has to do is cross over to our side. Those who surrender are known as Hoi Chanh. They gets amnesty and intergrated into a fighting group called the Kit Carlson Scouts. They go out and find their former comrades and shoot them. Helluva of a concept. These Kit Carlson Scouts know their shit though. They can tell you where the VC would hide supplies. Let you know if a village has too much rice for the inhabitants and therefore are feeding the enemy, lot'sa stuff.

Colonel Johnston sipped on his coffee. "How long has this program been going on?"

"Well Colonel, the South Vietnamese government has been doing this for years, quite successfully. There have been over seventy five thousand deflectors. Some deflectors have given us some pretty good scoop on potential attacks by the VC and the North Vietnamese Army. Just a few days ago an NVA Lieutenant, La Thanh Tonc turned himself in. He gave some info of possible attack on Khe Sanh, and Hills 861 plus Hill 881S. All in all, we've gotten some pretty good intel from the Chu-hoi program. The program comes at a basic cost of around $125 for each VC deflector. Of course thats minus the costs to pursue them, in equipment and men. Any Vietnamese who gets a VC to turn, gets a reward based on the value of that asset."

"Ya mean like a bounty?"

"That's right Gunny. Depending on the position of the VC or rank of the North Vietnamese turned in. Say, someone gets a guerilla platoon leader to deflect, that person gets $15,000."

Colonel Johnston spoke up, "In US money?"

"Well no Colonel, more like in Vietnamese script which has a lower value, but still a good haul for a farmer or any Vietnamese. Of course there are some that get turned in, receive the money and it's split between the VC and the person who turns them in. Then the VC scoots away returning to his outfit. Nice little profit for the VC. Some rewards have gone up to $30,000 Vietnamese script. There is some corruption, as with some programs like this. One report listed over 45,000 VC rifles turned in by the deflector, but resulted in only 3,091 weapons physically counted. So either the count was way off or a lot of weapons simply dissappeared and were sold. Who knows, the Vietnamese government works in mysterious ways."

"Ya know Lieutenant, in some ways I feel sorry for the average Vietnamese. When the communist took over North Vietnam, many voted with their feet and fled south. They just want to be left alone to work their rice paddies and such. The VC and North Vietnamese Army stepped up attacks and the average Vietnamese is caught between a rock and a hard place. If they cooperate with the South Vietnamese government and the US, the VC attack them, burn their villages and many times kill the village chiefs, his family, kids and even live stock and household pets. Now, if the average Vietnamese succumb to helping the VC and NVA either with food or temporary housing, the South Vietnamese burn theirs huts. We do the same thing to prevent shelter to the NVA. The unfortunate Vietnamese is caught in the middle. If they cooperate with one they get hurt, if they help the other they get hurt......just can't catch a break. Bad situation all the way around."

"That's true Colonel, but at least we try to help them by digging wells, building schools in rural areas, bringing doctors and medicines to many who never saw or knew a doctor."

"You're right Lieutenant, but for many it is a high price to pay."

Gunny spoke up, "OK Colonel I don't want to break up this love fest between you two but we need a plan to avoid casualties. It's seems that the shit is on and Charlie is gonna try playing it rough."

"Gunny, I feel bad for these Vietnamese but my duty is to our men. What do you think about coordinating with that Army unit accross the airstrip to lay out perimerter control every night. It will mean that most of our guys will spend at least half the night out on the wire and work during the day."

"With our limited man power, Colonel, it will be rough but we have no choice until we get some relief."

"Well Gunny, Lieutenant, seems we have the start of a plan. Lieutenant contact S-2 Headquarters of our intention. Any questions?"

"No Colonel. Oh Colonel one more thing. HMM 362, The Ugly Angels have been alotted two openings for combat promotion to Lieutenant. I was wondering if you have any names you might want to put down."

"Hell Gunny this one's partially easy. Put TC's name down, he's done a fantastic job in everything asked of him, plus he's a good role model for the men. I'd suggest you come up with a name also, you know your men better than I do."

"Aye, aye Colonel will do. Speaking of TC Colonel. He approached me today. Seems he's getting a bit nervous. He's coming to the end of his tour. It will make one full tour of 13 months and two six months extensions that he has been on. He feels like he is pressing his luck. We know that any crew members life expectance is about two or three minutes while hovering over an LZ during a firefight. At the rate YL-37 has been hit, TC thinks it's inevitable that he's gonna catch one. He's already received a Purple Heart and he dosen't want another. Says he wants off flight status as soon as possible. He knows Sean has been volunteering their bird for any mission that smells of a hot LZ. TC just dosen't like the odds and he wants out.

"Shit! OK Gunny, start finding a replacement for him.

Ch 33

TC found Sean sitting in the cargo door of YL-37 cleaning up from the last mission.

"Hey Sean, got a letter here for you. Smells pretty good too."

TC smiled as he smelled the letter, "mmmm,you know someone in Australia?'

Sean quickly looked up from what he was doing with a suprised look on his face. He grabbed at the letter but TC pulled it away, still smiling.

"Who ever wrote this smells pretty good."

Sean jerked the letter out of TC's hand, and with a smirk said," give it to me you asshole."

"Fine." TC backed away, "I'll leave you with your thoughts."

Sean looked at the letter for a while thinking it can't be her. How the hell would she know where to write? The envelope was light blue and had the wear of travel, small black scuff marks on the face of the envelope. Sean took out his knife and opened the letter along the top seam. There were four pages of finally written penmanship.

> Dear Sean,
>
> I imagine you are quite surprised to receive a letter from me. It wasn't that hard to find you. You see, one o my uncles is with the American intellegence as an advisor. All I knew

your unit was that you called it the Ugle Angels. My Uncle just checked out checked out the names of all Marine helicopters units in Vietnam. I took a chance and wrote. There was so much left unsaid for me when you left me at the airport. I didn't want to give you concern for worry so I didn't say amthing. The truth is I grew to care very much about you during your visit. I felt so comfortble and connected to you.

Felt like I've known you forever.

My heart wouldn't let me ignore what I felt about you. I must admit I was also concerned about how you might not survive Vietnam.

You said it was easier to put up a wall from those around you in case they left or were killed. This dosen't help those near you. There is a network of people who care about you. Shutting them out is not a solution.

All I ask is that you let people in, let

them be a part of your life.
a part of your life. For me I want to
know you better so I will write in the
that we might reconnect.
I deeply care for you Sean. Please allow
me to be a part of your life.
    Love, Joyce.

Sean looked up from the letter and stared out into the distance. Wow he thought, she took all that effort to find me, then writes a letter. He first felt a sense of euphoria. The letter brought up memories of a fantastic week in his life. Feelings for Joyce came rushing back. He too felt comfortable with her, like he knew her forever. Her whole person was that of a women he would cherish. Then a shadow came over those thoughts. All his initial reasons for being aloft were valid. She lived over 2400 miles from Boston. Plus who knows his chances of returning to the world in what ever condition he may find himself. No, the wall he put up was valid, it would protect him and her. Yet the thought of her, the scent of her perfume on the envelope and his minds picture of her were to strong too ignore. She was a presence, even if it lingered in the back of his mind. He sensed this would not go away and he would write back. Sean folded the letter and stuffed it in his pocket. He took a rag and wiped his hands, stood up and shut the cargo door to YL-37. Guess I'll hit the beer hut he thought.

By the time Sean got to the beer hut it was 1700 hours. He found TC, Dolman, and Rubio over at their usual table. TC and Dolman were laughing out loud trying to catch a breath. Rubio sat there with an irritated look on his face.
"What the hell is going on?"

TC looked up at Sean. "Rubio was just telling us how he almost lost his side arm." With that, TC slapped Dolman on the back and started to laugh again. Dolman was wiping tears from his eyes from the laughter.

"Whats so funny about almost losing your side arm?"

Dolman pointed to Rubio. "Rubio go ahead tell Sean how you almost lost you side arm." Dolman slapped his knee and continued laughing.

Sean was smiling now just because Dolman and TC were laughing so hard and Rubio was just sitting there silient and kinda pissed.

"Well Rubio what happen? What about this side arm thing?"

Rubio turned to Sean. I'm not sure I want to repeat it 'cause you'll do exactly what these two assholes are doing." Hearing that made TC and Dolman laugh more.

"C'mon Rubio clue me in."

"OK. Only because these idiots will tell you anyway." TC and Dolman kept laughing.

Sean was starting to chuckle just because of TC and Dolman.

"Now don't you start too, I haven't even told you."

"Alright Rubio, alright. It's just kinda hard not too laugh with these two guys around laughing."

Rubio began his story. "I came back from a flight and needed to take a crap real bad. After the chopper was shut down I ran to the shitter real quick. It was dark inside the shitter but I found a hole. Inside I took off my side arm quick and placed it beside me. I sat down and began my business, and oh what a relief that was. After I was done I took some toilet paper and wiped myself. Stood up and reached for my side arm.....like I said it was dark in the shitter when I went in. Reaching for my side arm all I found was the hole next to me.

Without Rubio saying anymore, Sean got a visual and leaned back in his chair and started to laugh

"You asshole, I thought you weren't gonna laugh. You're no better than these two jerks."

TC and Dolman were laughing again at the second telling of the story.

"I'm sorry Rubio, but I just got a visual of your face when you realized what happend to your side arm."

"Oh Sean, thats not the best part" TC chimed in. "Go ahead Rubio tell him what happened next."

"Shut up TC, I'll tell him soon enough!"

Sean spoke up. "What happend next? Did it get worse?"

Rubio turned his head in disbelief. "Ya....when I realized I dropped the fucking pistol down in the shitter I knew I had to get it out. Since it was dark, I went to get a flashlight. I mean it was dark in there and it was getting darker out side. I went and got a flashlight and came back to the shitter. And wouldn't ya know it, when I opened the door there was a guy sitting over the hole taking a shit where I dropped my pistol."

Sean joined TC and Dolman in a loud burst of renewed laughter.

"Aww fuck you guys. Tell ya a simple story and ya make fun of me."

"Nooo, Rubio." Sean said. "It's a funny story and that's why we're laughing. C'mon go on what happened next?"

Rubio took a swig of beer, then wiped his mouth.

"Well like I said, I opened the shit house door and there was a guy taking a shit over the very hole where I dropped my pistol. Well what could I do? I pointed the flashlight at him and asked him if he'd mind moving over one spot. The guy looked at me like I was crazy. He said why should he. I had no choice but to tell him."

Sean asked, "what'd he do?"

"Aww, he burst out laughing just like you assholes. It took him a while to settle down and move over. I got the side arm out and left. I could still hear him laughig as I went to the flight line."

"Hell Rubio , what did you do with the pistol?"

"Drenched it in aviation gas to get the smell and germs off it. Afterwards I went and took a long shower. Man what a way to end a night."

"Ya" Dolman spoke up. "Sounds like you had a crappy night." With that,TC, Dolman and Sean burst out laughing again.

"Ah , fuck you guys, I'm leaving." Rubio downed his beer and tossed the empty can on the table as the trio kept laughing. Out the beer hut door and Rubio was gone.

TC, Dolman and Sean decided to stay till closing time.

Ch 34

It was 0500 hours when Sean was awakened by Tommy Collins.
"Shake it out Marine. We're due on the flight line in thirty minutes."
Sean slowly woke, rubbing his eyes. "What the hell is going on and why
are you up so early? Hell, we hit the rack about the same time. Are Rubio
and Dolman up yet?"
"Ya they're down at the flight line. Sgt. Bonville rousted them out first,
then got me."
"What going on?"
"Khe Sanh got hit last night. It's under siege. The 26th Marines have been
receiving mortars and lot'sa artillery. Shit is hitting the fan. Looks like
Charlie and the NVA are launching an offensive. The 3rd Marines on Hill
881, about 3 kilometers east of Khe Sanh, are also under attack. The
North Vietnamese infiltrated along the Ho Chi Minh trail. We have to
resupply Hills 881 & 882 and pick up troops at Khe Sanh. Gonna be a
hellu'va day. Should be right up your alley. So roll out of the rack. I'll
see ya on the flight line."
Sean threw back his blanket. "Shit, the one time I could use some shut
eye." He looked down to see he was still in his fatigues. He smiled and
said out loud to no one, "well hell at least something is going my way."
Sean laced his boots half way up and made his way out of the hootch and
down to YL-37. When he reached the flight line there was plenty of
activity already going on. He walked by Rubio and Dolman, gave them a
wave and continued on over to YL-37. TC was just walking up with the
two M-60 machine guns. He had a pistol belt slung over his right
shoulder. When he spotted Sean he yelled out. "I got your pistol to speed

things up. Check out the rotor head and do a quick preflight. I'm heading up to the flight shack to see what pilots we're flying with today.

Sean took the pistol from TC and put it in the helio so it wouldn't get in the way when he was on the tranmission deck. Everything checked out with the rotors so he climbed back down. TC came back. "Looks like we're in luck. We have Col. Johnston and Capt. DeWay."

Sean felt good about that. Both pilots were experienced and could handle a chopper with ease. Now all he had to worry about was not getting shot.

The pilots did the pre-flight, put on their amour flak vest and climbed into the pilots seats. A run up of the engines, check of the tail and head rotor blades movements and YL-37 was ready for taxi. The chase bird, YL-39 with Rubio and Dolman, followed them onto the runway and both choppers took flight. Once in the air the crew of YL-37 locked and loaded their weapons. They settled back for the travel to Khe Sanh to pick up supplies and troops. During the flight Sean thought of the letter from Joyce which was folded up in his shirt pocket. He started to think perhaps she was right. Maybe he should ease back on his idea of staying detached from people. He still felt it was a good option of not getting close, especially since he was likely to get killed. But then again, who do you rely on? When do you ease your guard up? He felt a bit confused. Even being close was a risk. What could he provide her? It was just an R&R romance. One week out of his life, but oh what a week it was. He could never remember feeling this way about a woman. Then he thought, what could he offer her? She was from an old wealthy family. A differant social strata. He was just some schmuck from a working class Irish family. He had nothing but the clothes on his back, forty bucks every two weeks and the Marine Corps. He had nothing, she had everything. Reaching into his shirt pocket, he took her letter out, looked at it once, tore it up and tossed it out the window. Naw, better not get too close and lose that. The pieces of her letter trailed out behind the chopper, drifting into the Vietnamese jungle folage.

Khe Sanh was approached up through a large valley. It sat high over the land around it. Surrounding Khe Sang was a ring of hills. The hills were a fair distance away but could still be used by the NVA to lob artillary shells down on the base. Col. Johnston contacted Khe Sanh for landing and wind directions. He was informed to make a quick landing but be prepared for an aborted landing if the NVA started to shell the base. Tommy Collins and Sean could listen to the instruction on the intercom. Both were gratful Johnston was at the control. If anyone could make a quick landing, it was the Colonel. YL-37 came in low, followed by YL-39. A quick flair and the bird was on the ground and taxiing into the protective barriers. They passed by a smoldering C-130 cargo plane that was hit the day before with mortar rounds as the plane was landing. The wreckage was off the runway and split in two. As soon as their helicopter entered the protective barrier everyone got out quick and hugged the side of the barrier waiting for the shelling to begin. Ten minutes went by and nothing happened.

Col. Johnston spoke up, "well guys looks like the NVA must be at lunch, lets be quick and get over to the bunkers." Both crew members and pilots of each helio made a run for it.   Once at the bunker Col. Johnston turned to the crews.

"You guys head over to the chow hall and get some grub. Capt DeWay and I will head to S-2 to get a briefing."

TC said, "let;s see what's on the menu today. Wonder if they make powdered eggs taste better than those at Phu Bai."

The chow hall was down a ways from the bunker. The road was a foot deep in mud from the moonsoon rains. The four men gave up trying not to step in mud, it was everywhere. As they trudged along their boots got caked with mud. Reaching the chow hall they scraped the mud from their boots and entered. Grabbing a tray Rubio sarcastically said, "oh boy, powered eggs and shit on the shingle, what a delight." They had been overdosing on the SOS for weeks at Phu Bai because of disruption of supplies from Da Nang and poor flying conditions. Each Marine watched with a distorded face as the SOS was slopped over the powered eggs, making a plop sound. They made their way to a table and sat down. Dolman looked at three Marines sitting at the end of the table.

"Heard you guys have been having it rough these last few days? What's your outfit?"

The Corporal of the group turned his head. "Third Herd man. We're gonna catch a ride to Hill 881 this afternoon."

"Third Marines huh. Well, we're your ride. Be heading out right after chow I suppose. We're waiting for our pilots."

Shoveling another spoonful of SOS into his mouth the Corporal kept chewing. "It's been a bitch here man. Fucking NVA have been shelling us for the last three days. They hit that C-130 yesterday. No one survivded. Poor bastards ended up crispy critters. Also hit part of the ammo dump, but the base has enough ammo for a month. Too bad they didn't hit the chow hall." The Corporal laughed showing the food in his mouth. Dolman looked away in disgust and pushed his tray away.

The pilots entered the chow hall and walked over to the four Marines. "OK guys we got a full day" Col. Johnston said. We're gonna bring some troops and ammo supplies up to Hill 881. Eat fast we'll be heading out in twenty mintues."

Sean put his fork down, "I've had enough of this swill anyway, I'm done." They all gabbed their trays and got up.

Dolman turned to the Corporal. "See you guys in twenty minutes. Should be interesting to load the chopper and take off without getting hit."

"Naw" The Corpral said, throwing another spoonful into his mouth. "Them fuckers don't wanna mess with the third herd." He laughed again looking at his comrades.

"Good luck with that", Dolman said. "Hope you can run fast with all your gear." He followed the other crew members out of the chow hall.

All four crew members met up with the four pilots at the S-2 hut. Col. Johnston spoke up. "Here's the plan guys. We'll be taking some Marines and ammo up to Hills 881& 861. We're gonna run out to the

birds, start her up and taxi fast over to the ammo dump. The Marines
we're taking will run out with a box of ammo each and jump in. If we
don't take any fire, six other Marines will run out and throw in more
ammo. Then we're gonna taxi like hell and take flight before any mortar
rounds come down. Got it?" All four nodded. "Good, let's go."

All seven men ran behind Col. Johnston out to the plane barriers.
Once there, each chopper crew did their pre-flight and the birds were up
and running. So far so good.
Col. Johnston got on the intercom. "We're all set to rock and roll guys, be
prepared for anything."

The two choppers did a fast taxi to the ammo dump. Six Marines
came running out carrying an ammo box. Tommy Collins saw the
Corporal that Dolman had been talking to struggling to run with his gear
and ammo box. Dolman was right he thought.
With all men and ammo aboard, the two birds taxied fast down the
runway. Sean heard the distinct sound of mortars rounds hitting the
runway behind them. Mmm, he though, the NVA must've of finished their
lunch. Looking back at Khe Sanh he felt sorry for the Marines there
because the helicopters drew mortar fire. He could still see mortar rounds
hitting the base.

Both choppers, passengers and supplies headed east to Hill 881.
Within a half hour they approached the outskirts of 881. The Hill stood
high over the surrounding landscape. The top of the hill was brown, no
folage. Deep trenches had sandbags piled high around them. As there
was little room for the entire chopper to set down, Col. Johnston came in
sideways doing a slow, crabbing motion, flairing slightly to settle the
right landing wheel on the top side of the hill. The helicopter sat with one
landing wheel on the hill and the other hovering in air. Sean looked out
his left side window and sighted right down the hill. Damn he thought, if
we get hit and we'll just tumble down the hill. Marines rushed towards the
choppers. Some men had no shirt on, those who did have shirts were
caked with dried mud. They each took a box of ammo out of the chopper

and were followed by the passengers. Once unloaded, YL-37 took off to make way for the chase bird. This process continued five more times. By the fifth trip back and forth to Khe Sanh, Hill 881 and hill 861 it was starting to get dark. Col. Johnston came on the intercom.
"Men it's too late to head back to Phu Bai and besides we're low on fuel. Sorry to say but well be spending the night at Khe Sanh."
Tommy Collins began shaking his head and throwing his hands up in the air he looked over at Sean . Sean felt the same way. The last place he wanted to spend the night was at Khe Sanh.

 Arriving at the base was the same as upon first arrival. A quick taxi into the barriers and a run for the bunkers. Fortunately no mortar rounds hit the base. All four crew members and four pilots found a transient hut to sack down in. Later, they hit the chow hall where the same menu was on display, except for the added baloney sandwiches. Sean had enough of the eggs and SOS. He grabbed four sandwiches and a cup of coffee. The other crew member, did the same except for Rubio who had SOS poured over his sanwiches. After chow the men met the pilots back at the hut. All of them were exhausted and sacked out quickly.
Within hours the lights of the hootch came on. An S-2 officer walked in, "Col. Johnston?"
"Mmm, ya over here".
The S-2 Lieutenant said "sorry to roust you out sir but we've got a situation".
"Whaa..what would that be Lieutenant? And what time is it". The Colonel was still rubbing his eyes and yawning.
"It's 2230 hours Sir. We got a Marine night patrol that ran into a company of NVA. They're in a bad way sir, they have casualties and possibly some KIA. Pinned down, real bad, they need evacuation sir."
"Why don't you call in some gun ships and let them take the NVA out?"
It's too risky Sir. The Marines are too close to the enemy and its pitch black out there. The gun ships might hit our own men."

"OK , Lieutenant, we'll saddle up. C'mon men we got a mission and Lord help us."

    The crew and pilots were out by the bunkers in twenty minutes.

"I see no reason for us to sneak out to the choppers, It's so black I can barely see you guys. So neither can the enemy, but lets hustle anyway just in case."

Col. Johnston paused and turned to the men behind him. Ahh...anybody want to go first?" He smiled, "no takers huh, ok follow me." All eight Marines ran like hell out to the barriers. Within, fifteen minutes the two choppers were up and heading down the runway. Tommy Collins loaded and locked a belt of ammo into his M-60 machine gun. He could see that Sean had done the same thing and gave the thumbs up....ya he was ready. The intended landing zone was ten kilometers east, just in between Hill 881 and Hill 861S. The LZ was located by an abondoned village that had a small busted up old church steeple. Just five miles west of the LZ Col. Johnston made the call.

"Zoolu 3, this is Alpha 1, what is your situation over?"

No answer, but lot'sa static.

"ahhh, Zoolu 3 this is Alph 1 over."

There was more static on the line before a garbled voice came on the mic. "Alp,,,Alp,,,,say, Aph 1 this is Zo...1,   I say..Al..pha 1 , thi..s , is Zoo...lu 3 over.

"Zoolu 3 you're breaking up, switch to channel foxtrot, over." The Colonel put down his mike to wait the response.   Channel foxtrot was the secondary radio channel assigned during his initial briefing when he arrived at S-2 this morning. Without giving away the assigned channel, he could alternate channel communications if necessary to avoid detection in case Charlie was monitoring the gab between the choppers and ground troops.

Finally Col. Johnston and the crew of YL-37 heard, "Alpha 1, this is Zoolu 3, can you read me?"

"Zoolu 3, Alpha 1 here, what is your situation?"

"Alpha 1 , we have four KIA and eleven seriously wounded. We have a total of fiftteen men. Have been taking serious fire but have nothing now. Might be a good time to extract, over."

"Zoolu 3 we'll take eight on the first chopper and the rest on the chase bird. We want in and out in as fast as possible so hustle when we land. Pop a smoke and I'll confirm the color."

"Roger that Apha 1, popping a smoke."

"OK ground I have an orange smoke, now pop some flares to light up the LZ for us.

Sean heard the chatter between ground and Col. Johnston. Looking out just to the west of the LZ Sean saw the flares light up in the sky. The flares were shot off using a mortar tube. Once in the air at a specific height the flare would ignite and slowly float down on a parachute. Within a half mile of the LZ Sean kneeled on his seat and got ready. YL-37 approached in a circular motion to confuse the enemy about where exactly it would land. Sean looked at the outline of the LZ. The scenery appeared like an abstract painting he once saw. The church had no roof so you could see in. The walls slanted downwards from each side. Inside the church were broken parts of pews and seats. Most of it was still smoldering. Beside the church was a tree with four broken branches all different lengths without leaves. The ground was void of foliage and looked like a construction site, brown dirt everywhere. It was on the final approach when it happened.

As Sean was looking out, everything slowed down like a motion picture trick of sorts. The men on the ground appeared to run in slow motion. Even with his helmet on he could hear the flare make a popping sound as the chute opened up. It made a soft whistling sound as it floated down. Sean tilted his head slightly to make sense of what he was seeing. Everything was in slow motion. Then quick as a blink, the action resumed at a faster speed. Tommy Collins opened fire first. Sean looked out and saw the white rifle flashes from the NVA or Charlie or whoever was out there. He raked the outlining bushes and tree line. The ammo belt he had

previously put together showed a dotted red line, helping to zone in his
rounds. From above, YL-39 was also providing fire cover.

The Colonel brought the bird in fast and nailed the landing. No sooner
were they on the ground than eight Marines carried four stretchers out to
the chopper. Two of the Marines went back and picked up three body
bags. All of this happened while taking fire from the tree lines. As they
were running back to the chopper, one Marine went down causing the
other to drop the body bag. The one Marine covered his head and didn't
want to move. The other had been hit and was lying motionless. Sean and
Tommy Collins were using up belts of ammo. Sean turned to grab another
ammo belt when he saw Tommy Collins jump out to help the Marine.
Damn he thought, he's gonna leave us exposed without the other M-60
firing. Sean could see Tommy Collins rush up to the wounded Marine and
help him towards the chopper. Along the way he kicked the other Marine
to get him moving. The kicked Marine lifted up the body bag and dragged
it towards the chopper. Sean watched in horror as Tommy Collins went
down in a twirling motion ten feet away from the chopper. It appeared to
Sean as if in slow motion, just like moments before landing. His own
movements seemed slow and methodical as he ran to the cargo door. His
mind was processing, not now, don't leave me, don't you die on me you
bastard. Sean lifted Tommy Collins M-60 up out of its cradle, he jumped
out of the chopper and laid down fire in the direction from where Tommy
Collins got hit. The Marine who had been kicked threw the body bag on
Yl-37. Sean motioned for him to get Tommy Collins. The Marine looked
scared and unsure. Sean pointed the M-60 at him and gave every
indication of what would happen if he didn't. The Marine did what Sean
wanted, he went back, picked up Tommy Collins and put him on board.
Sean got on and placed the M-60 back in it's craddle and continued to lay
down fire. As the chopper started to take off the scared Marine who was
kicked jumped in. Sean motioned for him to man the other M-60. It was
then Sean felt the impact on his thigh. He looked down and saw his
trousers turning red. By now YL-37 was up a hundred feet and circling

the LZ, laying down cover fire while YL-39 extracted the remaining Marines. When YL-39 took off and was in flight, Sean reached quickly for the medical kit. The scared Marine they had picked up grabbed it away from Sean. It was then that Sean saw that the guy was a navy medic assigned with the Marine Corps. The medic ripped open Seans trousers pant leg. Seans thigh had been grazed but still had a nasty wound, almost like someone sliced his leg with a knife Applying a bandage over the wound the medic looked up and smiled, Sean just nodded. The medic went back to the M-60 and sat down.

The whole evacuation took less than nine minutes, way more than it should have. Sean got on the intercom, "Colonel, Tommy Collins has been hit, me too but I'm good. We have a corpsman onboard and he's working on Tommy Collins. I'm not sure how bad the other Marines are, but looks like they're in a bad way Sir."

"Sean this is Capt. DeWay. The Colonel has been hit and he's unconscious. We're heading back to Khe Sanh, we're kinda running on fumes and have no choice. It's gonna be a cluster fuck if we have to ditch, so say a prayer."

Flying at 3000 feet, YL-37 and YL-39 were miles from the hot LZ and Sean could rest back and light up. From the dim red light of the corpsmans flashight, Sean saw one KIA was partially covered. He took a good look at the dead Marine. It was a colored kid, looking like he was sleeping. He had a serene look on his face. Sean thought the Marine was a good looking kid, and didn't seem to have a scratch on him. What a shame. Here was this kid, killed in action and his family in the states didn't know he was dead. They were going about their business having no idea their son, brother, boyfriend, whatever, was dead. Their world was going to be shattered in a big way. This one kid, loved by his family, was coming back dead. Their loss would be hard. They would hurt for a long time. Sean felt that it was another reason not get close to people because they get killed or leave. The loss always hurts. Yet it was a fact this kid was loved. He had some one who cared about him. Perhaps Tommy

Collins was right, it's better to love and lose than to never know that feeling. It's part of life, one goes with the other. There is no joy in isolating your feelings. Sean took a last drag on his cigarette and threw the butt out the door. He watched the small flame disappear into the darkness.

Both choppers made it back to the base with little fuel to spare. Marines on jeeps drove out to the choppers, unloaded the wounded, then the KIAs. Sean jumped out and leaned against the side of the helicopter. He watched as Col. Flanagan and Tommy Collins were taken to the field hospital tent. The medic corpsman walked by. Sean stuck his hand out. "Sorry about pointing my weapon at ya back there but I needed to shake you up."

"No problem guy, I was pretty shaken up to begin with, only been in country two

weeks. I was so scared I didn't know what to do."

"Jesus", Sean said, "baptism by fire huh?"

"Ya..this was my first patrol. I thought we were dead for sure. You can't believe my feelings when I heard you guys coming in. God, I went from dead to alive."

"Well you're not in any better shape, we're at Khe Sanh. Chances are the base will be receiving a lot of shelling and you'll more than likely be on more patrols."

"Ya, but tonight I'm safe and thats good."

"You're right about that Marine, take care, and thanks for the patch work on my leg."

The Marine walked away and Sean turned back to the chopper. All of a sudden he felt alone, outhere by the chopper without TC. God, I hate this feeling, he thought.

Morning came quickly. Sean turned over and rubbed his eyes. The hootch was empty, that made Sean sit up fast. Just then Rubio and Dolman came walking through the door.

"Morning Marine, how you feeling." Rubio sat at the edge of Seans rack, Dolman sat opposite him.

"Hows the leg?" Rubio looked down at the bandage on Sean's leg.

"Kinda forgot I got hit. Guess it can't be too bad or that corpsman did a great job. What the hell time did you guys get up? Where's Capt. DeWay?"

Dolman spoke up, "we got up early. You were snoring like a bastard, a hard sleep. DeWay was already gone, so we just went to chow."

"We know anything about Tommy Collins and Col. Johnston?" Sean asked.

"They're both doing OK considering their wounds. We ran into Capt DeWay at chow. He said we'll be taking TC and the Colonel to Phu Bai in an hour or so." Rubio sat back.

Sean was up and dressed. "But who's going to fly the empty seat? The Colonel is out, so I suppose the Captain will fly right seat."

Rubio smiled. "Seems there's a Warrant Officer who's a qualified pilot, he was visiting his kid who's a grunt. He came in before all this shit happened and couldn't get out. So they made him an acting S-2 officer. We're gonna give him a lift to Phu Bai in exchange for his flying left seat. So get ready to rock and roll in an hour." Sean left Rubio and Dolman in the hootch while he went to chow. He could hear Rubio yell out behind him. "They have the same shit for breakfast!"

    After chow Sean got his gear and met up with the other crew members and the pilots at the helicopters.
"What happened to the shelling?"
Rubio walked over to Sean. "We don't know. The Captain thought for sure we'd take some shelling coming out to the birds. Maybe Charlie is waiting for us to move out of the bunkers and then shell us. Who knows, we'll find out as soon as we start loading and attempt to take off."

    Both choppers were up and running. They moved quickly over to the medevac area where an ambulance drove up fast. Tommy Collins and the Colonel were loaded on quickly. Within minutes YL-37 and the chase bird YL-39 were heading down the runway and taking flight. Oddly enough they didn't attract any shelling. That was a condition that Capt. DeWay reported to S-2 via radio. Sean laid back against the back of the seat and sighed. Finnaly getting out of that hell hole he thought. He lit up a cigarette and looked down at Tommy Collins. Both TC and the Colonel were wrapped warmly. Each was sedated to make them more comfortable on the flight to Phu Bai. He looked down at TC and smiled. He liked the guy from the first time he meet him when Sean arrived in the squadron. Sean was amused rembering how TC helped deflect the Gunny's attempt to chew out Sean for not reporting directly to the overhaul hanger. Then there were all the bull shit sessions at the beer tent. And most of all, the advice TC gave Sean about adapting to 'Nam and also helping him with flight procedures. Ya, the guy was good to Sean, and Sean appreciated it. Sean felt a bit leary about what was to come. Surely, TC would not be flying for a while. Then again, neither would he until his leg got better. Then what? Would he and TC be flying together at all? What the hell was gonna happen? He didn't like the thought that he might not fly with TC again. Or for that matter, when he'd see him again. That feeling of losing someone crept over Sean. That loss when someone leaves, gets killed or rotates back to the world. He hated it when someone left. Just like when Camron left. You bond with a guy. You got his back , he's got yours. You work, eat , and drink together every day, every week , every month. Ya get to know a guy. It's familar and keeps you grounded from all the shit that happening around you. Then one day you walk into your hootch and the rack where that Marine slept is empty. No pillow, no blanket no gear. Gone! Your anchor to reality is gone. Naw, dosen't seem to make sense to get friendly with those around you. But then, like TC talked about, if you don't make friends, bond with people then you have nothing. Ya need others to get through life. Sean was slowly coming to that realization.

He looked out the cargo door and watched the scenery go by. What a beautiful country he thought. Too bad people were fighting over it and control of the people. Fucking politicians no matter what country they were in, they made simple things complicated. Well it wasn't his problem, he was just a Marine doing his job. He finished his cigarette and threw it out. They'd be in Phu Bai in another forty five minutes.

They landed at noon. Taxied over to the medevac area where Tommy Collins and the Colonel were placed into an ambulance and taken to the base hospital. Both choppers then taxied over to helio bunkers and shut down. Sean spent the next half hour straightening up YL-37. Finally satisfied things were squared away, he limped to the overhaul hanger. Sitting at his desk was Sgt. Bonville.

"Hey Sean, welcome back. Heard you guys got into some shit up north."
"Ya we took some hits up by Hill 881. We were on an emergency extraction. TC and Col. Johnston got hit real bad. They're at the base hospital now."
"Whoa, no shit? Well things have been interesting here as well. Fucking NVA attacked Hue' City. They're fighting it out tooth and nail, bad shit that. You've been gone a few days and it all happended shortly after you guys left. They said it'll be going on for a few weeks. Saigon was also hit along with a hundred other smaller cities throughout Vietnam. Old Ho Chi Minh is making an attempt to take over. Yet from what I hear, he's getting his ass kicked. Oh, they caught us off guard with the cease fire for Tet, but that's where he made his mistake. North Vietnam thought

everyone in the South would rise up against the government. Well that ain't happening. Most of those people left the North when the commies took over. They didn't want the commies then, and they sure in hell don't want them now. Sounds like the NVA and Charlie came down with a hit list."

"What do ya mean?"

"Well just that! A hit list. People to eliminate, mostly government people, teachers or any one helping the South. Hell they're killing whole families; papason, momason, babyson, pets, livestock, everything. They're showing no mercy."

Sean was in disbelief. He felt like he was out of country when all this was happening. Being isolated up at Khe Sanh, they were out of the loop. They had their own problems in Khe Sanh. This is what he wanted, to be flying, to get in on the day to day action. Sure he had some scuffles but this was the big time and he was gonna be sidelined. He felt they're not gonna let him fly till his leg was better. What a crappy time to get hit.

Sean turned to Bonville, "thanks for the infomation Sargee, guess I go get some chow, shower and get some sack time."

"Take it easy Sean. If ya get bored I could use some help."

Sean smiled, "maybe."

Ch 36

It was two weeks after Sean returned from Khe Sanh. On that day he hit the rack and slept through to the next morning. He only got up once to piss, but then he hit the rack again. On the next day when he reported to the flight line, Gunny Simmons had a talk with him.

"Sean I have some good news and some bad news, which do you want first?"

Sean was kinda suprised by the question. "Guess I'd rather get the bad news first, get it out of the way."

"Look Sean, Tommy Collins is rotating back to the states. He only has four months left on his enlistment and by the time he's healthy he'll be ready for discharge anyway. Aside from that, he's taking up a spot, as long as he's on the rooster we can't replace him. I need all the men I can get. It's a hard thought, but it's reality. He's been informed and resigned himself to that fact.."

"Jesus Gunny, he was hit bad but I thought he'd come back and serve out his time in 'Nam."

"That's not gonna happen Sean. Tommy Collins is looking at four months of rehab. Hell, Col. Johnston is not much better, only his enlistment is years off. So he'll be back in three or four months."

"So what's the good news Gunny?"

"Well, in a week or so I can get you back on flight on status. That is if you want it."

"Hell ya Gunny, that's the only reason I came over here, to be flying and get in on the action."

"Ya I know Sean, your reputation precedes you. You made that clear the first week you came here. Isn't that where the "bad ass Ugly Angel" comes from?"

Ah.... Gunny you know how the guys are quick with the labeling. I think it started out more as a joke but I couldn't shake it."

"In any regard, since YL-37 has both crew members out of action, that being you and TC, when you get back to full duty you'll assume crew chief of YL-37."

At the news Sean's eyes got wide. "You mean I get my own bird?"

"Yup. Right now another crew is using the bird. But you have seniority on them. Besides it only seems right."

"Well hell, thanks Gunny, that's the best news ever."

"You deserve it Sean. You've shown your colors and I have confidence in you. Also, Tommy Collins recommended you." The Gunny smiled at the last news.

"Guess I'll just have to go and pay my respect to Tommy Collins and thank him."

Sean limped out of the Administration shack and walked towards the base hospital.

In time, Sean's leg was looking good and didn't disable him. The Gunny got Sean back on flight status and assigned him a new replacement. The new FNG, came from another squadron but was qualified as a door gunner. The new kid was Jeff Crawly. Nice kid from Pennsylannia. Jeff was about 5' 8 " and weighed 165 lbs with clothes on. He had a full head of blonde hair and for his height and weight, had ripped muscles, thin and wiry. The kid was like a sponge and soaked up everything. He was eager to learn and did what he was told. Sean had no complaints about this kid.

Inspite of the heavy action taking place in 'Nam because ot the Tet offensive, YL-37 had been given a few easy runs. The Gunny wanted to see how these two guys worked together, otherwies he'd assign a different door gunner. Things seemed to be working good for the new crew of YL-37.

Sean sat down with Crawly one day and let him know what he was in for.

"Look Crawly I have this thing about going on tough assignments. Ones that flight crews draw maybe two or three times a month. But I ask for, and go after the tough ones, your night medevacs, the emergency extractions, any thing with night or emergency I go after. If this is a problem for you let me know."

Crawly looked at Sean like this is what he expected. "Look Sean , a few of the guys in the beer hut already told me what I'd be in for flying with you. I'm OK with that, I just want do the best I can." Crawly flashed a big pearly smile. With his blonde hair and build Sean thought Crawly belonged on a surf board in California instead of in 'Nam.

The big smile also reminded him of some one else. Someone far away in Australia.

"OK Crawly, then we understand one another. I'll have your back and you'll have mine. We should do alright as a crew."

After the talk with Crawly, Sean sat back in the chopper and thought about Joyce. He was feeling bad about tearing up her letter. At the time it seemed the right thing to do, but now he wish he'd kept it. He realized he was softening his stance on reacting to people he knew. His thoughts were more to embracing those around him. He felt if he never saw a person again at least he made the best of being a friend instead of being a bit aloof.

Lt. Janhs, the S-2 officer approached Gunny Simmons in the admin schack. "Say Gunny we just received a report from HDQ S-2 that the NVA and Charlie are planning a raid on a small village just north of Hue' City. A place called Phong Dien. Ya ever hear of it?"

"Ya, seems to me we took fire from a friendly LZ in that area. A friendly LZ according to S-2." The Gunny looked over at Lt. Janhs and gave him a pissed look. Lt. Janhs realized Gunny was referring to errors on intel that mistakenly labeled an LZ friendly instead of hostile. Both knew errors would be made, but anything that put his men in harms way pissed the Gunny off big time.

"Ya..ah..well Gunny there is a small hamlet near Phong Dien."
Gunny Simmons turned and looked at the Lieutenant, "thats the place, now I remember. Thats the little shit hole we got hit in."
Lt. Janhs went on, "well the villages have been giving us intel on VC movement and some how the VC got wind of it. Now they gonna retaliate so HQ decided the best thing to do during Tet is to move them."
"How many people are we talking about Lieutenant?"
"About thirty that we know off plus some small live stock."
"Livestock? You mean like fucking animals?"
"Ya Gunny, these people can't exist without their animals. It's how they exist, and lord knows they don't have much as it is right now. These animals keep the family alive, it's their way of life. Without the livestock there is no family, there is no village. It's a big thing for them, very important."
"Shit, why don't they just ask us to evacuate a circus, maybe a fucking zoo. My guys are taking a chance of being hit just for some stupid animals?"
"It's more about people Gunny but without the animals they won't leave."
"Ya, Ya, Ya , they can't live without their animals, and for that we might get shot at. Stupid way to run a war. OK, Lieutenant how many choppers are we talking about?"
"If all goes well, I think maybe four birds would do the trick. Two or three runs and we'll be done. Oh and there was some major flooding in that area so the village is partially under some water, maybe a foot or so. Choppers might have to hover loading everything."
"Oh great, this keeps getting better. It's 1130 hours right now. I'll send the choppers out after lunch. At least the guys will be flying on a full stomach."

   At 1300 hours four helicopters were taxiing out onto the small iron mat runway. YL-37 was selected to be lead chopper followed by three other birds. Sean felt fortunate he drew Capt. DeWay as a pilot. DeWay was battle tested and knew how to fly into a zone.

Within thirty minutes, the four choppers were approaching Phong Dien. There was a small patrol already on the ground, ready to assist with the loading. Capt. DeWay called ahead and a smoke canster was popped which helped in indentifying wind direction. YL-37 came in low and saw immmediately that the only clear landing zone was under water.

"Great! Just fucking, great!" DeWay muttered. The chopper came in on directions from the ground crew. Just then DeWay heard on the radio from the Marines on the ground that a large group of NVA were headed their way.

"OK Sean get ready to take fire, we're expecting company. Just grab the people, fuck the animals, I'm not getting shot for some chickens."

"Got'ca Captain."

YL-37 came in low and hovered just off the water. Seven Vietnamese came running through the water carrying their meager belongings. The ground crew helped load two women and three kids. A third women held a baby in her arms. Her husband was carrying a pig. When they were at the door of the helicopter, Sean motioned no pig, no pig, with hand gestures. The villager shook his head and motioned that the pig has to go with them. Again Sean motioned to throw the pig and only the mother and child could get on, not the pig. In the next moment Seans jaw dropped as the farmer grabbed the baby from the mother and threw it into the flooded water. Sean froze, not believing what he saw. He pulled out his pistol and pointed it at the farmer. The Marine on the ground stepped in between them, grabbed the pig, tossed it on board followed by the mother and farmer. The Marine motioned to Sean to let it go. Sean still held the pistol in his hand when the chopper started to take off. Fortunately only two evacuation flights were done before the NVA was near the villages. The flights were successful, the villagers and the Marine patrol were evacuated and no one took fire. Sean was still in a slight daze from seeing the farmer throw the baby into the water. Even after landing at Phu Bai, he was still shocked by the farmer's action. He let Crawly clean up the chopper while he went for a debriefing. Later that night at the beer hut, Rubio and Crawly walked over to Sean.

"Hey Sean, heard you saw some weird shit today."

Sean looked up, took a swig of his beer. " I don't understand these people, they're animals, no respect for life. That fucking farmer just threw his kid away like it was a piece of trash."

Rubio spoke up, "did they cover that in the debriefing?"

"Ya they said it was the war. That the only thing the villages had to keep them going was the livestock. Lt. Janhs said that, to the villages, a baby is a burden, livestock is valuable. With the pig the family could eat for a month, sustaining the whole family. Without the pig, or other live stock the family starves. The baby was useless, couldn't work in the field, couldn't be married off to benefit the family. To their way of thinking the mother could always have another child. But any livestock is expensive and hard to come by, invaluable. That pig was more valuable to the family than the baby. That's a hard cold fact of life for these people. Then you factor in the war and these poor people are fucked three ways to Sunday. That's what we're dealing with over here. But I just can't get it right in my mind. Hell, I would've of shot that farmer."

"Ah Sean it sucks being here. We have different values than these people. They have their world and we have ours. We're here for thirteen months and then we're gone. Back to the world. They have to stay here and live with the war, the killing. They're just poor farmers in a poor country. Nothing we can do about it."

"Maybe so Rubio but it still sucks. I'll think of that poor baby for years, what a waste. I can take the blood, the killing and all the carnage but seeing that farmer throw away his kid. I'll never forget that." Sean thought of putting that emotional wall back up. Something to protect his mental state from bring destroyed being over here. But then Tommy Collin's words came back to him, 'don't isolate yourself from the world, it'll just make things worse for you. It'll keep you from the good.' Sean reached for another beer and shook the entire day out of his head.

Rubio broke the silence, "Oh Sean, you got another letter while you were up at Khe Sanh. I grabbed it for you and almost forgot I had it." Rubio pulled the letter out of his pocket. "Smells real good too." Rubio gave a wise ass grin as he waved the letter under Sean's nose. Sean turned his head quickly towards Rubio, "give me that you asshole." Looking at the postage, Sean could see it was from Australia. His felt a bit flushed and excited but didn't let it show. "I'll read this later, lighting in here is poor."

"Sure it is Sean, sure it is", Rubio said as he leaned back with that same wise ass smile.

It was still light out when Sean left the beer hut. To make sure he had some privacy he headed down to his bird. He opened the cargo door and sat in the entrance. He pulled out the letter, holding it in his hands, he looked at the postage again, turned the letter over then just stared at it. He wondered why she wrote again. Was it to chew him out for not writing? Naw, that would not be like Joyce. He just looked at the letter, remembering when they were together. Finally he had to read it. He took out his K-bar knife and carefully cut along the envelopes top. Reaching inside he pulled out three perfumed pieces of paper. Wow, he thought, she really had beautiful penmanship. Contained in the folded papers where two photos. He put the letter beside him and viewed the two photos. One was of Joyce sitting on a beach towel with her arms behind her to brace herself up. Her knees were drawn up slightly just like a magazine model. He remembered how fine she looked in that bathing suit. There was nothing wrong with her anatomy. The second photo was taken by a couple walking by. Joyce asked the women if she would take our picture. The photos made him wish he could just be back there, enjoying the best week of his life.

Sean put the photos down and picked up the letter, unfolded it and began to read.

Dear Sean,

I got pictures back from our trip to Bondi
Beach. Thought you might want a copy
selected two of the best. I thought we made
a very nice couple, don't you think? It was
so great spending the week with you. I don't
remember when I had such a great time.
I keep a picture of us on my desk and the
girls in the office ask me who you were,
what you were like. I think some are
curious because they never met you.
I also think they may be a bit jealous.
Did you get my last letter? I know maybe I
should not of written but I just felt I had to.
It made me feel closer to you. If you could
at least just write and let me know you are
alright.
Sometimes I get a terrible thoughts that
maybe you have been injured. I know it's
silly, but I just want to know you're alright.
I still care very much for you and wanted
you
to know. I would feel better that

you're OK. So please put aside your Irish stubborness and write! If for no other reason than to ease my mind that your are well. With love

Joyce

Looking at the letter Sean stared out into the dusk. He put the letter up to his nose and inhaled. A ton of memories came flooding back, and for a brief moment he was back in Australia with Joyce. For this one moment in time he was out of this hell hole. He put the letter down and realized he was smiling. No sense feeling this good and being alone. He decided to head back to the beer hut to let Crawley and Rubio buy him some beers. He put the letter and photos in his right breast pocket, stepped down from the door and walked briskly up to the beer hut.

The Gunny turned in his chair when S-2 officer Lt. Janhs entered the operation shack.

"Morning Gunny."

"Whats up Lieutenant."

"Just wanted to update you on Col. Johnston and Tommy Collins."

"How are those guys doing? Last I heard they're taking it easy down in a Da Nang hospital."

"The Colonel is doing fine, should be back with us in about two months. Tommy Collins is real good, and will be transfered back to the states, then discharged when it is appropriate. And get this....., he's gonna get a Bronze Star for saving those Marines."

"What about Sean? He was part of that team and laid down fire covered for Tommy Collins. Dosen't he get anything?"

"Afraid not Gunny. The brass felt he did what he was suppose to do. He will get a Purple Heart though."

The Gunny looked shocked, "did what he was suppose to do? Hell if he didn't take the initiative and provide Tommy Collins with cover fire, plus get that corpsman to do his job, Tommy Collins would be history."

"I know Gunny but the brass thinks that was what he was suppose to do. Go figure."

"It's all bull shit Lieutenant."

"Gunny, I also have the recent report of NVA activity on Tet from HQ S-2."

"You mean those assholes who give us bad intel on friendly zones? What do those fuckers want?"

The lieutenant ignored the Gunny's wise crack.

"It's a summary of the recent Tet attack. There was a lot of shit going on that we didn't know about."

"Like what?"

"Well we knew that Hanoi reneged on it's agreement for a Tet cease fire they agreed upon last September. They had planned all along to use the agreement as a ploy to stock supplies and men for an offense."

"So Lieutenant, ya think thats why we've had all that action starting back in early November?"

"Ya Gunny, they wanted to probe our defenses to see how prepared we were."

"I would've thought after getting their asses kicked they would'a changed their mind. Don't ya think?"

"Kinda Gunny. The North Vietnamese thought if they attack, it would result in a mass uprising against the South Vietnamese government. But that didn't happened.

Guess Ho Chi Minh and the rest forgot, or choose to ignore that many people in the North had voted with their feet when they fled the North after the Communist took over."

"Say Lieutenant, schuttlebutt has it that the NVA took a severe beating during this attack."

"Ya, that's included in this report. It also highlights that there is division in Hanoi's war policy."

"What do you mean?"

"Well, seems the North Vietnamese are having a difference of opinion regarding whether to seek a peace agreement or continue on fighting."

"No shit, sorta' like our fucked up leaders, huh Lieutenant?"

"Sort of. The North commander Gen. Vo Nguyen Giap was more in favor of a settlement. Whereas, a political leader, Communist Party First Secretary Le Duan was more militaristic and wanted to continue the war."

"Jesue Lieutenant, just like a politician. They don't fight but design crappy policies and let the military bear the brundt of military action. I swear there is no military guy that wants to go to war and get shot or killed. We'll do it to protect our country but the politicians come up with policies that get us into war." The Gunny shook his head.

"Wow Gunny, it says that Gen. Giap, the so called military leader, had no part in the planning or initial operations of the Tet offense. When the shit hit the fan he did command the operations after the Tet offense began."
"Damn Lieutenant, that would be like our commander, Gen Westmoreland not having a say in our operations."
Lt. Janhs flipped through some pages. "Speaking of Gen. Westmoreland, he and his staff underestimated the Hanoi's ability to advance a massive attack with the assets the North had on hand. It states here that the poor showing of the South Vietnamese was more due to the Vietnam's military issuing recreational leave to half of their forces because they thought there would be a temporary cease fire. Thought their troops could spend the Tet holiday with their families When the NVA attacked, the South had half their forces on duty. Man, Hanoi threw close to 80,000 troops at the South."
"Hell, Lieutenant, the South was not unprepared, they were overwhelmed."
"You got that right Gunny. There is still fighting going on in Hue' City, just 8 kilometers north west of Phu Bai.
Holy shit Gunny, listen to this. A capture NVA document, Communist Document 1892, states there was a hit list of people to execute during the attack. When the NVA attacked Hue' they had a list of teachers, civil servants or any one in the upper social stratum. So if you were a leader in the community, your ass was grass."
The Gunny looked at the Lieutenant.
"You mean they were gonna wipe out any one in a social position or who worked for the government, not soldiers?"
"That's what it says here Gunny. Damn! Our guys found mass graves of people. Many with their hands bound behind them. Some were tortured or clubbed to death, others were buried alive. It's estimated over 3000 people were found in those graves."
The Lieutenant looking at the pages, walked over to the Gunny. "Hey listen to this, some foreigners were found in those graves. Some West

German Cultural members who taught at the Hue' University Faculty of Medicine were executed.
Jesus, the NVA basically were executing every one. Some kids as young as 3 or 5 years old were found at a place called Da Mai Creek bed. The bastard showed no mercy at all. Everyone was a victim of brutal revenge. If you weren't fighting for the North you were an enemy of the revolution, as they called it."
Gunny Simmons spoke up. "The NVA and the VC are no better than the Nazi's."
"Oh, oh Gunny."
"What?"
Lt. Janhs looked at the Gunny. "Some American journalist took a photo of a VC in civilian cloths being executed. The VC had his hand bound behind his back. The picture shows the VC making a distorted face as the bullet went through his skull. Seems the shooter was the Saigon Chief Police, Gen. Nguyen Mgoc Lan."
The Gunny looked up. "Why the hell does a Police Chief have the title of General? I mean isn't Chief of Police enough?"
"Says here the VC was actually a Vietcong officer, Nguyen Van Lem. He was a captain in charge of a so called, revenge squad, captured at the site of a mass grave containing the bodies of several Police families.
The Chief Of Police who shot the VC was quoted as saying, "These guys killed many of our people. I think Buddha will forgive me".
"Ya know Lieutenant, that guy has balls."
"Only problem is Gunny, the shit will hit the fan when this appears across the front page of newspapers in the states."
Just goes to show ya Lieutenant, a picture doesn't tell the whole story. He should have been executed. He was in civilian cloths. He had no distinctive military signs or characteristics. Everything required by the Geneva Convention of 1949. This VC was basically a mass murderer during war time. But I think you're right, it's gonna look bad."
The Lieutenant was now sitting on the edge of Gunny's desk.

"Ya mind Lieutenant?"

"Oh sorry Gunny." Lt. Janhs stood up.

"We still have the 1st Marines cleaning up in Hue'. The Army First Cavalry and the 101st Air Borne are outside Hue', blocking NVA escape from Hue' and cutting off their supply line. Guess we'll be getting some more missions from that operation. Right Gunny?"

"We definitely will Lieutenant, we definitely will."

"Guess I'll go back to S-2 and log in these reports. Take it easy Gunny."

"Adios, Lieutenant."

The Gunny looked at the Lieutenant walking out the door. Not a bad guy he thought. It's just a shame he's an Annapolis guy. They're always so full of themselves. The Gunny always felt Annapolis guys thought they were the smartest people in the room. Besides, except for a few, the Gunny just didn't like officers. Only enlisted men earned their pay.

The Gunny turned back to his desk to finish some paper work when he spotted Sean walking by. He shouted, "SEAN! SEAN! Come in here." Sean stopped in his tracks. He leaned toward the shack putting a hand up to his eyes to block the sun. He barely made out a figure inside but thought perhaps it was Gunny Simmons. He walked towards the shack, opened the screen door and went inside.

"Morning Gunny What's up?"

"Hi Sean, have a seat."

"Oh Crap, what did I do now?"

The Gunnny looked up, "nothing, nothing, I just want to update you on Tommy Collins. The Lieutenant from S-2 was just in here with a report on TC and the Colonel."

"Oh, S-2? You mean those guys who give us wrong information about so called friendly landing zones?"

The Gunny smiled, "Ya those guys. Anyway, Tommy Collins is being medevaced back to the states and from there he'll be discharged. The Colonel has a few more months of rehab before he'll be back with us. In the mean time, Capt. DeWay the excetutive officer will be the acting

Commanding Officer. That's more information than you need to know but I did want to clue you in on Tommy Collins. I know you two were a pretty tight team."

"Damn Gunny, I was hoping to see him before he left, I may never see him again. Seems when I get tight with someone they get killed or leave."

"I know Sean, but thats the way of the military, it is what it is."

"Ya I suppose, but it sucks. It that all you wanted to see me about Gunny?"

"Well that and I wanted to know how the leg is doing. You've been on a few missions and I was curious how you're holding up."

"Oh it's good Gunny dosen't bother me at all. I keep a bandage on it because even a little scratch over here last for every in this heat and I didn't want to chance an infection. But I'm good to go. These tit runs I've been on may be good experience for Crawley but it's kinda boring."

"Sean, how many times have I told you that every mission is important, even simple supply runs. If we don't resupply those grunts out in the field, they're in deep shit."

"You're right Gunny, it's just that I get bored just sitting in the chopper flying around dropping off ammo and c-rations. I'm ready to get back into it."

"You know Sean, some people think you have a death wish, thats why you want to fly all the bad ass missions into hot LZs. I would think you'd get scared at times."

"I don't have a death wish. I just figured as long as I 'm in this country I can get hit by an incoming mortar round or a sniper shot or any number of things. So instead of being scared I just assume my time is up and I don't worry about getting hit. Besides, during a mission the aderenlin is pumping and thats all I feel. It's after the mission, when I have time to think about it, I do get a bit scared. So I go to the beer hut at night with the others and have a few beers. It helps me sleep and not lay there thinking about the day's mission."

"Yeah, I've heard a number of you guys are at the beer hut quite often. That's not a good thing, but eveybody has their way of coping with this place, and it's not my business how you do it. Well, if your legs is good then you're back in the lineup for every mission. Thats about all I have for ya. Now get out of here so I can do some paper work. This place is becoming like a train station with people coming and going."

"OK Gunny, thanks for the info on Tommy Collins, I'm gonna miss that guy."

Sean walked out of the shack and headed to the beer tent to tell Crawley the good news.

Rubio walked over to YL-37 and handed Sean a grease gun. "Thanks for lending me your grease gun. Don't know where the hell mine went to. I bet some jackass stole it."

"No problem guy, glad I could help."

Sean and Rubio sat in the cargo door bay of YL-37 and lit up a cigarrette.

"Oh, oh, Rubio, here comes Crawley and boy is he gonna be pissed."

"Why? What's up with that, why's he pissed?"

"I sent him to ask Sgt. Bonville in the overhaul hanger for a can of Torgue."

Rubio looked at Sean, "Oh you bastard, ya didn't. Thats one of the oldest jokes out here."

Sean smiled and chuckled, "ya I know, I figured that him being the FNG he needs to have his balls properly busted. Not only did I send him for a can of Torgue but I specified it be a one pound can of Torgue."

Crawley's face was that of an angry person when he approached the chopper.

"You asshole, think you're pretty funny huh?"

"What's the matter Crawley? You look angry? And where's my can of Torgue?" Sean turned and smiled at Rubio.

"It's not fucking funny. Bonville crewed my ass out, telling me not to be such a stupid shit and to get the hell out of his hanger. Said if I didn't know that Torgue is applied with a wrench and not out of a can then I shouldn't be working on helicopters. And if I came back anytime today he'd kick my ass. Said he was tired of these bullshit games you guys play that involve him. He also said he'd deal with you later Sean."

Rubio laughed, "you're in the shit house now Sean. How many times have you done that to him?"

"Seriously, it's the first time I did this. Tommy Collins did it to me when I first flew with him. Said it was a rite of passage to screw with the new guys. I didn't think it was gonna work so well."

Rubio and Sean burst out laughing while Crawley just stood there and fumed.

Sean threw the rag he was holding inside the chopper. "C'mon you guys it's lunch time, lets get some chow before the line gets long."

All three were walking to the chow hall when they heard the Gunny's voice.

"Where you guys going?"

Sean stepped forward. "Hi Gunny, we're just going to get some chow."

"Well you guys should've gone sooner. I got an emergency medecac and it can't wait.

Got'a call from the 1st Marines in Hue' for medical evactuation. Some of theirs guys got hit pretty bad this morning cleaning out a pocket of Viet Cong held up in a building. They got some serious wounded and requested emergency medevac. Now go down and get your birds ready."

"Well there goes lunch", Rubio threw his cigarette butt on the ground.

"Crawley, run up to the chow hall and get some sandwiches and get back to the chopper real quick. I'll get things ready. Rubio and I will be waiting for you, now go." Sean slapped Crawley on the shoulder and turned to Rubio.

"C'mon man lets get things rolling." Turning abruptly, the pair headed back to the flight line.

Sean preped YL-37 for flight. He had the rotor head greased, inspected the chopper's airframe to insure no cracks and gave a once over of the engine. He made sure the cargo area was free of dirt which might fly up during flight and get into their eyes and squared away the inside for taking on stretchers or body bags. He did everything within his power to make sure the chopper would encounter no problems. Some of what he did would be duplicated by the pilots themselves during pre-flight. But Sean trusted no ones inspection except his own. In that way he could control a high level of rediness. Crawley still hadn't returned yet and the pilots had not arrived. The longer Sean waited by his bird the more anxious he became. Looking in at the ammo he felt he could use a few more cans. He ran to another chopper nearby and took two cans of ammo and placed one by each of the M-60 machine guns.

Time seemed to drag by. He could feel an uneasiness about being unprepared, so he went and got two more cans of ammo, again placing one by each of the M-60s. Finally Crawley showed up with the sandwiches. "Where the hell have you been?"
"Damn Sean I've only been gone fifteen minutes. The lines were long so I went to the back of the chow hall and made the sandwiches myself."
"Fifteen minutes?" Sean looked at his watch. He realized that the delay in taking off caused him to be uneasy and he let anxiety creep into his mind. Usually on a mission things happened quickly. The mission was assigned, he'd go to the chopper, get it ready, the pilots would show up and they were on their way. But even this small delay of fifteen minutes made him antsy. He realized this was the first time he got anxious before a mission. This never happened to him before and it gave him concern.

The pilots finally showed up and Sean was pleased to see Capt. DeWay and a new co-pilot Lt. Stints. After a pre-flight by the pilots, YL-37 was cranked up and rotor blades turning. The chase plane was YL-39 with Rubio and Dolman. Good, Sean thought, a reliable crew on the chase plane. Both planes took off at 1300 and headed northwest towards Hue' City.

When the City was in view, Capt. DeWay called the 1st Marine Radio man. "Bull Dog One, Yankee Lima on approach, pop a smoke to identify your location."
A red smoke appeared just inside and west of the city's main center by an old church.
"Bull Dog One, I spot a red smoke, confirm."
"Yankee Lima, roger on the red smoke."

Sean wondered why many of his mission took place by old churches that had been destroyed

DeWay spoke to the crew, "OK guys watch out for Charlie or any other bastard that shoots at us. Your call on when to fire."
Sean keyed his mouth piece, "copy that Captain."
Without hesitation Sean motioned to Crawley by placing two fingers up to his eyes and then pointing out the door. Crawley nodded, indicating he knew to be aware of ground fire.
Much of the Old City was smoldering. Few buildings escaped the constant rocket, mortar and tank shelling. It was a shame that the 'Old Citadel', that was Hue' City was in rubble.

YL-37 came in low and fast, flaring out at the last minute for a text book landing. Marines carrying stretchers with wounded came running towards the chopper. Crawley kept watch on the choppers' port side while Sean assited in getting the first stretcher on board. This guy was all messed up with his chest bandaged. Bad sign, must be a severe chest wound. He was going stateside if he survied the ordeal. The next stretcher carried a Marine that had no legs beneath the knee cap. Sean could see viens and jagged bones hanging out from where the calf muscle use to be. The Marine had a tourniquet on each thigh to prevent further bleeding. Sean thought this guy must be juiced up on morphine to endure the pain. The next three Marines on stretchers were not in any better shape. It was impossible to tell where they were hit because of all the blood. Another Marine hopped on board. His left ankle was dangling and held on only by his boots. There was no hope for the last Marine, he was in a body bag. Sean grabbed two corners of the bags and as he lifted he could feel sloshing of liquid inside. A Marine with no visable wound got on. Sean was just about to throw him off when he saw the corpsman insignia. It was then Sean realized it was the corpsman from Khe Sanh. How the hell did he get down here? The corpsman busied himself with the wounded.

A Marine with a ground radio waved YL-37 off. From his seated position, Sean could see that Rubio and his bird were also taking off. At a hundred feet in the air the head hair of the Marine with no legs started to emit white smoke. Sean immediately thought, oh fuck, phosphorous particles, this guy must of been hit near a phosphorous mortar round. That shit could easily ignite a plane in flight. Sean quickly reached around his seat and pulled out a small fire extinquisher. He pulled the pin and aimed the hose on top of the mans head. A white substance covered the man's hair. Sean figured the man was so juiced up he wouldn't feel a thing. Just when he placed the extinguisher back behind him, the chopper took a fast downward move to the left. The maneuver was so sudden and violent it caused the corpsman to fly backwards against the bulkhead of the chopper. Sean held on fast and noticed Crawley was having trouble staying upright. YL-37 continued to spiral in a left downward pattern. Captain DeWay was on the radio, "mayday, mayday, we've been hit, no control."
Sean braced himself for the inevitable. They were gonna crash.

It didn't take long to drop two hundred feet. YL-37 turned and spun around with the rotor blades breaking apart as they hit the branches of the trees. Sean heard the crashing of the chopper and tearing of the airframe as the chopper descended downward thru the trees.

Except for the sound of branches falling, metal creaking, hissing noises from the engine, everything seemed suprisingly silient. Sean was still waiting for the pain of the impact. He thought there had to be some major injuries. He found himself on top of the legless Marine. Crawley was in the back corner of the chopper. He had two of the wounded on top of him. The corpsman was laying nearby. Sean started to move and felt the pain he had waited for. He saw a bone protruding through his left thigh. Damn he thought, why it it always the left leg. As bad as he thought it was, there was enough trama to the leg that he could move even with the pain. He realized that serious pain would be coming soon.
"CRAWLEY! CRAWLEY! YOU OK? CAN YA HEAR ME?"

Crawley moved a bit then stopped. Sean thought the man done. Then he saw Crawley push one of the wounded Marines off himself. He moved a bit more, then shoved the other Marine off him. He struggled to get up to his feet. Sean was astonished to see Crawley move like that.

"You OK Sean?" You hurt?"

"Got a busted leg. Dosen't hurt too bad yet, but it will anytime now. See if the corpsman is OK."

"I'm OK, I'm OK. Just not moving till I 'm sure nothing is broken."

"Well get your ass over here, I got a broken leg, need a splint or something. And get some morphine ready in case the pain starts in."

"But I have to check these wounded."

"Bullshit corpsman. You help me then you help them. We got to set up a quick preimeter before Charlie, the NVA or whoever hit us, comes looking for us.

Crawley and the corpsman got Sean out of the chopper and onto the ground. The corpsman set a splint and gave Sean a vile of morphine to inject in case the pain got to much. Sean got up and could move by holding onto the chopper. With his leg in a splint and wrapped tight he could remove his M-60 off it's mount and onto the ground twenty yards away. He went back dragging his left leg and got two cans of ammunition and laid them besides the machine guns. He was moving OK with the broken leg, slow but moving. The pain was not any worse than when he first noticed it.

"CRAWLEY!" He shouted.

"Ya, over here."

"Check on the Captain and Lt. Stints."

"I already did. Got the Captain out, he's over helping the corpsman out."

"What about Stints?"

"He's dead. Probably on impact. DeWay has a good lump on his head, otherwise he's OK."

"Grab the other M-60 and place it on the other side of the aircraft, maybe twenty yards away. Get that Marine with the ankle thing and set him up at the front of the plane. When the corpsman has the wounded out on the ground and settled, get him a weapon and put him by the tail rotor. See if the Captain has any instructions."

"Will do. Oh, Sean should I load it now?"

"What?"

"Should I load my pistol?"

"What? You dumbass! You're flying around in a combat zone with an unloaded weapon?"

"Well I wasn't sure when you wanted me to load it."

"Do I have to wipe your ass too? What the fuck, you gonna throw your pistol at Charlie? Load the god damn thing! And get out of my sight....go see the Captain!"

"OK"

"Ya, OK my ass. Unloaded pistol, that beats all!"

The perimeter was all set up. YL-39 was circling overhead to provide fire cover. No one was sure when relief would come. Rubio had wounded on board that might not survive, but they couldn't leave YL-37 by itself. There was no way to have radio contact with the grounded crew of YL-37. Hue' was three miles away through heavy brush. It would take awhile for any help from the 1st Marines to reach the crew of YL-37. Sean looked around at their position and noticed for the first time that they had crashed on the edge of a Vietnamese graveyard. Four foot high mounds of dirt marked a grave. Each one had a headstone planted on top of the mound, some had small rectangle stones on the grave. Sean thought the Vietnamese were not gonna be happy about them crashing next to their graveyard.

About five hundred feet above their position, YL-39 was circling them. Sean felt good that it was Rubio who was covering them. Without warning Rubio opened fire at a target in a tree line seventy yards from Sean's directions. Capt. DeWay and Crawley came running from the other side of the aircraft and took positions twenty yards apart. Crawley had his M-60 angled so that there would be a cross fire with Sean's towards the tree line. The cross fire provides better coverage with both machine guns overlacing the area for maximun fire power. DeWay had an M-14 rifle with an automatic setting. He could easily pump out twenty rounds from his magazines. The Marine with the broken ankle turned his attention to the tree line with his automic weapon. The effectness of all weapons would be enough to deter a head on attack on their position. Rubio's fire coverage raked the area beneath the tree line. Whoever was over there was taking intense fire from Rubio. Sean saw movement in the brush. He spotted a couple of pith helmets with grass stuck in the sides as an attempt to camouflage the individual.

"Here they come Sean, they're NVA, open fire." Capt. DeWay began firing as soon as he spoke. All four men poured fire power in the direction of the helmets. Sean could hear rounds hitting the side of the downed helicopter as the approaching force returned fire.

"Damn Capt. There must be a company of NVAs coming at us."

"Just keep firing, they can't advance without taking casualties and we're in no position to run."

The Marine with the broken ankle yelled out, "I'M HIT, CORPSMAN! CORPSMAN!"

The corpsman was dragging the other wounded Marines closer to the chopper out of harms way. He ran back and attended the newly hit Marine. Sean thought he'd never want to be a corpsman, too dangerous. Those guys earn their pay and more.

The automatic weapon fire from the tree line was intense. Rounds were kicking up dirt making rocks lethal projectiles. The knee high grass was withered down making the crew of YL-37 more visable. Mortor rounds hit half way between YL-37 and the tree line. Slowly the NVA were walking the rounds towards the Marines.

DeWay yelled out," this is gonna be real bad."

That's when Sean felt a tremendous impact to his left hand. It was enough of a force that it threw his whole arm backwards. Stunned, Sean looked at his hand as it turned a solid red. "Shit!" He knew it was going to hurt real bad. "CORSPMAN! CORPSMAN! The corpsman ran over to Seans position and pulled wrapping out of his bag. He sprinkled some antiseptic power on the wound and bandaged it tight. "That will have to hold ya for now." The corpsman ran off to the other Marines.

Sean thought once his M-60's ammo belt ran out he was gonna have a hell'ava time reloading. He wished they had some grenades, that would give them more options to hold off the NVA. Then he thought of the Marines packs that were thrown onboard the chopper. There might be some grenades attached to them.

"Captain. Do'ya think you could check the choppers for grenades, the wounded Marines might have some in their gear?"

DeWay got up and ran to the chopper, grabbed two bags lying near the wreck and ran back hitting the ground hard.

"We're in luck Sean. We got eight grenades. Ya think you can throw one?"

"I still got one good arm, throw me a couple."

"Alright Sean let's throw them at the same time, 1..,2.., throw."

The grenades landed forty feet away with a loud VOOMPF. Crawley and the other Marine were providing cover fire. Rubio was still firing down from above.

"OK, that should at least give the NVA some hesitation. Let's try and get more distance.

"1..,2..., throw." Again the grenades went flying, further than the last the time. There was a louder crash of an explosion.

"What the hell was that? That wasn't our grenades and it wasn't the NVA's." DeWay shouted at Sean.

"Listen Captain. I hear a tank."

"Ya but whose?"

There was a second loud explosion, but this time it was closer to the treeline.

"Either the NVA are stupid and zeroing in on their own guys or those are our tanks."

Multiple explosions went off, hitting the tree line and shatering tree branches and any cover they gave.

A US ARMY tank broke through a tree line just east of YL-37's position. "Holy shit Sean, they're our's. They must be part of the 82nd Airborne covering operations just outside Hue'."

"Hell Captain I didn't know the Airborne had tanks."

"Uhh, they're attached to the 82nd they have these M551 Sheridan light recon tanks with 152mm guns. Very effective for what they are used for, and I'm glad to see' em.

"Well I don't care who they belong to, I'm just glad they came. I don't think we could 've held out much longer."

"Don't mind telling ya Sean I was worried myself. Wow, look at them bastards chew up that tree line. I almost feel bad for the NVA. They're catching hell."

"Better them than us, right Captain?"

"Fucking eh!"

The tanks advanced on the tree line demolishing any opposition. A company of 82nd Airborne troops followed up behind the tanks. Capt. DeWay spotted an Army Lieutenant coming torwards them. He got within ten feet and waved.

"Hey guys, we thought you could use some assistance."

"Hell, are we glad to see you!" DeWay extended his hand out and shook the Lieutenant's hand.

"Not sure how long we could've held out if you hadn't shown up."

The Army Lieutenant took off his helmet and scratched his head. "We got a call forwarded from your chase helicopter. We came as quick as we could. It wasn't hard finding you, we just traveled to where your chase plane was circling."

"Well, we're just glad to see ya. We have a few seriously wounded Marines here."

"No problem Captain. Our corpsman will assist yours in patching them up. There arsome choppers on their way here now from Phu Bai. I believe thats your's squardron."

"Yup, that's our base."

Helicopters could be heard coming over the horizon.

"Hell, here they are now Captain."

The Army and Navy corpsman took care of the wounded and got them ready for evacuation.

Capt. DeWay went over to Sean. "How ya doing Sean, they got you fixed alright?"

Sean stared up with a strange look.

"Ohhh....Captain, I'm feeling reaaal gooood! They gave me some morphine and I got a good buzz going on here. Hurts a little but I'm OK."

DeWay smiled. "I can see you're in good hands so we'll get you loaded into the choppers and get ya out'ta here. In the mean time just relax."

"Gotcha Captain." Sean laid his head back down and closed his eyes.

Four helicopters came in two at a time. All wounded were loaded and were now headed back to Phu Bai. The last chopper took Capt. DeWay, the Marine with the broken ankle and Crawley.

Once at Phu Bai, an ambulance took the wounded to the base hospital. Capt. DeWay was the last one standing around and headed to the operation shack. The Gunny came walking out of the shack towards DeWay.

"Christ, what the hell happened Captain?"

"Ahh hell, we were pulling out of the landing zone and about to make our get away. At about a hundred feet or so we got hit. They must've hit the hydraulic system because I lost control of the stick. All I could do was a controlled crash. Thank God there were trees, they helped soften our fall. Bad thing about Lt.Stints though. Poor bastard was only in 'Nam for a month. He bought it real quick."

"Anyone else hit besides the Marines you picked up?"

"Ya, Sean sustained a broken leg. Then he got shot in the hand. He seems alright, but ya never know."

"Sounds kinda cold Captain, but he wanted action and he got it."

"I know. He'll have time to think about it while he's recuperating,"

"Gunny I think he's gonna be out for at least twelve weeks, minimum. Plus he's got that hand wound. Who knows how long he'll be gone."

"I think you're right Captain. They'll probably send him to Da Nang and then medevac to Japan. If he comes back, chances are he'll be assigned to another squardron. Maybe up by Quang Tri below the DMZ."

"You know Gunny he's not gonna be happy about leaving HMM 362."

"Oh your right Captain, but that's the way the big honchos work. There is never a gaurantee you'll return to your old outfit."

The Gunny and Capt. DeWay went into the operation shack to file a brief on what took place 'causing them to get shot down.

At the flight line Rubio walked up to Crawley.

"Glad to see you're alright. That was some bad shit you guys got into."

"Hell Rubio, I was so scared I almost shit my pants. Thank God you provided that cover fire, or we'd be dead right now."

"Ya at first, when I saw you guys moving around, I thought you'd be OK. But then I spotted troops moving towards you and knew they weren't our guys, so I just opened up. Our pilot radioed in that you were down and asked for assistance. Our guys were all tied up inside Hue' City. So they transferred us to the 82nd who were closer to you. As soon as they were on you we bugged out. We had serious wounded that needed medical attention. As it was, we lost one in flight. Poor bastard didn't have a chance. I heard Sean got hit , huh?"

"Ya, twice, well kinda, He got a broken leg when we crashed and then he got shot in the hand. But he hung in there firing his M-60. I tell ya, I'll never bad mouth the Army again. Those guys saved our ass. They're alright in my book."

"Good to see ya OK Crawley. How 'bout we meet at the beer hut?"

"Sounds great, I could use a beer or two."

Rubio found Crawley and Dolman inside the beer tent at their usual table.

"Hi gents, seems like I'm the late one."

"Naw, we just got here a few minutes ago. Sit down, we've plenty of beer." Dolman pointed to one of the four empty seats.

Rubio sat and wiped his brow with his cover. "Damn what a day. Not sure if I want to go through more like that."

Crawley was holding a can of beer and looking down at the table. "Not sure if I was any help today. Felt like I kept pissing Sean off and then he goes and gets hit."

"That's got nothing to do with you Crawley." Rubio took a sip of beer. "Sean was under pressure, ya'all was his responsibility. He was just venting and you were handy. I'm sure he was feeling helpless. I know I would've."

"I hope so. He was on the ball though, issuing orders, providing cover fire."

"Look Crawley, you held your own. I mean this was your first time getting shot at plus
you got shot down and all. That's more than what happens to many guys that's been here longer than you." Dolman belched. "So feel yourself luckly man, your still walking."

Rubio looked around at the empty seats. "Ya know at one time we filled this table. Now it seems like one by one people are leaving. First Ford gets killed, then Camron rotates back to the world, then TC gets hit and now Sean. Christ I might start sitting at another table.

Dolman Spoke up. "Be careful what you wish for Rubio. Remember those guys at the next table? They're not here anymore either. Went stateside in a box."

"Oh great Dolman, I feel so much better, NOT!"

Dolman smiled, took another drink of beer and belched again.

Rubio raised his beer can for a toast. "Well guys as Sean would say, 'here's to those who wish us well, the rest of them can go to hell." All three men took a swig of beer.

"I wish all of them guys luck where ever they wind up. I'm gonna miss those bastards, ain't gonna be the same around here."

With that, all three raised their beer cans, drained them and threw the empties into the corner of the beer hut.

Ch 39

Opening his eyes, Sean blinked a few times trying to make out what the hell was twirling above him. As his vision cleared he made out a white ceiling fan.

"What the hell?"

"Morning Marine, how you feeling this morning?"

Sean turned his head to make out a nurse in blue scrubs.

"Where the hell 'am I?"

"Still a little groggy huh? That's the sedative they gave you. Things will clear up."

Sean vaguely remembers being taken off a helicopter and put into a vehicle. I'm at Phu Bai. He looked around and realized that Phu Bai didn't have a hospital. If it did have a hospital it wouldn't look this good. He noticed the nurse was a Navy Lieutenant Jr. Grade. Nothing was making sense to him.

"Give your self time, things will come back to you."

Sean shook his head to clear out the cobwebs.

"What the hell did they give me, and again where the hell 'am I?"

"You were given a strong pain killer. There was some trama to the nerves in your hip because of the crash and it was causing you a fair amount of pain."

"What'da ya mean hip. I thought I hurt my leg?"

"Well you did, in fact it's broken. But when you crashed, you landed on your hip pretty hard. The whole side of your left leg is back and blue, which is normal for a trama like yours."

"But my leg is broken, right?"

"Oh yes, they had a difficult time setting the bone. It was splinted pretty bad. The doctors didn't want to injure any nerves in the leg. The setting took a while. Yet, it's the nerve in your hip that's causing you the most pain. It'll take a bit but we're positive in time things will improve."
Sean reached down to uncover his left leg and saw his hand heavily bandaged.
"Shit, that's right my hand got hit."
The nurse was looking at him.
"Sorry, I've been in the field for a while."
The nurse smiled. "Don't concern yourself, I have two brothers and they're not angels."
"How long have I been here?"
"Oh, you came in about two days ago. You were medevaced to Da Nang and then here.
"Two days ago? No way. I don't remember no two days."
"Don't worry Corporal, it will all come back to you in pieces. You were in a lot of pain. because of the nerve, so you were given a strong sedative to make you comfortable. You woke a few times talking gibberish. Nothing made sense except....."
"Except what?"
"You mentioned a womans name a few times."
"What name?"
"Do you know a Joyce?"
Sean looked up at the ceiling fan and placed his good arm under his head.
"Ya, kinda."
"She's not your girlfriend?   Someone from back home?"
"No just someone I met a while back."
"Don't worry Marine, drugs make people say the strangest things. You just relax, the doctor will be in to check on you later. But right now take these pills to help you relax."
"Help me relax? Hell, I'm in bed and I've been in and out of sleep for two days. I don't think I can get any more relaxed."

"I know, but when the pain starts you'll be begging me for something. This way we stay ahead of the hurt. Rest and time is what you need." Sean took the pills and a few sips of water. The nurse started to leave but turned and walked back to Sean's bed.

"Look Corporal, lots of you guys come back and are a bit disorientated. Then things start coming back to you. Most guys just block it out. Many are in denial, get emotionaly detached. Some try and deal with it, others just stay that way. I've seen too many of you stay that way. All I'm saying is give your self a chance. Let others in, it'll be better in the long run."

"I hear ya sister, a buddy of mine tried to teach me that."

"Ahhhh Corporal, it's Lieutenant, not sister."

"Sorry about that Lieutenant, I've been out of touch for a while. I lack a bit of social graces."

The Lieutenant smiled. "OK, you relax now."

Sean waited for the nurse to walk out then spit the pill out into his hand. I'll decide when I need a pill, not some Navy nurse he thought. He placed the pill on the bedside table and laid back.

A sharp pain went through his hip. "Oh shit!." He reached over quickly and grabbed the pill and swallowed it down. "Better safe than sorry", he muttered. A drowsiness came over him and he fell asleep.

The sun was shinning low through the window when Sean woke. His head throbbed a bit, somewhat between a head ache and a hangover. His mouth was dry and his tongue felt like cotton. "Fucking pills, what do they have in them." He reached over and grabbed the water glass and took a long swig. Damn he thought, water tastes so great at times, hope they never stop making it. Just then a doctor walked in with a chart, "Morning Corporal, Sean isn't?"

"Yes Sir, Sean..., Sean Michaels."

"Well Sean, how ya feelin'? Leg any better?"

"Legs OK I guess, but you'd be a better judge of that. My mouth feels like I haven't brushed my teeth in days."

"Yes, well, it was a bit of a challenges getting your leg repaired but we did a good job, if I say so myself. You had a shattered fermur. It's not so much it was broken but it was also shattered. It was quite a job piecing it all together. I'm more concerned about your hip. There may be a some nerve damage but we'll monitor that. Do you have any pain in it?"

"I did have a sharp pain just before I fell asleep last night, but the pills the nurse gave me did the trick."

The doctored smiled. "Those pills really do a job on ya, also makes your mouth feel like crap. I suggest you drink lot'sa of water, OK?"

"Yes Sir."

"You're out of observation mode now so tommorow you'll be moved to the main ward. We'll keep you in bed so not to aggrevate that hip. Might be a hairline fracture we can't see, but it's more about any permanent nerve damage Any questions?"

"Mmm, just one sir."

"What's that?"

"Where the hell 'am I? Da Nang, Okinawa, where?"

"You don't know?"

"Doc, I've been in and out of sleep for two days. Where 'am I?"

"Son, you're in Japan."

"Japan? Why the hell 'am I in Japan?"

"Space Corporal, space. In 'Nam they patch ya up quick and send ya to either Japan or Okinawa. The bed spaces in Vietnam are for those who would be back in the field within a month or less." The doctor smiled. "We can send you back if you want."

"No, it's not that Sir. What about my outfit? Do I go back to them? What happens when I'm better?"

"Not my call son. I just patch'em up. And I have to tell ya, you're gonna be with us for a while. So enjoy your stay. Take care Corporal."

"Thanks Doc."

Sean laid there and wondered if he would ever see HMM 362 again. What about Rubio, Dolman and Crawley. All this time he put up an emotional defensive barrier because guys he leaned on got killed or left. Now he was the one to leave. It didn't feel any better if they left or he did. That familar bond was gone. That one thing he depended on to keep his mind intact was gone. He now felt alone in an unfamilar place with no one he knew or could depend on. The one thing that kept guys in a combat zone going was gone. You depended on your fellow Marines to cover your back. You looked out for him and he looked out for you. Now he knew why he set up a wall, to prevent himself from getting too attached to others. Even his brief R&R with Joyce tore at that emotional wall. Why get too attached to some one when it's only brief, and does no good. Although the nurse made a good point. Do you block people out, be in denial or deal with it and let people in? Like Tommy Collins said, not letting people into your life is no life at all.

Sean could feel the throbbing in his head coming back. He closed his eyes and tried not to think. Sleep came easy.

The US Naval Hospital in Yokosuka, Japan was a 47 bed facility. Sean was excorted half way down the ward by a naval corpsman to an empty bed. The corpsman was a heavy set guy with a big smile.
"Here ya go Marine, your home for the next month or two, or however long it takes ya to mend."
The corpsman helped Sean off the gurney and onto the bed.
"Now that wasn't hard, now was it."
"No. Thanks guy."
"Name's Smith, people just call me Smitty. You just make your self comfortable and get to know your neighbors."
Sean looked around and thought that's gonna be hard. Next to him was a Marine with bandages on most of his body.
"What happened to him?"
"His tank was hit and he got some bad burns. He's mostly sedated because of the pain. There's plenty of guys here with some bad ass shit. We take good care of them and eventually they get better depending on their injuries."
"What if they don't get better?"
"Oh, they do, some just need lot'sa rehabilitation, some physical, some mental. But they do leave here mostly to the states."
"What about the rest?"
"Oh, I guess they return to Vietnam or get transferred to another duty station."
Sean looked to the bed on his left and saw a guy whose profile ended at his knees. There was no evidence of legs and his head was bandaged.
"Whats this guy's story?"

"He came in a few days ago. Not only did he get his legs blown off but the helicopter he was in got shot down."
"Say what?"
"He was medevaced out of Hue' City and the helicopter he was in was..."
"Ya, Ya I heard that. It can't be the same guy!"
"What are you talking about?"
"I was shot down medevacing some Marines outta Hue'. One of the medevacs had his legs gone below the knees. Then his hair started to smoulder and I used a fire extinquisher on him."
"This might be your boy. He had some chemical burns on the side of his head. Doctors couldn't make heads or tails out of it. They just treated it and let it go at that."
Sean thought 'this is creepy, I meet up with a corpsman in Khe Sanh and he shows up in Hue'. Then I pick up a wounded Marine in Hue' and he ends up here. This is weird.'
The corpsman had already gone when Sean turned back around from looking at his neighbor. The rest of the ward was pretty much what one would expect of a place dealing with wounded. Beds in a long row on both sides of the room. Most beds were occupied, some showed signs of having been laid in but were empty. Sean made the connection between the wounded he picked up and where they eventually ended up. Looking down the ward he noticed a guy in a wheel chair coming in his direction. The guy was slightly older than most on the ward. He was smiling and looking at Sean. It was then Sean's eye widened.
"Colonel Johnston! How the hell are ya?"
"Hello Sean, I got word from Lt. Janhs in S-2 that you might be here. I asked around if anybody who just came in had a Boston accent named Sean Michael, and here I'am."
"Damn Colonel, it's good to see you. How ya doing?"
"Pretty good. They sewed me up good and bandaged my chest like a mummy. But I'm on the mend."
"What about Tommy Collins?"

"Aw, it's a shame Sean, he was transferred out yesterday back to the States."

"Shit, ya mean I was here when he was here?"

"Looks like it son. He would've liked to have seen ya before he went. He had some good words to say about you. He thought you did a great job after he got hit. Said you took care of business and got everyone back safely. Well, under the circumstances at least without further damage."

"He was a very good teacher Sir. I'm gonna miss his presence."

"You guys were a good team Sean. It's a shame that got broke up, but that shit happens."

"So what about you Sir? What's the story, how long are you gonna be here, you getting shipped out to the world."

"Whoa, one thing at a time. They have me over in a ward for officers. I was told yesterday that I'll be shipped to Hawaii for further treatment. Seems I have a round lodged near my spine and they wanted a specialist to go at it. After that I go to the States.
From there I'm not sure. My wife wants me to take a desk job in Washington DC. I'm not in favor of that. I'm a pilot and I'd like to be around a squadron somewhere."

"Hey Colonel, maybe they'll make you the Presidents chopper pilot."

The Colonel laughed, "highly unlikey Sean, everybody wants that position. Naw, I might end up in New River, North Carrollina. Many pilots from 'Nam are ending up there."

"Where ever you go Sir I'm sure you'll do well."

"Thanks Sean. Well look, I just wanted to stop by and say hi. You need to rest a bit and I need to get back before they report me AOL." The Colonel leaned forward and
whispered, "I wasn't supposed to leave the ward because of my wounds, but I was going stir crazy."

"Thanks for coming by Colonel, you were always one of the good officers."

"Ok Sean, take care guy. I wish you the best."

The Colonel turned his wheelchair around and started to head back to the direction where he came, but stopped. He shouted over his shoulder, "if you ever get near New River, stop in and say hi", he continued on to his ward.

"I will do that Colonel."

The sight of the Colonel was blocked by the mingling of people coming and going in the ward.

Sean felt good to see a familar face and didn't feel as isolated as he did the other day. The rest of the day was spent reading a new book, M*A*S*H. He thought it was a stupid book about three Army Doctors in Korea. He just came from a war zone and felt stupid reading about a differant one. It wasn't long before he fell asleep.

The weeks went by fast for Sean. His days were spent half in rehabilitation and half in the recreation room where most of the guys hung out during the day. He still had some discomfort trying to walk with crutches without getting a sharp pain in his hip. The severity of the pain lessened the more he tried walking, The doctors felt this was a good sign that any trama to the hip might just be decreasing. A diagnosis was anywhere from bursitis, an inflammation of the bursa sac surrounding the hip, to a herniated disc caused by the heliccopter crash. Slight trama was also suffered by the spine causing pain to radiate within the hip area. At times Sean experienced sharp pain, at other times a slight numbness in his leg. Yet the more he walked and did some stretching the less he experienced the pain or numbness. The doctors did indicate that it might cause him problems in his later years. Sean felt that was so far away he could deal with it.

He finaly got the courage to write to Joyce. He felt guilty about not responding to her two letters and felt he at least owed her some type of explanation. The letter was three pages of his activities since returning to Vietnam. He was careful to minimize the news of his crash and injuries. The letter was finished with a promise to write again and danced around the issue of his feelings towards her so as not to raise any expectations. He thought the chances of returning to Australia were very slim so why bring up the issue.

During his stay at the Yokosuka Naval Hospital Sean made friends easily. He got to know his two neighbors real well. The guy with the missing legs was Robert, from New York City. He was due to rotate back to the states two weeks after he was hit. But now his injuries would delay that for another month or so till he got outfitted with prosthesis. Then there would be months of rehabilitation back in the states. Robert talked a lot about his fears of how his girlfriend might react to his injuries. They were engaged to be married before he was shipped to 'Nam. He said he would understand if she backed out. After all who would want to be saddled with a cripple.

The Marine on Seans' other side had to endure painful sessions of getting his bandages changed. Most times the bandages would stick to his burns even though they were treated with Antibiotic creme to prevent that. Compared to these guys Sean felt he got off pretty easy with his broken leg and hip pain. In a way he didn't feel worthy of being in their company.

Other times Sean would wheel himself down to the recreation hall and watch guys play ping pong or just watch TV. The guys watching TV would get upset when protesters were shown marching around the Washington Mall. The one thing that really pissed them off was CBS TV anchorman Walter Cronkite. After returning from a visit to Vietnam, he commented that the Vietnam War could not be won. That at best it would end in a stalemate. The Marines booed and threw whatever was handy at the TV. One Marine yelled, "we killed over 5000 of them bastards in Hue' alone. And we killed more in Saigon and other cities. Stalemate my ass!"

The Marines in the recreation room felt that the politicians and people in the States would start writing Vietnam off as a stalemate. The troops in Vietnam were winning battles, getting shot, getting killed and some TV anchorman called it a stalemate. It didn't make sense to the troops, especially after Hanoi failed during Tet and over 32,000 VC had been killed. That's not a stalemate to the US fighting men.

Sean never commented on the news, he was just tired of it all. By now he realized he just wanted to go back to the states and get discharged. He was done with 'Nam, let the bastards have that shit hole. He felt hatred towards the protesters, felt they were giving comfort to the enemy. The jerks protesting waved North Vietnamese flags, then burned the American flag. He thought if he ran into any of them he'd beat the crap out of them. Yet, in the reality of things, he just wanted to go back home and resume his life again. He was done with it all, seen too much carnage and destruction. He just didn't care anymore.

Ch 41

Thirty Eight Years Later, 2006

"Sean! Sean! Wake up hon."
Sean slowly opened his eyes and could feel a smile developing on his face.
His wife was standing before him.
"You fell asleep hon. What have you been doing? You have been in here
for quite a while, I was getting worried, you were so quiet."
Sean was seated in his favorite chair, a brown leather lazy-boy. He liked
that chair because it didn't bother his hip if he sat for a prolonged period.
On his lap were pictures of a time back in his youth. Pictures of guys he
served with in Vietnam. It seemed so long ago. How did he get to this
point so fast, where did the years go? In his hand was the reason for the
nostalgic trip into the past. It was an obituary of a good friend,
Sgt. Tommy Collins. The obituary was sent by an acquaintance he met up
with at a reunion of HMM 362 'The Ugly Angels'. At first Sean didn't
want to attend that reunion. He didn't want to see a bunch of old guys
standing around, bald heads, beer bellys with stories from a long time ago.
Sean wanted to remember them the way he left them, young. He didn't
want those images to be destroyed with new ones of old veterans. More
telling was that, seeing these old veterans would be a reminder that he was
one of them. Just an old guy who once spent part of his youth in Vietnam.
But his wife insisted. She said it would do him good to see the guys he
has talked about over the years. She usually got her way so he went.

When he walked into the Hilton Hotel bar that night his fears were realized. Standing around the bar were a bunch of old guys. Some wore hats with military insignias pined on them. As he approached the bar a guy called out his name. "Sean, Sean, over here."
Sean looked in the direction of an older surfer type dude. He had sparce, thin, dirty blond hair,and wore a Hawaiian flower shirt. Sean walked towards the man trying to figure out who the hell he was.
"Sean, except for a little weight, you haven't changed a bit."
The man stuck out his hand.
"Crawley? Is that you? What the hell happened to all that curly blond hair?"
"Ah Sean, we get old, even us surfer dudes. Come on Rubio is around the other side of the bar."
For the next three hours, Sean, Rubio and Crawley talked about all the times and conversation they had in the beer hut. The more Sean talked to them the more the years evaporated. It was like being back at the beer hut in 'Nam. They may have changed as they got older but hearing their voices brought the image of their youth back. These were the same guys, just with a few years of life under their belts. Sean was glad his wife encouraged him to go. Before the reunion ended that weekend Sean, Rubio and Crawley swapped addresses, agreeing to get together sometime after the reunion. But like many promises made at a reunion, neither acted on contacting the other.

Rubio was living in Texas and happened upon Tommy Collins at a VFW in Austin Texas. They saw each other on and off thru the years, telling lies and war stories about their time in Vietnam. Rubio knew Tommy Collins was not faring well at the time and attributed that to the reason Tommy Collins never went to the Ugly Angels reunion. Knowing that Tommy Collins and Sean flew together and were tight, he felt an obligation to notify Sean about Tommy Collins passing away. The obituary indicated Tommy Collins had suffered from a prolonged illness possibly from agent orange. Agent orange was a chemical to defoliate trees and underbrush denying the VC cover. It was rumored to cause all types of illness in Vietnam veterans. The article went on to list the remaining relatives and the usual military and social history of the decessed.

It came as a shock to Sean to read of Tommy Collins' death. The last time he saw him was when TC got hit, some thirty eight years ago. Where the hell did the time go?

After two months at the Yokosuka Naval Hospital, Sean was sent back to Vietnam to finish out his tour of duty. He was reassigned to HMM 161 located at Qua'ng Tri airbase. HMM 161 had the UH-1N Huey jet engine helicopters, quite differant from the UH34D piston choppers Sean was used to. Being the newest guy to the outfit, Sean was assigned to the overhaul hanger, which was alright with him. He had his belly full of flying into an LZ not knowing if it was friendly or not. The thing he didn't like was having to go on patrols with the perimeter guard. But that ended when the 2nd Battalion 1st Marines took total control over all patrols and ground activities. Sean just had to guard a bunker within the perimeter for four hours a night. Since he was an experienced helicopter mechanic and crew chief, most of his time was spent in the overhaul hanger. In a few weeks he would be transferred back to the world, his tour of duty was up. He was a short timer.

He received another letter from Joyce hinting about him coming down her way. With two weeks left in 'Nam, Sean felt responding wouldn't help the situation.

Eventually he rotated back to the states. Even now Sean could still remember what it was like to be standing there in Da Nang waiting to board a Boeing 707. He stood there with his travel documents tucked under his arms, happy to never see this shithole place again. Let the natives or whoever keep it. He first traveled to Okinawa to pick up his civilian clothing and seabag stored there. After a few days he boarded another Boeing 707 back to America.

Once back in the states for eight months he received orders for an early discharge. Seems his services were no longer needed and he was happy about that. During this time he did send and receive letters from Joyce. It was a long distance relationship that seemed to be going no where. She was a thousand miles away, living in a different social strata than he was accustomed to. To him, he saw no way to resolve those two differances and for now decided to do nothing. They continued to write each other with a vague promise to meet at some future date.

Like most guys returning from the military, he went back home and settled into civilian life. Working for a year as a Longshoreman, he saved his money. His goal was to attend college on the GI Bill. Afterwards he got a job as a CPA with a Boston firm. Yet the damp New England weather bothered his Vietnam injury so he decided to move to Florida. The warm Gulf temperature of Pensacola, Florida seemed to better suit his aching hip which flared up from time to time.

With his career established Sean eventually married. He and his wife raised two fine kids. Living in Pensacola Florida was enjoyable for them.

He was retired now and enjoyed working on his small ranch. It gave him great comfort working with the animals Their two kids were gone now and it was just him and his wife. He reflected back on the good advice given by three people, Tommy Collins, Joyce and the Nurse Lieutenant at the Naval Hospital. 'Let people into your life, don't keep them at a distance'. Sean followed that advice from the moment he was discharged from the Marine Corps.

It proved to be the smartest thing he ever did. Otherwise he would have missed out on the best wife a guy could have. Sean watched as she walked away. She flashed back that killer smile and beautiful blue eyes. Yes, he was grateful for a lot. The friends he made in 'Nam, a good career and of course his beautiful wife, Joyce.

THE END